Za'Varuk's Stone

Za'Varuk's Stone

Pleides Series: Book I

Adam Lee D'Amato-Neff

Writers Club Press
San Jose New York Lincoln Shanghai

Za'Varuk's Stone
Pleides Series: Book I

Writers Club Press
an imprint of iUniverse.com, Inc.

For information address:
iUniverse.com, Inc.
5220 S 16th, Ste. 200
Lincoln, NE 68512
www.iuniverse.com

ISBN: 0-595-20034-6

Printed in the United States of America

Dedication

For my wife Francine who puts up with my temperamental nature and rides out the maelstrom of my creative outlets, and to my daughter Elizabeth Tracy who inspires me to return to the fantasy of childhood dreams.

Part I

A common bardic song in praise of Darkwolfe and the Dragon Band in ages long past; of his quest for self, the gods, and his pact with Pleides

ONCE THERE WAS A LITTLE BOY, BY HIMSELF IN THE WORLD ALONE
HE TRIED TO MAKE HIMSELF FRIENDS
BUT HE WAS SO DIFFERENT
SO HE SAT IN A FOREST CLEAR AND PRAYED TO THE GODS THERE

(REFRAIN)
WHY AM I HERE, LIFE ISN'T FAIR, WHY AREN'T I LIKE ALL THE REST
I TRY SO HARD TO BE RIGHT, TO BE WHO I WAS MEANT TO BE

THERE WAS A STIR IN THE WIND, AND A VOICE CAME TO HIM
WAS IT REAL OR IN HIS MIND, HE DIDN'T KNOW BUT HE LISTENED
IT SPOKE OF MOTHER AT THE DAWN OF TIME
THE SEPARATION THAT BOUND US HERE

THEN A BUSH BURNED WITH FIRE, AND SPOKE THE NAME OF OUR FATHER
HE FELT HEAT DEEP WITHIN, AT THE CENTER OF HIS BEING
THE FOREST CAME RIGHT ALIVE, A LION STARED INTO HIS EYES

HE WALKED DOWN THE OLD PATH, DOWN TO THE ANCIENT LAKE
HE LOOKED DEEP INTO ITS DEPTHS, AND SAW THE BLUE LADY THERE
SHE HELD ALOFT THE SACRED SWORD, HE MADE HIS HEART BARE

THEN HE WENT ATOP THE HILL, THE ONE OF ELDER KINGS
HE MET THE GOD WITH ANTLERED HEAD, AND DONNED THE PAGAN CROWN
ALAS HE CALLED THE STORM AND RAIN
AND MADE A PACT WITH PLEIDES

1

Beginnings of Strife

The fire line of the burning circle of candles lay somber effect to the darkened hovel. Shadows played lazily upon the walls and danced to a tune that only the great mother may ever know and do. A small orchestra of crickets played at the outer walls and a wisp of morning fog blew in at the lonely windowsill. Gorden Tucker contemplated his small and yet undecided future here, squatting in a little wood and whicker chair at the room's far corner. His dark complexion and raggedy beard leant a downcast measure to the glare of what was soon to appear within the ensorcelled circle. His stick-like frame hunkered down in the undersized chair added to a comical aspect to this event; as if old Mr. Brady's scarecrow had walked in off the field and taken up residence in this child's seat and awaited the coming show. With a bored and whimsical yawn, Furball the cat stretched beneath his feet and clawed plaintively at the dry and tasteless floor.

A large circle was etched in chalk in the center of the room. At the points of the eight-pointed star stretched within its center sat small white candles with their flames flickering hungrily.

"How long is this suppose to take Furball?" Tucker asked as if the little feline would so happily oblige a ready answer. The cranky and less than friendly cat merely stretched further into comfort and ignored its current master with utter disdain.

Just this last span of several days (commonly called a five-day or *fist* for short) a rider had come into Grathmoor speaking of a terrible curse that was soon to come upon the town. Once the captain of the guards discerned that he wasn't entirely crazy, he was brought to Gorden Tucker, the town cleric, upon the rider's request. Since it was thought not prudent to bring him to the castle and stir up the resident clerics there, Captain Emory acknowledged his request and sent him on his way. Captain Emory also thought that the fewer disturbances to Lord Noblin the better; curse or no curse.

Gorden Tucker, while not wholly versed in curses and demonic infestations as the case may be, agreed to at least converse with the somewhat hysterical young lad and see what he was about. As was soon gathered, Pylreht a tiny fishing village up the Borneck tributary was annihilated just a fortnight ago by a rather nondescript man walking into town at sunset.

Apparently this man soon transformed into some kind of beast or demon and ripped the entire town limb from limb. Before all was completely lost in total bloodshed, the local mage, named Sabbath, sent the rider on to Grathmoor with a scroll of awakening to summon a beast of the lower planes to battle this unknown demon. Tucker, being versed in local beasts and demonology to some degree, thought this all very vague, but when a forward Grathmoor scout came riding in reporting of some horrible monster thrashing its way up the southern stretch to town, Tucker decided it probably wasn't too bad of an idea to go ahead and do a little summoning.

The candlelight continued its dance to unseen gods and pulled from the web of the goddess. Like two small pieces of the heart, at first discordant, soon they come into perfect beat and drone on like a war chant or master at the helm of a slave ship. Boom-da-da-da, Boom Di-dum, Boom-da-da-da, Boom Di-Dum. Soon tucker began swaying in rhythm with the sound no one else could hear. The little rickety chair squeaked with each movement and threatened to splinter into nothing but kindling beneath his adult frame. Furball sauntered off to a more private corner of the little shack near the matted straw, which was used as a bed, mewling discomfortingly, but otherwise not terribly concerned at the moment. His black and tan tiger stripes, so typical of the mysteries' brown tabby, soon became lost in the gathering shadows as the flames began to wane suddenly.

A preternatural stillness came in the low circle of flames. First nothing visible, then a misty blackness coalescing from some other worldly or magical plane appeared. Swirling darkness, amorphous yet purposeful was this sentient mass; seething its evilness and malicious intent. Tucker tried to rise from his little seat but felt completely paralyzed except for the intake of breath barely drawn from a captured diaphragm. His darting eyes edged with fear would have leapt from his skull and run far from the unknown depths of this manifestation had they the power to do so.

The little house began shaking, bottles on the shelves lining the walls rattling, some falling to the ground and spilling their contents of healing herbs and spell components to the earthen floor. The sign outside swayed rhythmically as if within beckoned a festive tune. The candle flames turned a wicked green and leaned in toward the mist as if to burn it away with their meager heat, flaring upward to ignite or perhaps enhance the artful display.

Furball apparently had enough of this craziness. How could any cat of proper upbringing sleep amidst such a vile clatter? He cast Tucker one last look, gave a meager meow in farewell and bounded through the small portal window into the night. He, mind you, would take his chances outside this humble abode and spend the wee hours of the dark morning to catch some mousy morning-draw meal.

The mist shape finally solidified into a brackish globe of black and green the size of a morning-draw melon, however Tucker had no desire to bite into this thing on this particular morning or any other. That's precisely what was about to happen regardless of the poor cleric's intent. The candle flames returned to their normal color and pointed straight upward for an instant and then winked out, leaving a vast sea of inky nothingness and a wickedly ominous sizzling sound in its wake.

The last thing Tucker remembered was the globe, just fingers from his face, and it seemed to smile voraciously. Then there was only raw relentless pain as if his whole body was set afire. Still paralyzed, he didn't even have the comfort of a good scream.

Furball was nearby hunting mice in the surrounding woods and grassy fields. He thought it was better not to dwell on what was happening to his master. I *am* just a cat after all. Holding his fresh kill playfully in his mouth, he still managed an all too non-cat-like grin.

* * * * *

It was a quiet glade just a short walk from Grathmoor proper. A small trail snaked through the West Woods and opened into a small grassy area with a fishing pond set at the southern end. Many townsfolk came here at all times of the seasons and took their chance at snatching a bass or two from the fruitful pond. The place was ringed by trees and offered privacy. It was here that the young man Seth Crownover, more commonly called Darkwolfe by those close to him and not overly bitter about his choice of chosen names, would come to practice his magic and swordsmanship.

Assuming a gleeful escape from his father's shop, Darkwolfe released his blade and summoned his inner strength to cast magic at the same time.

He parried left, then down, kicked out with his lead leg and thrust for the kill. He jumped straight up as if leaping a blade or staff, turned forward into a roll, came up and turned instantly in a spin with a backhand slash. He stopped suddenly as if blocked, pivoted downward for an attack to the knee, hacked back up toward the neck, and drove in with another spinning technique in the opposite direction, thrusting into the gut.

Immediately after the kill move, he swiftly turned and targeted a stump on the far side of the pond. The sun's reflection off the water distracted him at the last moment with its morning blaze of beauty and glory. His spell fizzled out in a small wisp of smoke and quickly dissipated in the gentle breeze.

A noisy gray squirrel and a lonesome robin, both momentarily breaking from their endless quest for food to observe his human foolishness, congratulated Darkwolfe's accomplishments. As if in feeling his rising anger, both animals quickly fled into the surrounding trees for cover and less observed humorous spectatorship.

Darkwolfe kicked the dirt on the pond's edge in frustration with his hard leather boots and whispered, "damn!" The semi-moist soil curled back into a deep impression of his anger. Glancing into the pond's surface, he took in his reflection and studied himself intently, wondering what he was really doing here and not listening to everyone else in his life that told him that he was crazy.

He was kind of thin but well muscled. Brown pants were tucked into his knee-high leather boots that had seen many draws laid upon them in his scouting expeditions in the surrounding woods and hills. A thick heavy leather belt was strapped around his waist and the hilt of his longsword, now thrust into its scabbard, sat above his left hip comfortably. To the front and right of the belt were many small pouches holding herbs, minerals, and other tid-bits used as catalysts for spells.

All things in existence are energy. It is the work of the mage to transform that energy and shape it with his will. While to some degree one can magic-cast without components, it is easier to use components as catalysts, and quite frankly most mages never make it to the level of free-casting. Either they do not have the proper concentration, ability, or out of pride and foolery burn themselves out. That is, without components, the mage is purely the catalyst and if not in harmony with his environment and the energy that he is channeling, he can sort of short circuit the energy and end up cooking his brain or over burdening his heart and never live to cast again. Because of the great discipline required in spell casting, mages as a rule never took another art upon themselves, such as invoking the powers of the blade or a god. It was considered uncouth and below them, after all, weren't mages the chosen of The Pleides?

Mages assume that drawing from the arcane knowledge and years that they have spent acquiring it, and utter control of the life force, entitled them to some greater hierarchical standing in the greater understanding of things. Did the devotional cleric deserve less, or the trained monk of the temples scattered across the face of this realm? Or even the paladin or thief or assassin who trained whole heatedly to achieve their perspective levels of mastery? Even the bard or artistic souls, did they deserve less? These were the questions that plagued Darkwolfe in his long search for his soul and what he sought to be truth. Was there not some level of divine infusion in any art or trade, which once suffered for, gave back ten fold in the name of understanding and wisdom?

Once Darkwolfe had decided to be both a warrior and a mage, he had outcast himself from both his groups of friends. Both the warrior guild and the mage class had decided that his presumptuous inclinations of following in the footsteps of some legendary figure were more fantasy than anything a real person could attain to. Few, if any individuals had a knack for both trades, and if they did, never pursued both.

The warriors thought the mages to be pure weaklings who used tricks more than any power to actually do anything of real importance. The mages sneered at the warriors as one would a bug or stupid ox, who, while having both size and power in physical abilities, were nothing more than brute strength manifested in human form. The mages certainly thought this was useful, but considered their warriors more as expendable bodies than human mechanisms of war.

The rogues weren't officially a class, since stealing wasn't particularly looked on with favor, but there were rumored to be some groups who gathered in the woods about the town. The assassins existed, but not openly. It was clearly known however that if someone needed to meet the dark lord, there was someone to do the deed for the right price. Gold that is.

The priests kept to themselves and while their chosen warriors, The Terra Paladins (protectors of the Earth—akin to the dragon band but wielded minor clerical magic as opposed to arcane magic) generally didn't enter into name-calling as a past time, but were known to humble many transgressors to what they called their holy law. Its been rumored that the black knights, purely evil paladins, existed but no one around Grathmoor, thank the gods, had ever seen one.

So that really left the warriors and mages squabbling about their own superiority; and Darkwolfe was caught in the middle. He loved and pursued both of these wonderful arts and strove to make every nuance special and meaningful in his training. Since he wasn't allowed to be officially trained anymore, he spent much of his time perusing the books that had collected over time in his father's curio shop. Thankfully, there were many non-famous or sought after treatises on lore, minor incantations, and martial arts. Apparently most of them were extremely outdated, but Darkwolfe got from them what he could and improvised variations of them to suit his needs.

This combination of might and magic were so true to his nature; logical strength. Mages were powerful with their arcane knowledge and deadly spells, but quite easily defeated in combat if overwhelmed or surprised before a spell could be cast. Warriors were great in combat, but could be disabled by even the lowliest of mages if time was available and the right spells cast. In fact everyone knew these arguments. However there were few with the aptitude and skill to actually do both.

Whether selection or training enlistment was the reason for this anomaly, who can say, but brawny lads always became warriors, and witty-scrawny young ones mages.

Who would ever think to break this time memorial mold? One might say that at that exact moment in time, Uranus wept with joy, for he was the god of innovation and free thought.

I suppose no one wanted a warrior who couldn't lift his weapon or wasn't strong enough to wear his armor; likewise, no one wanted a mage who couldn't read, memorize spells and their paired components, or not enough common sense to prevent blowing up half the town. So you see, Darkwolfe just figured the best of both worlds made the most amount of sense. Wasn't he both strong and intelligent? It just wasn't that easy though. He knew it would probably take a lifetime for him to be able to use both effectively in combination and in true combat. Especially since no one would or could teach him, and even most of his friends stopped hanging out with him because of his "supposed arrogance" and willful stubbornness to recapitulate some long forgotten tale through his meager peasant life.

He swatted away a mosquito with his right hand and breathed deeply, savoring the morning as if it were his first and last upon this wondrous plane. He settled back into his concentration, staring across the pond at the stump again. Darkwolfe found that void of nothingness-yet-all from which magical energy was drawn. There was a split second of utter stillness, bliss, and then a pair of red-glowing darts made of pure energy shot out across the still pond's surface and blasted into the tree stump sending splinters spraying up into the air. A resounding thud-thud came back to him as if someone were knocking on a door and then all was still again.

A small smile crept across his lean face and he brushed his auburn hair out of his eyes. A trickle of sweat dribbled past his temple and down his cheek. He took a leather tie out of one of his pouches and pulled his long hair back into a ponytail. His muscles were sore and magic nearly drained, but it wasn't often that he could slip away from his father to practice, and mastery wouldn't be gained by quitting as soon as he got a little sore and weary. His father owned a curiosity shop of sorts where antiques, mostly junk, and an occasional item of lesser magic were sold. Since his mother's passing, "Seth", his father's only son, took up most of the shop's work while his father slipped further and further into despair at the bottom of a potent bottle of strong drink. So while his father slept off a particularly long night of drinking and subsequent hangover, Darkwolfe slipped out to what he liked to call the training field, for a little practice. Most of his friends were strangers now except for one, and he guessed it was her who was making all that noise coming down the trail. Charlemette was never one for stealth, goddess bless her.

She came then out between a pair of spruces on the path from town. Her purple robes rustled about her ankles and holy symbol glinting in the sunlight between her well-formed breasts on a silver chain. Levanah's symbol was a waxing and waning crescent moon connected through the middle by a dragonspear. Yes, all of his friends were no more, lost to ignorance, except Charlemette, his close friend and aspiring priestess of Levanah, goddess of change, love, and illusion.

"Well met Lord Darkwolfe, how fare ye on this glorious morn?" She purred.

"Better than the best can ask for Lady Charlemette." He responded, taking a deep bow with a flourish of his arms. A moment passed and then they both burst out laughing.

"Lord and Lady right," she squealed, "more like a couple of peasants with big dreams of glory, self importance, and adventure."

"Aye! Adventure!" Darkwolfe adjusted his sword belt and glanced around the glade briefly as if adventure might be lurking behind some nearby tree before letting his eyes fall back upon the lovely Charlemette. She smiled brightly and for a moment her blue eyes caught his hazel orbs and there was a glimmer of something more than just friendship.

His eyes took her in. Her golden mane was startling, and a few loose strands danced in the breeze. Her cheeks weren't plump per say, but more than one aunt or grand'mamma had pinched them over the years.

Her gaze drifted down to his bare chest and abdomen. He watched her watch him and when their eyes met again she suddenly turned and took a seat in the grass a few heads off. "Well, don't let me stop your practice Lord Darkwolfe, but your father did ask where you had got off to and seemed in even a more foul mood this morn than usual. If that's possible." She added as an afterthought.

"Fine I won't be too long. I can seem to manage my sword forms and my minor attack darts, but I have a hard time doing both."

"Now you see why everyone is town thinks you a fool…" she hesitated. His eyes grew large and an angry scowl appeared. "I ah….mean that is…ah…well, they think it, I didn't say that I did." She finished emphatically. This had really been a sore subject for him and she now regretted saying anything. Such was her bane, always talking before thinking. It had been an endless cause of trouble for her. But its true isn't it!!! So she was fond of pointing out the truth, not sugar coating everything just to appease a few egos. So she shattered a few illusions when she told the truth, that was Levanah's realm was it not? Well she was adept at creating illusions *and* destroying them. So be it.

Darkwolfe drew forth his blade and took a few steps back away from where she sat. "We'll see who's the fool in the end now won't we?"

* * * * *

After the sun had fully risen that morning, Tucker found himself still sitting in the diminutive chair with muscles sore and joints quite stiff. He had a surrealistic perception of the world for many minutes, which reminded him of the time that he had challenged a dwarf from the quarry to a drinking contest and so miserably lost.

Dreams of fire and being burned alive were still fresh in his mind, but he looked at his arms and legs as he awkwardly came to his feet and found that he was very much still alive. His plain brown priestly robes of the great mother were a bit sooty and smudged with dirt, but otherwise intact except for the smudge of tomato sauce from the evening-draw meal yesterday eve.

Furball was curled up on some straw matting which served as a bed and appeared asleep; his whiskers twitched every so often as if in response to some cat dream that he may be experiencing or perhaps savoring a remembered mouse of remarkable taste. He pawed at the matting as a kitten would to a suckling breast.

Tucker saw that all the candles had burned out and the room was in good shape except for a few bottles and herbs that had fallen from the shelves. No tracks or markings appeared in the circle and the nine-pointed star was still complete. Tucker assumed that the spell had basically not worked and he had fallen asleep with a variety of horrific nightmares, but nothing to conclude that anything was essentially awry.

Gorden Tucker went about picking up the spilled bottles and herbs methodically and with much care, and the small cleric's hovel was again as previously considered normal, as if nothing the night before had ever occurred.

Breakfast was soon underway with tucker busily dancing back and forth with his usual cooking fervor. He started a little fire with his flint in a small hole for his flames, and proceeded to feed it enthusiastically. When he had finished his prancing and preparations, the meal consisted of some old hard bread, bitter cheese, and a glass of sweet cider that was brought up for him periodically from Pylreht. Pylreht, yes Tuck thought; what has happened to Pylreht. Anyone who may have witnessed the cook in action, might have wondered what all the prancing about was for, for such a simple meal.

* * * * *

Sabbath, a mage of much notoriety but possessed the title of town mage none-the-less, sat in his study in Pylreht. It was a warm and cozy little lair that he liked to think of as a temporary place of residence. For in his mind things would soon come around in his favor, and if things went extremely well, he would be dining in the castle of Grathmoor in Lord Noblin's steed by this time next month.

He was often known to do nothing without selfish intent. In fact, he had sat idly by and let a few lads die from a wild snake-beast before blasting it with a lightning bolt when he realized he'd probably be nominated town mage for doing so. Yet he truly felt sorrow for killing the poor beast, because he really had such high hopes of taming the creature and using it in his new torture chamber to suck the life out of unwilling informants.

Once he turned a man into an opossum for saying he hated magic and all mages. The pitiful warrior happened to have a little too much drink in him at the time and happened to be scouring the Wormwood's company for opposition. Sabbath was just finishing his evening-draw and decided to take the rather inadequate fool for desert. The man was a warrior after all, what else would one expect him to say about mages? In fact the warrior schools often taught their disciples to be condescending to mages to break the inherent fear of their unknown spells. It would be unlikely for one to charge a casting mage if one truly knew what they were about.

The act was soon forgotten after the long harsh winter that prevailed that season, and Sabbath's magic had saved many folk from freezing to death. If he had followed his true nature, most of the young children would be long since buried, but an opportunity in this town was noticed in its proximity to Grathmoor.

From what Sabbath had read in his necromantic texts, if he could assume power of Grathmoor and by nomination gain the crown, he could raise the field of undead soldiers to fight for him. This contingency was created to preserve the line of rulers within

Grathmoor, but Sabbath hoped to use this power to spread his rule and use the magical texts hidden within the vaults to eventually become king of all the region.

So in the end the good outweighed the bad to date and so he stayed within the town as tolerable as opposed to revered. Not that if the town wanted to get rid of him they could do anything about it anyway without making a plea to Lord Noblin, the nearest noble who resided in Grathmoor castle. If even word of such treachery leaked out, many feared the little town of Pylreht would suddenly become a ghost town at the hands of Sabbath the mage and his seemingly limitless power.

Sabbath had to congratulate himself on the progress of his plan thus far. The rider had delivered both his message and the spell-scroll to Grathmoor as instructed. Sabbath's illusions were perfect. The rider truly believed his townsfolk had been massacred, and when Tucker had cast his truth spell on him, the rider was telling the truth as far as anyone could tell. The projection of the monster coming down the road that one fateful night seemed real enough. Enough to cause that fool cleric Tucker to hastily call upon the powers of the scroll spell that Sabbath had so carefully constructed over the past year, and to release the curse of wrath upon the town.

Riders from Grathmoor would inevitably arrive and find Pylreht safe and sound. And the rider, well polymorphed into a rabbit could be fun of course, but surely he had been eaten by now in the woods up north. If not, a location spell would tell soon enough and perhaps it would be prudent to personally finish the job. Sabbath had to chuckle at the difference between the real world and how it was often perceived.

The Well of Magic, or sometimes known as the weave, was nothing but pure, limitless energy that drove all life and death in the universe. Holding all of existence in perfect balance and harmony was the essential construction of all things at least in the mortal realms of material perception. Surly there are more subtle energies that a typical humanoid can' perceive readily, and as well, more intense energies are of the magnitude of gazing at a star.

If one could examine a specific point in time, say now…what has happened? You are sitting wherever you are. Whether inside or out, if you stop to listen there are background noises. You may feel your surroundings; chair, bed, couch; hear—talking, clicking of the clock, or some resonant humming, even if its your own blood flow to fill the void. The saliva in your mouth, and even if your eyes are closed, given long enough, one will hallucinate to fill that void. And yes, it wants to be filled. It is the creator beyond all of the personal divine essences that we so devoutly pray to and ask for guidance; it is whole, beyond sexual segmentation, and all pervasive. It, not so different than a child, wants to learn. Yet it learns through us.

This energy is neither good nor evil, but its use and intentions make it so. Even then, what one perceives as good could be another's purest evil and vice versa, Ad infinitum. So what is reality but the sum of our perceptions. What is good and evil but how we coincide with one's morals and values. The gods and goddesses help discern these differences, but they are more concentrations of particular energy than anything else, though they do often enough visit the mortals in various guises and manipulate events through dreams, visions, and of course their faithful servants.

Yes, Sabbath D'Alrathe had to laugh; things were going just as he planned. He would bide his time. The curse he had released was concentrated in Tucker for now. Its energies composed of strife, envy, hatred, fear, and rage. In but a few short weeks Gorden Tucker, the proud cleric of the great mother, would spread it all over Grathmoor like some kind of venereal disease, and when Sabbath came to plunder the castles vaults and claim the magical texts, and items of antiquity for himself, who could stop him? For in all probability, most of them will have murdered each other long before he arrived. Sabbath could then assume the empty throne.

2

Seth

Darkwolfe began his sword forms again; blocking high, low, slash, spin, thrust. He became a dizzying blur, his ponytail whipping, and sweat creating a sheen coat on his torso and arms. He sped up even faster; thrust, parry, slash, parry low, reverse parry high, blocking across the middle to the right, then left, curving down to the right, middle, left, and a thrust, and in a climactic feat he gave a guttural yell, "hiyaaah", and a series of red energetic darts shot out of his outstretched hand in a flurry like angry hornets. They shot out across the pond and slammed into the stump with a "whok-whok-whok-whok" and sent the top portion of the stump splintering and spinning end over end into the trees behind it.

For many moments Darkwolfe just stood there in pose, like a statue. Charlemette looked on in true awe. He did it she thought; he's actually finally done it. Granted only on a small level, but that was a start.

Charlemette never outright questioned her goddess, but when a vision came to her in her prayers foretelling of her dear friend resurrecting the Dragons, and himself becoming The Capit Draconis (head of the dragon), she was more than a little skeptical. This great band of warrior/mages hadn't walked the face of Alcyone in thousands of years. Once a powerful group who sought out imbalance and rooted out creatures of evil; back when the evil demon horde ruled Alcyone, before their banishment to the inner core. Wherein it was foretold that the core would one day become breached and the dragons would be needed again, not to capture the demons as before, but to eliminate them once and for all.

Darkwolfe sheathed his sword feeling a sense of contentment that he hadn't felt at any other time in his life, then he plopped down next to the priestess of Levanah, sitting in her perfect purple robes upon the still dew born grass. "I'm exhausted", he said laying his head in her lap. A sweet aroma of lavender and jasmine assailed his senses bringing a sense of peace and contentment. Only memories of special dreams of him and the goddess could compare.

One time when he was drifting off to sleep, he found himself standing on a hill overlooking a ruined city. All the structures were laid to waste and may bodies filled the cobbled streets. Darkwolfe had looked around and saw the many spirits drifting in the air, and all so suddenly out of the masses came a blackbird with red tipped wings. It fluttered up and sat upon his shoulder, whispering within his ear. It told of things so secret that he would not learn quite yet, until ten-years, and so he forgot upon waking.

She stroked his hair peaceably, smiling softly. "Maybe it was appropriate to choose Darkwolfe as your Mage-Name after all," she insisted. Her thoughts drifted in and out to the past few months. She had received many visions and dreams concerning her dear friend. In summation, all she could proclaim, was that he was special and planned for something big, beyond all that normal people would expect. There was danger, love, and deception at its core. There was pain and murder, misgivings and lore. But all that could be said, plain and true, was that this priestess loved this man, through and through.

"I'm but an infant compared to the *legendary* 'Darkwolfe', *The* Capit Draconis, but all babes must take their first hesitant steps I suppose." He sighed softly as if to suddenly decide to reveal more to her than he had before. "Ever since I began reading the old books in the curio shop and came across the legend of Darkwolfe, I felt as though that was my destiny. I know it sounds kind of childish, in fact I know that is what stories are written for in some ways, —for readers to associate themselves with the characters in a personal way, but...well ever since I read the book and took on the name, much to father's chagrin and everyone else's for that matter, I've become to understand things. I don't know; it's weird. I could just begin to have feelings about things. Like when I said something about Mrs. Harris being pregnant, and while she was, it wasn't by her husband and boy that that lead to all sorts of trouble. I've learned how to keep my mouth shut about what I *see* since then.

Or when it was dark and I had to relieve myself out by the gorge, and fell off the cliff. I landed without a scratch and climbed my way out. I went back the next day to look. Charlemette, it was at least a fall of 10 men onto jagged rocks, and I don't know how I could have ever climbed out without a rope. There are many cases like this. I can't explain them, it's just that I suddenly have these powers and while I don't know how to control them, they're there none-the-less." He paused to wet his lips and check her response, looking up into her loving and compassionate eyes.

"I understand," she said. " I think you should explore these powers, but always with great care. Most must study for years under the masters to get these powers, using spell components to aid them. And, certainly not taming the sword as well. Many people are going to be jealous of you and may even try to challenge and kill you. Don't let on about your powers to anyone if you can help it, but also don't hesitate to defend yourself and kill if you have to. Hesitation or thinking about the act, or letting your emotions creep in will you get you killed for sure. If you remember the legends of Darkwolfe, he had much sorrow and blood on his hands. Think of the greater scheme of things, while as a priestess surly I know that all life is precious, a hundred or even a thousand is nothing compared to all life. We reproduce, and our souls return. Those that are laid down by your hands shall find peace somewhere, someday if it is the will of the gods and goddesses. You're my dearest friend Seth, Darkwolfe,...I'll never let anyone hurt you." And she continued to herself, *for all of Alcyone may depend on it.*

* * * * *

Benjamin Dover was a surly young lad of the warrior guild. His hair was blond and cropped short like most of his training profession, with a large round nose, and dull brown eyes. He was heavy set of about 250 lead and possessed the attitude akin to an ill-tempered boar. He grumbled to himself as he made his way down the lane to Gorden Tucker's house to get healing herbs for his mother. "I'm a warrior now, not some errand boy!" he exclaimed to himself. The streets were still empty this early and only the quiet facades of store- fronts looked on amusingly.

Grathmoor wasn't a huge town by any means, but the largest within at least a hundred draws in any direction. Pylreht the nearest of the lesser towns sat to the south along the Borneck tributary of the Salmon River. Borneck itself was further south. Rockshome lay to the north, which was a quarry supplying for all of the immediate area and was run by dwarves.

One would have to cross the large wooded areas to the east or west to arrive at any settlement of decent size though there were always bands of rogues, gypsies, and elven folk who resided in the woods proper. They usually however kept to themselves, other than occasional trade. A nearby rogue encampment was suspected as things now and then have gone missing, but the last capture and behanding of the thief seems to have been an appropriate deterrent.

Grathmoor was essentially a few lanes laid out in a grid-like fashion. Most of the shops and homes of poorer folk were wedged between the main road, which ran north to south, and the west woods. The richer homes lay between the main road and the east woods under the shadow of Lord Noblin's large walled estate to the north. It was simply called the castle because of it's relative size to most of the homes in town and the fact that no one in town had ever seen a true castle in the great lands far to the south and east like Sanctuary or Thor's Hammer. In actuality it wasn't much more than a stone stronghold or manor so typical in the greater lands of Alcyone.

Benjamin Dover walked on through the empty lanes peering at the many shops for lack of anything else to do but play with the hilt of his longsword. A smithy, a bakery, linen and clothes, jewelry store, curiosity shop...the thoughts of the upstart Seth came to his mind angrily and Seth's father the town drunk. He and Seth had been more than acquaintances but less than friends before Seth took the warrior-name of Darkwolfe. No, Seth was just another fool who was even too pretentious for the weapons masters to train anymore. To think himself worthy enough to follow in the footsteps of such a mythical legend was bad enough in just picking the name, but Seth had insisted on his studies of both magic and swordsmanship and consequent withdraw of training rights in both of the town's small schools. Besides, he wasn't even of noble blood.

Benjamin continued to grumble to himself, rounding the bend and came before the open door of Tucker's house. The sign on the door read, *Gorden Tucker, Cleric to The Great Mother: healing, consultation, potions, and herbs.*

"Yah, yah." Benjamin groaned walking in, swaying his bulk as if to impress a tavern full of warriors and women with his sheer size and muscles.

Tucker was fiddling with some of his potions on a shelf muttering to himself near the door and saw Benjamin shamble in like a walking tree out of the corner of his eye. Tuck lit up a little with a broad smile, smoothed out his plain brown robes, and straightened his bony frame. "Welcome young Ben." Tuck extended his hand warmly. Ben shook back in a bored fashion wishing he could be some place else, like getting some breakfast. In fact a stack of flatcakes, shredded potatoes, a little pork links, and an egg or two sounded really good about now. Ben decided just then that The Warm Nook, an eatery by day and Tavern by night, would be his next stop *before* heading back home with his dumb errand complete.

A discrete tendril of greenish smoke swirled around each man's forearm and then was gone. Benjamin felt a slight burning sensation in his stomach, but he passed it off to his hunger. "Here's a list of stuff I need Tuck, and I ain't got all day."

"The warrior guild sure doesn't teach you youngens manners now do they?" Tuck took the list, turned to grab a little burlap bag, and went about his work of filling the order from the shelves and table nearby.

Benjamin felt an overwhelming sense of rage begin to grow within him, and he suddenly wanted to kill something or someone just then. Tucker would have been impaled by Ben's weighty sword in the snap of one's fingers, but he was protected by the very curse that he was unknowingly spreading. For obvious reasons; how effective would one be in spreading the curse if he was run through by the first person he came in contact with and spread the curse to? Sabbath was certainly not a dumb mage and had thought of this when he had created the curse. No, chances were that Benjamin would fixate on the first new bit of anger or a recent thought of bitterness and feed on it. Yes, thoughts of Seth crept into his mind and began festering like an infected wound. Becoming angry and red.

Benjamin Dover took the sack from Tucker, paid his bill, and stalked back out of the healer's shop with murder in his eyes. Patient murder, for a man did have to eat now and gain his strength for the battle to come he reasoned.

* * * * *

Darkwolfe and Charlemette hugged tightly and she kissed him on the cheek lightly. "Let's just see what happens and take things slowly okay?"

Darkwolfe wasn't sure if she meant about the powers he was trying to explain or that something else he saw in her lovely eyes, "Sure", he said and left it at that. "Lets head back to town before my dad gets any more out of sorts. I need to get the shop opened and straighten things up before the morning-draw is through and the hundreds of wild customers start lining up at the door to buy all of the treasure we horde at the famous curiosity shop of Grathmoor." He snickered and waved his arms flamboyantly.

"I don't think you've had any customers or sold anything in four fists, but you're right we should get back." Charlemette agreed and put her arm through his. "Lead the way my Lord".

They wound their way back down the trail enjoying the morning air. The smell of wild mint, the coolness under the trees, and the warning of a jay telling all that they were coming through, all helped to set the sweet stage of peacefulness. Charlemette silently thanked the goddess for the beauteous morning and felt a warm loving feeling within her being in response. They enjoyed each other's company as always, both of their hearts racing now and then when their hips rubbed together or he brushed the side of her breast with his arm.

They passed oak and maples, tulip poplars, pines and even a few willows running the length of a small creek that fed into the pond from whence they came. Soon the scents of wood smoke and morning foods assailed them and the noises of civilization came to ear. Animals apparently carrying conversations on of their own spilled forth from outdoor pins and open barnyard doors of Mr. Brady's farm. They passed Tucker's healing shop and saw Furball sitting in the windowsill eyeing them and soon stood before the bright red door of the Curiosity Shop. The paint was old and chipping but the two story wood building was in good shape. The ground floor served as the business and the second floor had a pair of rooms where "Seth" and his father lived.

"I must attend to my morning prayers and duties to the goddess, but I'll stop by later to make sure you're keeping yourself out of trouble." She winked coyly then and strode off toward the castle swaying in that wonderful way that women seem to do. The priestesses of Levanah and Priests of Sin, the lord of magic, had a temple within the castle walls, and so it was there that she went to her devotions and to converse with Javonavich, the High priest about Darkwolfe's growing powers.

Darkwolfe fondly watched her walk down the avenue and turn toward the castle. He then took a deep breath and went inside.

3

The Fool

Robert Crownover was sitting at the cashier desk half asleep when Seth walked in. His wrinkled red shirt had stains of alcohol and vomit on it and was hanging loosely over his torn, black cotton pants. He bobbed lazily on the wooden stool and then caught his pray with drunken eyes. Somehow Seth had become the target of his father's misery and anger after his mother's death. Robert braced himself on the counter barely before he toppled over and fell to the wooden floor grunting with satisfaction as if he had finally accomplished some long forgotten goal.

Seth examined the room in an instant as had become his customary warrior instinct. To the left was a counter, behind the counter was his father having a taste of dirt and pine as he lay face down, and behind him was a wall rack filled with old axes, and swords and pole arms. Straight ahead was an isle leading straight to a stair well, which ran both upstairs to the living quarters and down to the basement where cases of old garbage, which was typically sold as premium stuff, was stored. To the right were many free standing shelves lined in isles of various items on displays. Closest were vases, and in the second row were smaller bits of antiquity, and far against the wall were cloaks and various pieces of clothing of multiple colors and origins.

"Where in… the hhhhell…," Robert Crownover began, and then had to steady himself on the counter and collect himself rising to his feet.

Seth waited patiently and came in and closed the door. He took of his gear and hung it on a rack that was concealed around the corner of the door, so no buyers would notice his stuff and mistakenly try to buy his clothes or sword and belt. Seth scanned the room routinely and came around the corner of the cashier's counter to face his dad.

"Why don't you go lie down dad, I can..," that was as far as he got.

Robert swung an arm at him and fell to the floor with a pathetic thud. No one moved for a good amount of time, in fact Seth started to daydream about his training this morning, when his father began to moan and crawl around the counter. Seth just let him. Hell, what was he supposed to do? Robert kept crawling as if possessed by some purpose and headed towards the front door.

Seth just watched. These things have happened before he told himself with complete assurance. Sure, dad would dredge around the shop for maybe an hour at tops creating somewhat of a mess and knocking things over, and then eventually, he would drag the old man up to bed. He would sleep most of the afternoon and leave Seth in peace to run the store. Which as a matter of fact, no one ever really came into, and gave Seth more than ample time to study the books on the shelves by the counter and practice with the latest weapons on the rack. He had gotten quite good with the various weapons and learned more from the books than most pupils of any class had learned in a lifetime.

Seth had never contemplated why these "useful" books happened to be here at his disposal. In fact periodically High Priest Javonavich would drop some off discretely knowing Seth's inquisitive nature would teach him what he wanted. This allowed the priest to guide the young man's development without getting directly involved. As well, Charlemette was close to the boy and helped to counsel him as an experienced priestess and friend.

Robert Crownover would wake up some time during the afternoon, profusely apologizing for his behavior, say how much he missed their mother and truly loved him, and then head down to the tavern to get thoroughly drunk and start the process all over again. A part of Seth just said screw it, let the old man wander out into the street and never come back. He loved him deeply and he held on to the memories of how wonderful things were when mom was still around, but a part of himself thought about the processes of nature. To some degree, if a member of a flock or group became handicapped, the rest of the group would leave him to die. This may seem cruel, but it actually made the group as a whole stronger. We are human after all and not animals in the basic sense, he thought. Shouldn't we show compassion for even our weak, and elderly? While these thoughts did linger in Seth's mind, a part of him was still purely naïve and thought that his dad should be sheltered and cared for no matter how much of a burden he became to society.

Seth's father once again gained his footing and learned against the doorframe. He rubbed his eyes as if to clear them. He coughed up some phlegm then and desperately flung the door wide and sent a wad of spit flying out into the street. "Hell boy, I think I need a drink." Without further adieu he slammed the door and headed out to The Warm Nook for maybe some warm wine to clear his head.

Sure. See- ya. Have a nice trip, see you next fall, and all that good stuff. It still just seemed hard for him to be so callous as his rational intelligence told him to be; his emotional self, still had a voice, and he wasn't sure how to handle these mixed signals for he found both to be mutually profitable to his well being. Somehow things just didn't seem to get as far as all that, and in fact got miserably worse.

* * * * *

The Warm Nook was a cozy little tavern, and appeared as if cast from the tavern-mold where perhaps all divine such constructs were spawn, for many taverns of its kind were scattered throughout the western stretches of Alcyone. It was a large rectangular room of old dark wood.

It was considered clean and rather bright compared to some of the wreaking dark filled caves that abounded in several of the larger towns and cities. Sizeable rectangular and circular tables were orderly lined. Straight-backed chairs were thrust beneath them like temple pillars, and even a couple of daisies were thrust in cobalt blue cups for added frill and gaiety.

While in good order, the beer and wine stains as well as pervasive lingering of old smoke made it perfectly clear that yes this was in fact a tavern where many spent their days and nights dulling the pain and hardships of life, or celebrating for any gods-given reason. The room at present was mostly empty at the time save for a large circular table right in the center of the establishment where sat Benjamin Dover and several of his warrior cronies who were presently indulging in a fine breakfast.

Ben was hunched over at the moment shoving food down his throat with both hands. The burlap bag he had gotten from Tucker sat on the table to his left. The longer the meal continued, the more Ben thought that hunting down Seth at The Curiosity Shop and killing him before he went home seemed like a good idea. Already the curse, as if a conscious being, was bored and anxious to spread its strife and bathe in the blood of murder. In fact it would have smiled had it the lips when John bumped feet with Ben under the table and the tendrils of green smoky fingers jumped into his being.

John was usually a rather even-tempered young man. He wasn't particularly strong or as stoic perhaps as Ben, but John was known for having good judgement and reasoning. In fact he dressed rather conservatively in plain brown leggings, and tan shirt. His eyes were likewise bark-brown, and his curly brown hair was shoulder length with the luster of tilled earth. In fact he was rather plain and Ben often took delight in calling him sir dirt clod. When he suddenly started getting the notion to stick his fork in Ben's eye, it was a rather remarkable show of will to restrain himself.

Sally Silkwood, a rather fine looking woman though perhaps a few pounds overweight, came over to their table to fill their glasses with water. The morning was quiet and so Sally went out of her way to keep checking on the men's table, more to keep herself awake through her flirting than to be overly courteous as wife to the proprietor. Ben was far from her most favorite patron because of his ill begotten manners. John was somewhat of a gentleman and the other two; well they were something all together different.

Will and Jacob were both competitors for her flirtatious affections, while also making a poor attempt at being discrete to keep her husband from braining the pair. Both wore vests of red and black, black cotton trousers, and high boots. In fact they even had matching hats sporting frilly feathers and studded bands. The twins were handsome in both appearance and their tongues, and that's just how Sally liked her young men. In fact she even fantasized taking the two to bed, but knowing Yertick's anger and the intent of his cruel axe he had hidden behind the bar, she thought her flirting even on the dangerous side, but anymore would probably get the lot of them killed.

Sally poured Ben's glass coming just inches from his shoulder. Next she came around to Will's glass. She might have escaped the curse for some time yet, but since here eyes were on the twins and not on where she was going, she bumped into Will's leg as she was filling his glass. The green smoky fingers coursed up her leg and caressed her sickeningly. She considered herself a lover and not a killer, so there was no immediate effect. However as she came around to the twins, her ample breasts became the conduit as she was so often fond of accidentally brushing them against the twins in teasing delight.

Yertick was no fool and observed these vile events before. It certainly made him a bit angry, but he thought it at least somewhat useful that his wife was able to get these men to spend their coin here. As some reassuring act to him, Sally came back toward the kitchen and gave him a wet kiss and smiled. She then headed back toward the rear of the building to see her son Jason off for his delivery rounds. Once the curse had settled in, Yertick had second thoughts on slaying the little bastards and went for his great axe.

In the rear of the building, Sally saw that her son was about to head off without the cheese that he was suppose to deliver along with the kegs of beer to the castle. "Jason, here don't forget the cheese. You know how delighted they are for our new recipe. Lord Noblin himself has sent a special request this time." She took the large block out to the wagon and set in the back with the rest of the delivery items.

"I almost did, sorry." He said sheepishly, flipping his long blond hair out of his icy blue eyes. He jumped up on the flat board, which served as the driver's seat and got ready to head out. He grabbed the reins and cooed quietly to the old mare Betsy.

"No problem luv, best ye get going now. You've got half the town to get to and the castle before mid-draw." She smiled pleasantly, but noticed an irritable fit of anger coming on for her son almost forgetting the cheese. As he began to pull the horse drawn cart away she tapped his leg farewell amidst a swirl of delighted green smoke.

* * * * *

The Curio shop fell into a blissful peace after Seth's dad had gone off to find a morning drink. Probably down to The Warm Nook, Seth thought. Chances were that Yertick would sell the old man some wine against common sense to make some coin; Robert had spent more than one day and evening passed out in one of the corners. Seth took the opportunity to look through the books he loved so much and settled onto the stool behind the counter.

Amidst the stacks, one book stood out in particular. It had a dark blue binding and appeared to be very old. Seth knew that this book wasn't here yesterday when he was working, but he had long since given up trying to discern the origin of all these wonderful books and just chalked it up to luck, good fortune, or even magic which of course he was so fond of. There was no title on the book, so Seth opened it up to the first page and stared upon a map.

It was a map of this exact area. It showed the forests and rivers that he was so familiar with, Grathmoor itself, and all of the surrounding towns, but one feature in particular caught his eye. Off across the eastern stretch of woods near the two horns sat what was labeled as the Dragon Temple. Seth had never heard of such a temple, but he did know that occasionally some of the local priests would make the trek to the holy horns of Levanah and Sin. These twin peaks thrust high above the forest floor and from afar looked like great beastly horns. Many of the Gods and Goddesses were depicted with horns as a sign of the moon and immortality, but Levanah of illusion and Sin of magic had particular affinity with this body and long ago this structure was erected to their glory.

"Hmmm..." Darkwolfe muttered. he flipped the page and began reading.

Long ago all the gods and goddesses had bound together to create such a place of paradise unlike it anywhere in the universe. Eight shining stars, eight systems of orbiting bodies and eight planets inhabited by the most wonderful creatures that the gods and goddesses had ever put forth. These planets were embodied with the spirit of the great goddess and called the eight sisters, or Pleides; whereon the seed of the great father spilled forth and there grew all manner of trees and beasts and human-kinds: Humans, and elves, dwarves and great reptilian beings called dragons, bears, and lions, and wolves, and cats, evil demons, snake-beasts, whales, seals, and.... All of existence was a balance of dark and light, evil and good, but to these beings were given the rights to choose for their rewards or misfortune as the fates would decree. For as they were set forth at the beginning, forever were they bound to reincarnate again and again until the end of time. To learn and evolve and perhaps become gods themselves one day. One time a woman then a man, sometimes committing terrible acts for selfish purposes and others good, but as the karmic law was set in place, everything came back to those who cast them forth three fold; for ill or for worse they would learn through their many lives and suffer. The Gods and Goddesses learn also, for living vicariously through these many life forms they gathered unto themselves great knowledge, and so all evolved unto total purity and bliss through opposites.

Darkwolfe pondered all this and marveled at how there were other worlds out there somewhere. It all just seemed so huge. Hell he hadn't even seen much more of Alcyone than this little tiny corner, and there were many such places...out there somewhere. It was just too huge, but he promised himself not to let this precious little book go and to study these deep words, meditating on them and hopefully to eventually come to some greater understanding of what all of this meant.

He flipped through the pages and became even more delighted. The next section appeared to be some kind of manual at arms. There were skillfully drawn pictures and descriptions of how to fight bare handed and these moves were strung together into set dances called *katas.* Further back there were similar forms with weapons of various kinds. Past that near the end was a little section, wherein was a little treatise on magic and some spells; many of which he had never seen or heard of before, but looked fantastic. His heart raced with excitement and he couldn't wait to start learning. The bell at the door jangled just then, and as an odd looking man in mix-matched clothing came in smiling, Seth slammed the book shut and hid it under the counter guiltily.

"Good morning fine lord, what may I do for you this glorious of days," Seth offered.

"Well met, I think I'll poke around a bit." He replied through his grin and began poking around the middle self where all of the little nik-naks were placed. "Oh,..Hmmm, yes I see.." he went on conversing with himself.

Seth was becoming interested in this odd gentleman, seeing his head bobbing about and his jester-like cloths flopping about as he moved.

"Quite a plethora of, er…stuff you got here young man." He made his way around to the clothing rack and held a brazier up to his chest. "Ok, this will do." As he made his way back around to the counter Seth could see that he had his arms full of various items and clothing. He plopped them down on the counter and continued beaming forth his pearly smile and looked about happily at the weapons on the wall behind the counter.

"Alright sir, lets see here. One old and quite lovely vase, fine choice I might add. A genie lamp, minus one genie. A witch's broom, and walnut wand. A fine bit of string, and one brazier. That'll be 30 Silver sir." Seth concluded and grabbed a little wooden box to put the things in.

The gentleman smiled and leaned forth on the counter. "Well I don't got any silver, but perhaps we might make a trade." With that he brought forth a deck of cards and placed them on the counter.

"A deck of cards," Seth scoffed, " that wouldn't even get you the brazier." He leaned back with arms crossed ready to do some haggling. He was much practiced at it and figured he could get much more out of this man.

"Oh these aren't just any old cards my man, these are magic cards of divination mind you." He shuffled the deck methodically and with expert hands, "here I'll show you." He finished mixing up the cards and placed them before young Darkwolfe. "You gust say a few simple words, *Show me the path ahead,* tap the top of the deck three times and presto one bona fide telling of the future. Of course interpreting what the bloody things mean takes some practice, but I'll leave that portion of the deal up to you."

Seth was a little leery of this strange man, but was always somewhat of a sucker when it came to dealing with magic items. It set his blood afire and head within the clouds. How could he resist? "Show me the path ahead," he spoke and tapped the cards three times. For a brief instant nothing appeared to happen, and Seth looked to the man expectantly. He smiled back and looked down at the deck. Then Seth felt it, that drawing sensation around his solar plexus, between his ribs and below his sternum; that pull of magic that he had grown to understand and love.

The cards then began shuffling themselves and three cards flew above the deck and spun about in a dizzying whirlwind. Seth could see the cards and was disappointed to see that they were blank, and as they settled down before him on the counter in a line, the first one became hazy and slowly brought forth a picture. First it was faint and hard to see any detail, but after a few seconds it became quite clear and awe-inspiring.

It read *The Seeker* and showed a young man in robes climbing a mountain with an identical mountain in the background. The sky was dark and misty, and the man held aloft a lantern to better see.

He looked to the second card, and the picture began to materialize before his eyes. It said *Strife* and displayed a field of war where many men and beasts were killing each other with sword and magic alike; next to the field was a creek bed filled with blood.

The last card then materialized as *The Charioteer*. There was a man in glistening plate armor with his faceplate down to hide his identity. On his breast was a large yellow snake in the shape of a circle with its tail in its mouth, set on a red shield background. In his hands were the reins of some type and in the background were many demonic beasts.

Seth didn't have a clue to what any of this stuff meant, and looked to the jester for help. "I can't help you lad, only time and familiarity with the powers of the cards can help you, but don't forget this first reading, it is always the most important. Now do we have a deal or what?"

"Sure Seth offered and quickly filled the box and handed it to the man before he decided to change his mind and keep these valuable cards after all."

With his typical smile that Seth had come accustomed to in this short little time, the man took the box and headed for the door. "Just a tip, my young friend, you may want to draw a card each morning and meditate upon it during the day. The particular powers of the card will show itself to you, sometimes to your much discomfort, but it will make future readings make more sense, and allow you to understand the interactions of these energies when you draw these three card readings. Just tap the deck each morning once to get the daily card and do so until you have learned the way. Farewell now."

"Wait," Seth yelled, "who are you?"

"Oh," he smiled, "just a fool."

4

A Taste for Death

Yertick hefted his axe angrily and made his way around the bar and toward the table of young fighters. His gait and demeanor, while certainly malicious in nature, was more of a man going to slaughter a beast for feast than one to commit warm blooded murder. The men were engaged at that moment in a heated discussion about that impudent little snot Seth. The stirrings were coming to a head in that soon the foursome were going to run over there and slaughter both Seth and his father for being such a loser and letting his son become such an idiot.

Neb the older of the twins by no more than 12 breaths met only quick oblivion as Yertick's axe spit his head in two and became lodged in bone somewhere around his sternum and vertebrae. The blood, brain, and bone fragments showered the other three at the table as if in some evil after meal rite. It left them stunned long enough for Yertick to yank his axe free with a yank and barbaric grunt and for Sally to issue forth a wail of despair to rival any undead queen.

Then steel was drawn as the three well-practiced swordsmen unleashed their blades and launched themselves at the burly proprietor with unbridled fury. John withdrew to avoid a mighty sideswipe of the axe and Niles likewise dove out of the wide arc to save his sword arm. Following the big swing, Ben hurled himself across the table and impaled Yertick's left shoulder with an arms length of steel. Yertick was able to push Ben back and sent him tumbling off the table, but it gave the other two the time and opening they needed and while John stuck his blade under Yertick's ribs and into his heart, Niles stuck his blade clean through his neck.

Suddenly Sally was tackling John to the ground and trying to pry out his eyes while screaming "No, No, No," over and over again. John and Niles had perhaps briefly considered restraining her. However, Ben had a different plan. He hefted the fallen axe, dripping with brain and blood, and hacked it into the stooping neck of the hysterical woman. Her head cartwheeled over, rolled in a lopsided fashion across the floor, and hit the bar with a dull thud; a bloody trail was left in its wake.

"Uuh, gross," John wailed beneath a river of blood and the headless corpse. He hefted it off and came up to his knees. He knew he'd remember that look of wild abandon on Ben's face for the rest of his life. He just didn't know that the rest of his life consisted of less than an afternoon

* * * * *

Jason made several stops on the way to the castle delivering cheese, smoked meats, and small beer kegs to those individuals who liked to have some on hand and not have to run over to The Warm Nook every time they had the desire for a sip of ale. He ran down his father's list making good time. It was methodical work, which became boring occasionally, but he did at least enjoy meeting and speaking with all the important people of the town. He even got to shake Captain Emory's hand last time he was up at the castle. He was courteous, said yes sir or ma'am, and shook hands with each person in a business-like fashion as his father had instructed him to do. He didn't have a contract or receipt like large delivery systems did like his father had spoken of in the big cities, but he said a handshake was just as good in a town this size.

By the time he rode up to the guards, and they waved him through to begin unloading in the courtyard, he had passed the curse on to no less than nine individuals throughout Grathmoor. Like a brushfire during midsummer, the curse was soon out of control; souls slipping swiftly on their way drew Death's gaze curiously and he looked upon the small town with growing interest.

* * * * *

Ben, Niles, and John hastily made their way out into the street and left The Warm Nook to the dead couple within. Now that the bloodletting had begun in earnest, the three men were trembling with their eagerness to continue, and Seth and his father were at the top of their list. Much to their delight, Robert Crownover was stumbling toward the trio in the middle of the street.

"Hiya there boys," Robert began running his hand through his hair before extending it to shake Nile's hand, "how about a drink for an old man a little low on coin these days?"

In a flash of sunlight reflecting off steel, Niles had severed his hand at the wrist. Robert half screamed half moaned, holding his bleeding wrist with his now, only hand. John took off his right leg at the knee. Robert fell to the street, wailing full force now and bleeding from two severed limbs. Ben stood over him, axe raised mightily toward the heavens, and claimed his second head of the morning.

* * * * *

Randolph Cummings was enjoying his breakfast now that it was quiet. This was good cheese that Yertick's boy Jason had brought by earlier. His nagging wife and screaming children had disturbed his morning meal and so he had methodically broken all of their necks. Yes, now it was quiet and he could enjoy his cheese.

* * * * *

Kara Fisher held a large pairing knife in her had. It was dripping a steady stream of blood to the wood planking of her bedroom with a *splat, splat, splat.* In her other had were a pair of bloody round objects. Upon closer examination one would realize that they were in fact someone's testicles. One needn't be a mage-master to figure out that they came from the groaning man on the floor lying in a growing puddle of red. "That's the last time you cheat on me," she whispered. At first her impulse was to slit his throat next, but then changed her mind. Watching him slowly bleed to death and suffer would be much more fun.

* * * * *

Before Jason had even finished unloading the cart, he enthusiastically shook hands with several guards including the great Captain Emory. Emory was a patient and goodly man, but Jason had irritated him on several occasions when he made his deliveries to the castle. With their hands still grasped and shaking, Captain Emory thrust his jeweled dagger deep into his chest. Many of his men applauded and cheered him on.

While not all of his men had been curse laden as of yet, none were brave enough to speak up against killing the boy. In fact they even yelled with greater fervor than some of the cursed when Emory shouted, "Let no mage within these castle walls live to see another day!!!" There was a chorus of yells and drawn weapons and then a storming of the castle began.

Javonavich could feel the presence of the curse, and it was very near. Both he and Charlemette twisted their heads like dogs to hear better when the commotion arose from the courtyard. "Go now," the high priest insisted, "out the back. Take yourself and Seth, and get on to the temple at the horns this day." He hugged her briefly and dragged her toward the back entrance to the castle. "May the God and Goddess bless you and guide you."

"And you," she said, and darted out into the trees not looking back.

* * * * *

Seth had wrapped the pack of cards up in a red and black silk scarf and respectfully put them in one of his pouches. He was intrigued about the appearance of this wonderful blue book and the fool with the cards. He came to a conclusion just then and took a moment to consider how he was going to deal with his father. He knew he had to get out of here. Out of this town. Away from this crazy shop, and from his drunken father. He had to go to the temple marked on the map in the book. But did it really exist? He had to believe it did. It just had too.

Should he tell his dad or just leave? He figured that it didn't really matter, and decided to not bother revealing anything to him; it would just make matters worse. What about Charlemette? Could he leave his only friend? If she was a true friend she would understand. He doubted he could talk her into coming, but he would try his best charm and see what happened. Like an avalanche that slowly shifts, building momentum, and then tearing down half a mountain, Darkwolfe was suddenly possessed to just go. He had to leave, and leave right now!

He raced up the stairs into his room and grabbed a large pack he often used when he went hiking in the woods. He shoved a spare shirt and trousers, a handful of throwing daggers, half a loaf of old bread, a small block of cheese, a water skin, and his blue book into the sack. "Good enough." He raced back down the steps.

Just as he reached the ground floor, facing the front door, it flew open with a loud bang, and framed therein stood Benjamin Dover. In one hand was a large battle-axe, dripping with blood and gore. In the other, dangling by a lock of matted hair, was his father's head. For a brief instant, his father's dead eyes met his.

* * * * *

Starsender, the resident mage-master of Grathmoor castle, was in mid lesson explaining to his five present students the intricacies of basic casting when there arose the great yelling of Captain Emory and his warrior guardsmen. All six of them hurried over to the balcony and peered out just as Emory was claiming death to all mages this day. It would have been a bit humorous if not for the severity of the situation, and Starsender quickly began issuing orders.

"Feather run hence and tell Lord Noblin what his guards are about. Jasper and Shroom grab the wands from the storeroom. You other two come with me. We need to give these louts something to think about before they get past the entrance hall. Now. Move." He raced off as the young mages scurried like mice. Starsender began casting as he walked, creating a shield around him, his burgundy robes fluttering about as if racing into a tempest wind.

Starsender and his two apprentices were soon at the top of the stairs that overlooked the entrance hall. Shouts were becoming louder beyond the closed front double doors. The entrance hall was spacious, lined on both sides with tall pillar-like statues carved into the likeness of various gods and goddesses. Levanah, Sin, Hermes the god of communication and travel adorned with winged feet, Vesta the virgin goddess in a demure robe, Aries the god of war with helm/shield and spear, and many more. Before the soldiers came in, Starsender quickly cast another spell. It was a ward often used to block doors and other portals. Upon completion of his casting, a shimmering veil settled over the doorway and then disappeared.

"Now when they come in, just keep casting your attack darts. It is a simple spell that you should be able to cast many times before exhausting your powers. Don't waste your energy on anything more complicated, because it may go awry—you are not use to real combat and may lose your concentration when someone is actually trying to kill you. When you are empty and can cast no more, run back to the lecture hall and await my further orders." There was a pause as they both stood there stupefied. "Do you understand?" He barked.

"Yes master!" they both yelled in unison.

There was a heavy thud and the double doors flew open and slammed into the walls. There was a horde of angry and well-armed soldiers on the other side, and they didn't appear to notice the mages standing up on the balcony. Then a pair of soldiers rushed in and the magical barrier flared into life. There was a flash of smoke and fire and the two soldiers blasted apart into burning limbs and torsos scattering about the entrance hall.

All eyes found the mages then and a flurry of crossbow bolts raced toward them. Several bounced off Starsender's shield harmlessly. One of the apprentices was smart enough to hide behind it. The other took a bolt in the cheek, two in his chest, and one stuck right through his left arm. He staggered backward and crashed into the wall. A fine painting fell off the wall as he collapsed to the floor, as if to bury him in some amount of grace befitting a mage.

The other pair of mages came rushing up with several wands each.

A dozen or so soldiers rushed in clanking in their armor. They took up positions behind the many columns to hopefully help block direct hits from various magical fire. The first apprentice then let loose a couple of attack darts blasting into one of the soldiers. It split apart his armor and did some damage, but the soldier grunted painfully and ducked behind the statue of Aries.

Starsender said, "Use the wands and keep them pinned down while I try and ruin their day." He immediately began casting again. The two wand bearers opened up with a virtual storm of magical darts buzzing down upon the soldiers, but most of them were merely taking chunks out of the statues and filling the foyer with a cloud of dust and flying debris.

Another round of crossbow fire took out one of the wand bearers with a gurgle and spray of blood as his throat was torn apart.

Captain emery had taken a man with him and come in through the kitchen door. There was a side stairwell to the second floor and it was here that he and his sergeant emerged to see Starsender and his apprentices raining terror down upon his men. The sergeant let fly a throwing axe, which lodged in the head of the second wand wielder with a loud bone splitting crack. Starsender was lost in his incantation, just as his cloud of noxious gas erupted in the entrance hall with a billowing stink, Emory impaled him with his broad sword triumphantly.

From the back hall, which led to Lord Noblin's chambers and the temples main access, came another host of men, priests, and priestesses. High priest Javonavich summoned a sphere of lightning. It erupted between Captain Emory and Sergeant Wren cooking them within their armor to a blackened, sizzling and unrecognizable lump of flesh and metal.

High priestess Amber looked down upon the many men choking within the hall. She looked back to Lord Noblin in his half-strapped on armor and pained look of confusion. "What is your wish my Lord?"

"Kill them. I don't know what is going on around here, but I don't dare take the risk of keeping these crazed men around stirring up trouble. They've apparently just seen their two leaders killed and still they come on. No, something else is afoot here. Kill them and then we will get to the bottom of this."

High Priestess Amber then summoned forth the magic from her goddess in a whirl of purple bouncing lights. They alighted on several of the statues below. Immediately they came to life in a rumbling fury of stone and deified wrath and began ripping the soldiers into nothing more than stew meat.

* * * * *

Darkwolfe was shocked beyond all belief. In that blazing moment as time itself stood still, many thoughts raced through his shock-enthralled essence. What happened? Did father attack Ben? Was Ben out of his mind? Why in all hell did Ben have Yertick's axe? Yertick wouldn't let anyone touch his axe unless...he was dead! Then Darkwolfe became very agitated. Something was very wrong. Sure his father was at this time gone to this world, and unless he didn't act and think quickly he'd be hanging out with his dead father much sooner than he had anticipated. He wasn't particularly afraid of death in itself, but he was mad. If he died now, he'd never get the chance to find all the answers he was just now starting to get some understanding of. No way, he wasn't going to die today.

He slowly slid his hand into the bag and reached for a couple of his throwing daggers. "What are you about Ben?"

"About," he laughed, "death of course." He flung Robert's lifeless head into one of the stacked free standing shelves and knocked a couple of vases to the floor with a couple of cracking pottery emanations. Ben hefted the axe and took a few steps into the room. Niles and John were falling in behind him brandishing swords.

Darkwolfe finally grasped a couple of daggers. He dropped the bag shifted a dagger to each hand and let fly. His main hand dagger sank into Ben's right thigh to the bone, but the left went high and clanked off the doorframe. It wasn't much in terms of damage, but it slowed Ben enough for Darkwolfe to try and gather his magical essence for a spell. He had done it in the glade, but now he was under true duress. Either he cast this spell, or he died. This sort of motivation worked and soon the fiery magma flowed and his attack darts sprang forth from his outstretched hand.

Ben saw it coming and dropped to the floor, dislodging the dagger in his leg in the process. The two darts shot toward where Ben's head had been, and met Niles' instead. His face caved in and one eye popped out onto the floor. He gasped with a dull hollow sound, and fell back into

John; the both of them tumbled down the three wooden steps onto the dirt street. John was slightly dazed. Niles was quite dead.

Darkwolfe then hopped around the corner and pulled a spear off the weapons rack on the wall. Thankfully he brought it around in time to keep the advancing Ben at bay. Ben slashed once, then twice, and broke the spear in two on the third swipe. "Shit," Darkwolfe yelped, threw the remaining portion of the spear at him and pulled a dull scimitar off the wall next.

John was then standing in the doorway with glowing embers of rage in his eyes. Darkwolfe knew he was in trouble.

Benjamin smashed the counter with a wild swing; splinters and glass flew everywhere. John thought he'd watch a bit and judge his quarry before plunging into the fray. Ben smashed again, Darkwolfe ducked under it and came pouncing back up and slashed with an over hand swing into his collar bone. It broke the bone with wonderful ease, but because of its bluntness didn't sink in and totally disable the enraged giant as he had hoped. A strong backhand sent Seth tumbling back into the weapons rack and collapsed the entire contraption of wood and weapons to slam him to the ground defenseless.

"Time to die fool..." Ben issued forth through infusing pain from his arm. He stopped as a flare of light caught his attention and looked toward the doorway. A blast of lightning issued forth from a hole in John's chest, raced across the room and destroyed a good portion of the stairwell. A blink later Charlemette walked in with her golden hair and purple robes. She was pissed and planned on killing the next thing she laid eyes on.

"What are you doing here woman?" Ben managed, unsure of what else to say or do. Before she had a chance to reply, Ben's eyes went wide and he fell back against the counter, hit the wall after a step, and tumbled out into the aisle and collapsed to the floor on his back. A short sword was driven to the hilt and sticking out of his stomach.

Charlemette rushed over to the counter. Darkwolfe was wiggling carefully to extricate himself from the stack of weapons without furthering his injuries. Already a spear tip had driven into his calf and bled painfully. Char helped him up and they hugged.

"Char I don't know what's going on around here, but all hell is breaking loose. I'm getting out of town right now, will you go with me?" he realized he forgot the charming part and smiled weakly.

"Sure, where do you want to go."

"Well, er ah," he thought to lie to her, but couldn't. He just cared about her too much, and she was his only friend, so he laid it all out on the line. "I found this book, and there was a map that showed this place up by The Horns, and there is this temple, and I just need to go there because I think maybe they can help me, or teach me, or both..."

"Alright, but we better leave now. There's even fighting up at the castle. You're right something weird is going on, and if this temple you speak of is real, maybe they can help us."

He was a little perplexed by the ease of this transaction. Wasn't he supposed to coerce her into going or beg her or something along those lines? Darkwolfe limped around the counter to retrieve his bag. His leg was bleeding more than he thought, and he was starting to feel lightheaded.

"Hold still," Charlemette begged, "let me heal you, or we're not going to even get out the door let alone to this temple of yours." She prayed softly to her goddess. There was a dull light of green and a tingling sensation in his leg. When the light was gone his leg was totally healed, and he jumped to getting his pack and sword belt strapped on. A moment later they were gone from the town and the screams of its dying.

5

More Unknowns

The two men lounged around the campfire much at ease. They figured they were somewhere east of Grathmoor as far as the map they had could indicate. One was a strong soldiery type, but his tunic held the markings of The Terra Paladins and indicated that he was much more than some plain warrior. His hair was black like night itself and he sported a thinly trimmed and neat beard. His face was stern and chiseled through many years of devotion to his cause. Firelight flickered in eyes that held some distant pain in their brown swirling depths.

The other man sported Black studded leather armor though most of it lay at his side. He was cat-like in his grace even though he merely sat idly. One might mark him as an assassin or rogue but with the two classes one could hardly tell or distinguish the two until often enough it was far too late. In terms of their companionship, this did seem an unlikely pair. The Cat's features were slim, yet hardened like any true feline, and a mischievous grin that he now sported could be counted on often enough for the permanent creases in the man's facial expression.

"Come now Sir Gedrick, do you really think this temple really exists?" He leaned forward with a long stick and picked at the fire lazily.

The paladin thought for a minute, "You know my superiors wouldn't have sent us off many fists into these untamed lands on foot on a wild goose chase regardless of what you've done Cat."

"Sure , sure, but doesn't curiosity get the better of you some times, eh?"

"You know what happens to curiosity and the cat now don't you." The paladin replied in his deep baritone voice. "Perhaps it all seems pretty strange I must agree but they must have some motive that we don't know just yet."

Cat stood up then and walked around the campfire restlessly. "I know you probably don't think much of me for trying to steal the orders treasure, but hey we all have to make a living, even if you can't understand my thoughts on the matter. I know my penance was either to rot in a jail until I was of a ripe old age, or accept their spell of servitude, but why exactly are you here I wonder?" He came to a stop in his pacing and looked down on the paladin.

Sir Gedrick was slow in responding. "A girl..." he hesitated.

"I knew it was a girl," Cat cried in glee for the merriment of such intrigue. "You're not some order of celibates are you?" he asked scornfully.

"No, nothing like that." He replied quickly.

"Well, like what?

"I'd rather not get into it exactly." Sir Gedrick choked back.

"Oh come now, you've got my curiosity going now. What was it, some forbidden fruit perhaps, or young lass? Hmmm?"

"No definitely not some little girl, I would never even dream of such a thing."

"Well pray tell fine warrior, tell Cat your sorrows. 'Tis only fair. Seeing how you know my story. If we are to travel together, the least you can do is be forthcoming."

"Fine, it was a particular girl. It was the High General's daughter in fact. Sure she was young, but of age for courting. We went a little too fast, and when the maids found us lying together, I was lucky I wasn't killed or thrown in the dungeons or something. The girl tried to save herself from her father's wrath and said I forced myself on her.

Thankfully the mage-master said she was lying, but for penance I was sent on the mission to deliver a message to the temple. It just so happens to be a temple that no one has ever heard of and they stuck you in a servitude spell to accompany me instead of letting you rot. Fine, so be it, I've had worse assignments, but don't think of leaving or.."

"Or attacking you or anything else of an act of harm, blah-blah-blah-blah-blah; yah I've heard it all a hundred times. If I go against my vows I die. If I run off and abandon you I die. If I'm away from your side for too long I die. If by some miracle we come back from this crazy mission and the council sees my actions as favorable, they will lift the servitude. I know the deal. But beyond that, what do you really make of all this. It does seem a little cloak and dagger to me don't you think?" The Cat began circling the fire again

"Perhaps, we should get to the horns in a couple of days, and then we'll know for sure. If nothing is there, we turn back and all we've wasted is a little adventure across the boring parts of Alcyone and got to camp out a little. Trust me things could definitely be worse.

Charlemette and Darkwolfe had overheard the exchange between the two men and motioned to each other quietly from the trees. Charlemette seemed intent on approaching the men by the insistent pointing of her finger toward the campfire, and Darkwolfe thought the exact opposite as he kept pointing off in the other direction. The stubborn gaze in her eyes told him that she wasn't about to give in, and he finally acquiesced to her will nodding okay. They both made extra noise rustling the bushes to alert the men as they slowly approached their fire.

Sir Gedrick Jumped to his feet and assumed a wide footed stance staring off into the trees where the noise had come from thrusting forth his huge two handed sword. Cat crouched low into the shadows with a short sword in one hand and a dagger in the other. They both stood motionless as Char and Darkwolfe emerged from the woods into the tiny clearing where the campsite sat. Darkwolfe held both hands up and open for all to see and said, "Good evening sires and well met." Charlemette did likewise standing next to her friend, but ready to cast a spell if the two meant any trouble. She had been told to look for a couple of travelers, a paladin and an assassin, but one could never be too careful in the East Woods of Grathmoor.

"Who are you and what are you about," questioned Sir Gedrick, still holding his pose and ready to attack.

"We are travelers from Grathmoor, heading east to…the two horns, and only wish to share the fire if you would so humbly welcome our company." Darkwolfe offered.

"Fine, come about." Sir Gedrick insisted without moving from his stance a bit. Darkwolfe and Charlemette came closer into the firelight and sat near the fire boldly as if these two men weren't prepared to rip them asunder in mere misunderstandings or evilness alike.

Darkwolfe undid his sword belt and laid it away from himself as a show of peace and the two warmed their hands by the fire. "How came you two to these parts? "Char inquired, smoothing out her robes comfortably and beaming forth her most hearty yet information seeking smile. Her eyes quickly took in the nature of the two, and testing odds, these were the two she had been told about by High Priest Javonavich and Lady Amber.

"Just a little hunting, that's all," Cat offered and sat across the fire from the two new strangers next to Sir Gedrick who also lay down his sword and took a seat to offer peace and conversation.

"I have hunted here often," Darkwolfe added, "these are fine woods with a bounty of deer to be had, just beware the snake-beasts for they are likely drawn by blood and have been known to take a man down unaware while he was busy skinning his kill."

"True enough," Sir Gedrick offered, and while coming to his knee, offered his had in friendship. "I am Sir Gedrick of the Terra Paladins from Thor's Hammer, it is a pleasure to share my fire."

Darkwolfe grasped it warmly, as if in an instant bonding with the man, he chuckled merrily, " If you'd like I can show you some of the good hunting spots about these parts, you men have traveled far just to collect a little meat haven't you?"

Cat swayed gently with the fire, the connection with his fire goddess (Bastet) flowed within him and spoke softly within his mind that the strangers were peaceful and able to be trusted. In that regards he considered, "Hi I'm Cat, nice to meet you." He extended his hand with ready grin in Charlemette's direction and scooted a little nearer.

Char accepted the hand and met his gaze levelly, insinuating that she wasn't some dull lass to be swooned by his charms and he quickly took the hint and diverted his attention to Darkwolfe. "Hi, I'm Cat."

Darkwolfe took his hand with a firm shake and smile and settled back onto the dry earth and scattered pine needles. Just because Cat was bound by a servitude spell, didn't mean that he couldn't cause a little mischief. By telling the two strangers of their destination, it might spark some interesting conversation and even lead to some information as to the exact where abouts of the temple that didn't exist. Situations like these were always a little difficult for Cat to decide. For on one hand it was fun, it was exciting and all that, but on the other, if he somehow violated the spell parameters without even knowing it, it wasn't like he could say, "oh sorry, I didn't really mean it and all that," he'd just simply crumble into a pile of dust in the middle of a sentence and these two strangers wouldn't even have a clue as to what in the heck had just happened.

He decided to take a chance. "Were headed to the Dragon Temple."

Sir Gedrick's jaw dropped and looked at him in shock. Nothing happened however to the assassin, so Sir Gedrick quickly recovered and rationalized that it must somehow be in their best interests to talk to these two strangers about the temple. Maybe they could even point the way.

"'Tis true I must confess, we're really not hunters, we've come from Thor's Hammer with a message to The Temple of the Dragon." He said emphatically as if that would explain everything.

"That's incredible," Darkwolfe sputtered, "we're heading to the temple also. Well, not on any official business mind you, but I want to train there and Charlemette is my… well she's my wife and we're going there together." He smiled at Char hoping she wouldn't mind the little lie, and was confounded when she smiled back as if it was the most natural thing in the world for him to profess. This shocked him somewhat and stalled his forthcoming dialogue with the pair of campers.

"Marvelous," Cat uttered, " now we've got a foursome of adventurers heading for a temple that doesn't exist," and he stood up and continued to circle the fire as he had before.

"No it does exist," Sir Gedrick persisted. "We've got a map, and we know its at the two horns, we just don't know exactly where it is." He piped.

"Oh we've got a map too," Darkwolfe issued, and produced the blue book with the map. Sir Gedrick also brought forth his map from his bag, and the two were exactly the same. There was a lot of silent eye glaring over the next burning of several logs, and then the lot of them fell fast asleep.

In the morning there was a simple breakfast of the two groups' stores and then they were back upon the trail in full force. While not spoken, it was apparent that both groups merely wanted to get to the temple as fast as able, and accomplish whatever it was that they were each set out to do. There wasn't any malevolence between them per say, but each of them felt that something entirely odd was occurring and placed blame for it's manifestation on the other party.

They made good speed through the woods that first day together in the morning following the animal trails, for no man-made trail made itself apparent. By mid-draw they found a small clearing and decided to stop to rest.

"What do you make of this," Darkwolfe asked of Sir Gedrick. Before them were many tracks in the drying muck.

"Looks like wild snake-beast tracks to me," he replied. "We best be careful. I think we can handle one or two, but more than that and we're in trouble." The two looked about into the waist high scrub and further forest line. "Lets just sit tight and then we should have one of us scout ahead as we continue. Better one of us takes the full blunt of the attack than all of us. We can draw straws if you like, that's how us knights usually choose point."

"We'll take turns. I'll go first, and next rotation you can take it. Sound fair enough."

"Fair enough," he replied, and they all sat down to rest.

A while later just as they were picking up their gear to head back off toward the unknown temple, there emanated a mixed grunting and hissing noise from the bushes around them. Sir Gedrick and Darkwolfe exchanged knowing glances and drew their weapons. Charlemette, noticing the intent of the two men and began chanting, and Cat drew his short sword and dipped his dagger in a vial that hung at his side.

Immediately three snake-beasts emerged from the foliage grunting and hissing wildly. These monsters were essentially wild boars bearing ten-inch tusks and where there fore shoulders were, emerged twin snakes that bore deadly venom. The beasts eyed the party hungrily with saliva falling from their tusks, and the snakeheads whipping about wildly.

Char's spell completed and an euphoric feeling came over the party as if they could defeat any monster or number thereof. Sir Gedrick charged into one beast, Cat another, and Darkwolfe charged in to the last leaving Charlemette standing in the middle of the confrontation.

All of the fighters did all that they could do, to initially hold back the onslaught of the flailing poisonous heads. One charged Darkwolfe in a rush and as it passed he danced to the side and severed one of the snakeheads.

Sir Gedrick parried left and right just to keep the beast at bay, he nicked a couple minor wounds but gained no upper ground.

Cat jumped about in a lovely display of dexterous feats and soon had several stabs into the beast and one snakehead lying limply.

Darkwolfe turned and laid a vicious gash along the side of the beast on its next rush.

Sir Gedrick then fainted back, the beast rushed forward, and he came down with an overhead strike severing the boar head and most of a front leg in his mighty strike.

Cat's beast also leaped forward, he rolled backward and drove his poisoned dagger into the belly of the beast; his wicked poison took mere blinks before the beast lay still and dead.

The next rush came to bear on Darkwolfe and both the lonely snakehead and the tusks bore down on him. At the last second he leap frogged the thing and drove his sword deep into its spine as it passed. The remaining snakehead barely missed sinking into his leg. He lost his grip on the sword, but the beast only made it a couple of strides off before it succumbed to the wound and lay down to die.

Shortly after the whole affair had started, the confrontation was over. They all looked at each other with admiration and newfound friendship as they saw each other's worth and strength in a world of mostly unknowns.

"I apologize, "Charlemette began, "I should have thought of this earlier." She began chanting a spell then and the three men just looked on curiously. When she was done there didn't appear to be any effect.

"What was that all about?" Cat questioned.

"It's a useful spell that allows me to detect creatures in the area. Like there is an opossum in that tree over there, and a raccoon back down the hill. It has a limited range, but should pretty much stay in effect most of the day. It should give us a bit of an initiative next time something decides to attack us."

Cat, anxious as ever, said "Alrighty then," and started off toward the temple again. The rest of the party followed his lead.

Darkwolfe looked to Sir Gedrick, admiring his mighty armor and sword, "Looks like Cat wants point."

"Yah," he chuckled and clapped him on the shoulder like an old friend.

* * * * *

Sabbath had cast his spell to help astrally project his being. Some individuals with strong natural psychic abilities could separate their spiritual self from their physical bodies at will. Many people did this accidentally while sleeping and saw themselves looking down at their sleeping bodies. This may happen once or twice in a lifetime for those individuals with innate abilities that had never been nurtured. While other people never experienced this in a lifetime and ruled out the existence of such a phenomenon based on their limited version of perceptual reality. These last accidental projections often caused anxiety and fear, and the individual snap right back into their bodies and instantly wake. For mages, casting this spell helped separate the physical and spiritual bond and allowed the mage to fly about in the astral plane spying or observing events from afar. However, there were a few dangers involved.

For one, the mage was essentially unable to protect his physical body while projected. Sometimes a mage would have a guard or apprentice watch over him, but Sabbath wasn't the trusting type. He considered himself to be the master of deception and betrayal. If he was capable of such things, what would keep someone from doing it to him? If he was set over a mage to watch his body while he projected, he would kill the mage and take all of his magic. Everyone had the potential for such actions, but none he felt with his level of love and conviction.

A second option, which he preferred, was to simply set magical wards to prevent anyone from getting to his body. Not that he thought anyone in this pathetic little town would have the gall to actually come into his, let alone try to harm him. Never the less, he was always cautious and in so being had saved his life many, many times.

Sabbath D'Alrathe settled on his bed and left his body instantly. He floated up through the roof and hung momentarily within the swaying treetops to orient himself. He felt coldness pervasively throughout his being from residing outside his warm corporeal form, but such freedom and weightlessness that came in separation, made each projection exciting and like the first. Had he lips he would have smiled like a giddy child.

He sped then northward toward Grathmoor. Trees flew by, and many minor tributaries to the Salmon River. He flew through hills and valleys, and then the town came into view as if seconds later. Traveling at such incredible speeds always made such trips brief. Sabbath had even raced up to the moon once on a whim, and even such a trip which he imagined was much further than he could fathom, only took a few breaths as well.

What shocked him about the town, was how quiet and still it was. For a moment he thought his secondary spell he had cast to allow him to telepathically hear sound, even though his physical acoustic receptors were many miles away, had failed. But no, there were a few bird sounds and the rustling of the wind through the trees and brush.

Drifting around the town like some disembodied apparition, he methodically began searching the streets and houses of the common district. In quick order he began coming across a number of bodies in the street and houses. One old man lay in the street headless and without a hand or leg. A whole family was dead in one house including the children; it looked as though the father had committed suicide, driving his chest onto a propped up pitchfork. The local tavern called the Warm Nook had a couple of bodies within it.

Sabbath noticed with some interest that there were some bodies in a place called The Curiosity Shop which had been blasted by some kind of magic. One man's face was ruined, and Sabbath had seen many a person hit by attack darts to recognize their work. Another man had a hole blasted through his chest. By the scorched flesh and charring of the crumbled stairs he concluded that it was some kind of lightning spell, but magical or clerical in nature he could not discern.

He continued down the street and found Tucker's house at the end of the street. Tucker sat in his little whicker chair with Furball on his lap. He petted the cat rhythmically and Furball issued forth a dull purr. Tears streaked down the cleric's face. His face was red and swollen and Sabbath imagined that the man wasn't taking to the present condition of the town too well.

The cat's ears perked up and it cast its emerald feline gaze in the direction of Sabbath's form. Only cats or creatures native to the astral plane could see another form therein. There was a potential danger from such creatures, but by and by they usually left travelers alone. As well if a situation arose, just by a mental thought one could snap back to there body and instantly awake. Cats on the other hand had a natural affinity for this plane and were often pets to mages, who, with a keen sense of perception, could recognize when there was an astral presence about.

Furball had just recently been taken in by tucker as a stray, so the priest didn't take notice in the change in the cats demeanor. That and the fact that he was lost in turmoil and pain of not being able to help or prevent the slaughter of the town's inhabitants.

The cat and Sabbath eyed each other for several breaths. Then it became clear to him; overlaid with the corporeal body of the cat was another astral figure, some other being; one that exuded raw evil. A telepathic voice came to the mage's mind.

{Nice curse you have here mage. It has been a long time since I have seen a mage construct such a thing with any competency.}

[Who are you?]

{I am known to mortals as Za'Varuk}

[What then are you?]

{I am demon, long since banished to the inner core}

[Well then if you're banished, what are you doing here in the guise of a cat?]

{Aaah yes, what indeed. There is a breech in our prison, weakened with time and neglect. I am one of the strongest of my kind and so far the only one smart enough to figure out how to trick the prison to be able to project out of it. Others will perhaps in time, but true escape is what I'm really after. Sure I could wait another century or so until the prison dissolves itself, but what fun would there be in that. The world is ripe for destruction now; the races have grown weak. That's why I want your help in releasing me}

[Why should I help you? You're a demon. You'll just kill me as soon as I finish my end of the bargain.]

{Why kill you when I have a world to conquer? We won't be releasing all the demons, just me. It will take me a very long time to personally destroy Alcyone, and by that time you'll be dead by natural causes knowing the limited expanse of human life. And if not, well that just gives you enough time to grow strong and prepare for our conflict. You see, you can say no, I'll just find another mage to work with, but I can see the evil and power lust in you. What great power could we give to each other? Make no mistake one day one of us will eventually die, but that is decades from now—let us look to the immediate future.}

Sabbath considered thoughtfully. It did sound like an opportunity of a lifetime. Although he did have his curse after all, why risk making a deal with a demon that was even more malicious than Sabbath himself.

{Your curse has been thwarted you know. Most of the town is dead for sure, but I know the castle was your real goal; it still stands strong as ever, except maybe minus a mage and a few apprentices. It's still far too strong for you to take directly. I'll take your curse into the castle and help you claim it for your own as a show of good faith.}

Sabbath acted as if considering the proposition, but in truth he had already made up his mind. He watched the shadow of the demon wavering behind the façade of the cat Furball. Tucker still sat idly stroking the cat/demon.

[And how do I release you once you have won me the castle.]

{Its more of a treasure hunt than anything else, but let us worry about the details at a later time. Do we have a deal?}

Sabbath didn't want to seem too anxious, but he couldn't believe his good fortune. Grathmoor?—bah, with a demon at his side he could be king of Thor's Hammer.

[Yes. A deal it is demon Za'Varuk]

{So glad, so glad to meet a human with such a black heart. Maybe there is some hope for your race after all}: it followed with rumbling laughter.

A swirling ball of green light and shiny blackness emerged from Tucker as the demon assumed control of the curse. It settled into Furball, and immediately contaminated Tucker with its swirling tendril of wispy green smoke. The cat jumped down then and bounded into the street.

Poor Tucker somehow was very angry with himself. Wasn't he a priest of the great mother? All these people in town in pain, dying, or dead and he had done nothing to help them. He heard their first cries as they began murdering each other. He was afraid once he saw what was going on; pure madness. Fathers killing their children, wives killing husbands, friends killing friends; it was total chaos and beyond the realm of any rational thought. Tucker ran and hid in his house until finally the screams had stopprd and the town quite literally became as quiet as the dead.

Tucker was a worthless priest and hated himself for it. He got up suddenly from the chair and went to a pouch hanging from a nail on the wall. There was a large red X painted on the side. Within the large pouch were many little ones with labels scrolled on them. Deadly nightshade, poison hemlock, foxglove, and a handful of others. He poured them all out on the table in a big pile of dried leaves and powdered roots. He began shoving them down his throat as quickly as possible until suddenly he began convulsing and spitting up and soon crashed to the floor in a contorted configuration of blissful death.

As Tucker's spirit left his body he was not instantly whisked away to the planes where spirits dwelt between incarnations. Instead of Tucker spending the next portion of his existence dwelling on this incarnation's actions, hopefully learning from his mistakes and evolving his soul, the great mother had another mission for him. He heard no words or saw no form, but as he floated in his old cottage above his corpse he suddenly knew what he had to do. He knew all that had been "thought" between Sabbath and the demon. The whole transaction was like a mental picture burned in his memory, and he quickly fled his house and then the town, and raced toward two horns to enlist a small band of heroes in the service of the goddess.

6

Castles and Companions

The West Woods, which were relatively flat and held a variety of dense trees, soon entered into rolling hills where pine and other conifers became more prevalent. In the distance the two horns could be seen thrusting up into the sky, piercing large pillowy clouds as might be more fitting a bull let loose in a bedding store than out in the lovely wilderness.

The small band of companions picked there way toward the two markers through trees and hills with little or no conversation. Darkwolfe was lost mostly in his own mind, contemplating the strange killings in Grathmoor, especially his now gone father. The whole affair seemed bizarre and Darkwolfe wished he knew what or who was behind it all. He would love to see justice served for the loss of all those lives and particularly that of his only family.

Sure his father had been a drunk and treated him miserably over the past two years, but deep down he knew that his father had truly loved him. Now he was gone, wherever death's gates led, and he was all alone in the world except for this small band that traveled together to some mythic temple. His lovely Charlemette, the strange one called Cat, and last this honorable paladin who treated him like a true friend.

Sir Gedrick tromped along in his armor as steadily and as quietly as possible. Plate armor was extremely good defensively, but made somewhat of a racket and even more so now as the party made a steady pace. Years of wear had made him quite accustomed to it, and while the minor enchantment placed on it made it much lighter than normal, its constant drag had added bulk to Sir Gedrick's muscles.

Over time he came to be the warrior he was now; ferocious, strong, and able to split men with his huge sword in the name of the great mother. He had finally slung his sword over his shoulder in its scabbard after hours of a threatless environment and both strong arms swung at his sides. He was growing fond of Darkwolfe's willful demeanor and sense of purpose and honor. In fact in some ways he reminded him of a paladin friend within the order whom until now had only existed in Sir Gedrick's mind. He wasn't sure precisely what it was about the young man from Grathmoor, but he just seemed so real and genuine, confident in his convictions. Not like the paladins who more often than not were so steeped in their religious ideologies that they soon lost site of what they were suppose to represent in the first place. Whether Darkwolfe would be able to be persuaded to come with him back to Thor's Hammer and the headquarters of the order or not would have yet to be determined, but in the meanwhile he did at least enjoy him as a traveling companion. Cat wasn't too bad, but he was bound by servitude was he not? Who really knew where his loyalties lay and at what price betrayal could be bought.

Cat enjoyed playing games. Even when on a thieving expedition or an assassination, while it was work, he always tried to play it out as a game. When the ultimate steal was accomplished a great sense of excitement would come over him, and while the stolen goods where what put food in his mouth, he enjoyed the act itself more than the goods as an end in themselves. He enjoyed killing somewhat less, but only agreed to take jobs where the person being eliminated truly made the world a better place without them continuing their part in it. The paladins had discerned this relative goodness of heart and taken this into consideration when choosing cat to accompany Sir Gedrick on his Quest and binding him to servitude.

While the rest of the party marched along like a bunch of boring zombies, Cat was practicing his stealth and surprise attack with a flair of mystery and a mischievous grin. His name was very befitting his movements and soon the other party members lost track of his location. He went from tree to tree, stooping beyond a little outcropping and sometimes slithering along the ground like a big black snake. He would come upon a squirrel and touch it amusingly, the poor animal would chatter in fright and scale the tree or fly off in agitated anger. He didn't do this maliciously, but out of fun and, well, just because he could. This helped him hone his skills that made him very good at his profession.

He would sneak off to one side of the general line that the companions were traveling, and then back to the other side of them with equal grace. Seeing how close he could come without being detected. He used all of the natural shadows from the great trees, and masked his movements by the wind and other natural phenomenon of audible discretion. One time he came around a tree and stood suddenly in Charlemette's path, causing her to jump and utter a little squeal in fright. Cat thought it was entirely comical the way her face wriggled up and her eyes bugged out like an opossum suddenly caught in a circle of torchlight, but upon seeing the condescending looks of both Darkwolfe and Sir Gedrick, Cat decided to just bother the wildlife of the forest instead. Still he didn't understand their temperament, he was bored during this long trek after all, what did they expect him to do? Should he just trudge along like the other trio of undead? He thought not.

After her little scare, Charlemette took a moment to concentrate again on her location spell. While the spell she had cast would last all day, it took most of her concentration to weed out all of the life forms it picked up and figure out which to ignore and which could potentially be dangerous. For instance, earlier in the day they had come across the path of a bear on one of the lower slopes of a hill. It wasn't close enough to be of any particular threat and she decided not to mention it to the party. If she blurted out everything she sensed in these woods teeming with life, not only would it take them an extra week to make it to the horns, but also it would virtually serve no purpose what so ever. She did think it would be useful in terms of dinner, in that while spotting many deer and rabbits along the way, she would at least send the men off in the right direction to hunt when they set camp.

After a moment her concentration for the spell came back. At first she didn't respond to the warning the spell yelled at her. Ahead in the trees and also on the ground surrounding them were many creatures, elves as far as she could tell. Before she could yell out a warning it was too late.

* * * * *

Sabbath left Furball to his long walk to the castle, while he swiftly flew across the town and was there in but a few blinks. He had a notion to believe what the demon had told him about the curse, but trusting such a creature was like setting oneself on fire and believing the impending rain would extinguish the flames. While examining the castle seemed prudent, watching the cat/demon spread the curse and witnessing the downfall of its inhabitants would be finer than any play performed in Sanctuary or Thor's Hammer.

There was a large pile of bodies in the courtyard piled several high. Old blood had pooled on the cobblestones and stacks of wood and canisters of oil were close at hand for the evening's funeral pyre. From what he could tell, 20 or so of the guards were dead. No mages were present in the pile but of course their privileged status would at the very least earn them a separate burning. A pair of the more elite guards stood near the gate, as most of the regulars apparently now lay dead. They wore heavy chain shirts beneath a blue and white tunic emblazoned with the Noblin's black hawk crest. Sabbath thought perhaps the demon had lied or at least exaggerated about the failure of the curse, but upon seeing another pair of the elite marching along the outer wall, confirmed that the curse had only taken out the regular guard. From what Sabbath remembered of the infrastructure of the castle, he still had to contend with a rather large group of elite guards, Lord Noblin's personal guards, the priests, and whatever mages the castle held.

He flew through the front double wooden doors and examined the battle scarred entrance hall. There was rubble everywhere that was easily deduced to have come from the many statue-like columns lining the hall. Many of the statues were cracked and had large chunks missing from them. There were scorch marks on many, also the walls and floors held similar displays. There was dried blood everywhere and still a foul stench hung in the air that was commonly know to mages everywhere as a leftover effect of a disabling area effect spell. Obviously a great battle took place here involving magic and warriors alike. The remains of the soldiers out in the courtyard and the remaining of Lord Noblin's hold on the castle told plainly the outcome. What begging question was how many mages survived the battle? The warriors were not too much of a problem for one of Sabbath's prowess, but the mages and priests were another matter; they were his greatest problem to face, and the sooner they were taken care of the better.

Down another long hall and through another series of double doors brought Sabbath to the council hall. The room was a huge rectangular block of stone. The floor was covered with various rugs made of furs of bears and lions and other less known creatures. The heads of several large stags were mounted on the walls, their great antlered racks told of Lord Noblin's skill with the massive long bow he was so fond of using. A central running table of polished maple ran the length of the room and at the head sat the resident Lord with a silver chalice of wine in one hand and a jeweled dagger in the other.

He had short-cropped black hair and a ring of a beard circling his mouth. He had hard brown eyes the color of a weathered beer keg, and they currently displayed both anger and confusion. He sported high red velvet boots, satin black pants and a frilly white shirt with puffy cuffs. "I just don't get it…why?" he stammered. Many of his good men and mages were killed. Most of the town was decimated. He was ruler of not much more than a hall of would be nobles, a few holy clerics, and a lonesome apprentice mage who sat by himself mumbling as if still in shock from the previous battle. As if to find a release from his torment, Lord Noblin slammed the dagger down with brutal force and drove the dagger several knuckles into the table. There it sat wavering for a second and then resting still as if testament to the severity of the situation. Captain Emory's dagger's last voice to the wrong doing the curse had laid to his good name and honor.

High priest Javonavich with two of his alcyotes, and High priestess Amber with one of hers, sat along one edge of the table. The lone mage sat by himself on the other side babbling, and no less than five of Lord Noblin's personal guards formed a standing ring around him. All wore leather armor of black. This armor was not as strong as chain or plate, but these men needed to move, and move fast when danger was about. Their mobility and great skill with their personalized weapons were more than enough for any threat and had proved so for more than two decades.

"What say you high priest," Lord Noblin began trying to establish some sense of normality to this meeting.

Javonavich clasped his fingers together and arched his eyebrows as if preparing a speech about holy fortitude to his followers. "Well all of the dead guards including Captain Emory did possess some kind of sickly magical residue. It's hard to determine the exact nature of its origin, but I can assure that this was the cause of the revolt. Your men have always been much more than loyal, and it would make no clear sense to attribute this behavior to normal means. However, the origin of this magic is near impossible to trace. If it is the construct of some mage, he is certainly quite adept, but then again I can not even begin to guess who would be a likely suspect, or what would motivate this person to release such a vile thing. Some mages are renown for doing nothing but creating hideous weapons and then releasing upon a town or city, but always for a huge price. As far as I know, meaning no offense of course my lord, no one has ever tried to go against your rule or for that matter had ever wanted this isolated community. In sum, I'm at a loss. My best guess is that someone or some group is trying to take over Grathmoor. They are obviously to small in number to attack us directly, so have therefore resorted to magical means. Why? I don't know. But if someone has gone to such lengths to acquire or personally construct such a weapon, they will not give up after one set back. And if you think about it, it has not really been that great of a set back. Most of the guard is dead and all but this one apprentice is gone as well. What you see is several score of guards and a few priests to hold back any attack." The high priest finished, contemplating for a minute, then sat quiet as if satisfied at all that he had said.

"Well what do you propose should be our course of action? I know how to deal with a regular battle, but magic is a little beyond me. I respect the thoughts of my honored advisors." As if almost asking forgiveness in his lack of power in the matter, the noble Lord spread his hands in futile grasping or attention to the matter.

"With your permission my Lord," high priestess Amber began, " we think it would be necessary to cast a spell of protection to bar this magic. It would probably only be large enough to make this very room a sanctuary from this force, but if things got out of hand, or if certain individuals who were inflicted brought here, they would at least be safe or harbored from the magic while within its sphere." As if that would be enough to begin such an action, she stood grasping her holy staff and went to the side of the room where there was enough of an open space to begin the magical rite.

"But of course, do what you feel is prudent in this matter." Turning to one of his personal guards, " tell all to let no one leave the castle and no one enter until this matter is properly dealt with." Instantly he ran off through the doors to inform the guards, stepping lightly on his feet like a fox through familiar woods.

Sabbath watched all of the proceedings with great interest and puzzled over how he was going to tackle this paramount decision. If the curse couldn't get into the castle, then all was for naught. Somehow he had some satisfaction in knowing the cat/demon would find a way. He didn't stress too much about it, for if the demon wanted freedom after all, this was his problem, not Sabbath's.

* * * * *

A good score of elves in woodland clothing appeared as if out of nowhere and held bows taunt upon the party of adventurers. The mere presence and intent made the party freeze in a decisive manner instead of reaching for their weapons. Darkwolfe had never actually met an elf and a part of him was interested, which pushed his fears at bay. The books he had read in the curiosity shop told of a proud race. They certainly weren't fond of the so-called human invasion of the planet, but placed them as honorable and beyond full-scale slaughter, even when humans had invaded upon their land out of expansive ignorance.

"Well met humans, what interest do you have in these parts of the woods? You are well away from your normal settlements." One lead elf spoke and flourished a shining long sword with practiced ease. His thin manner could easily be mistaken as weakness, but Darkwolfe noted his agile movements and instantly realized that a confrontation would be a quick and definitive end for he and his friends.

"We have come from Grathmoor dear elven lord. There is a plague of madness upon the town and we journey to the dragon temple for divine guidance in ridding the region of this evil." The words flowed quite smoothly, but he wondered where exactly they had come from, for he had never been much of a spokesman.

"We have sensed the trouble in your town. Our magic has discerned a great evil in Grathmoor, what more do you know of it?" The elf apparently did not feel threatened and lowered his sword and approached within a couple span of the young warrior –mage.

"We know only that many of the inhabitants have gone out of their minds and started killing everyone. I wish I could say more, but this information we do not have; this is why we seek council of those who may tell of such foul deeds." Darkwolfe shifted his weight and tried to gather his magical energy in case a battle was to come about. If he was to die this day he decided at least one or two of these elves were going with him.

"Stand at ease my friends," the elf spoke and held his hand aloft. Cat sitting in the bushes sighed with relief as he noticed suddenly two elves standing behind him. One loosened his bow and another lowered his sword. While somewhat unnerved by their stealth, he had to applaud their ability. For until they had somewhat purposely made themselves known, he had no idea that they were directly behind him. Just prior he was considering charging into the clearing and attacking the lead elf. Now he knew he wouldn't have made more than two steps before being skewered by an arrow and a long shiny sword.

"From what I know of your folk, you are a goodly race and I beg to pray forgiveness in my ignorance, but I believe in this instance we are on the same side. If whatever evil has infested Grathmoor succeeds, it can easily work its way our here. I confess to deny why it would be so, but if this temple at the horns exists, it seems to be a likely target for anyone seeking power over the region."

The elf sighed considering and finally sheathed his sword, "I assure you it does exist, and if what we feel is true, and what you say is accurate, then we all would benefit from a thorough briefing of the matter. I apologize for affronting you all, and you especially my lady," he bowed politely to Charlemette, "but I beg you follow us to our camp where we may converse in detail of all that has transpired and what we see as an appropriate direction for diffusing this evil."

Cat walked out into the open, much to the sudden surprise to his own party, "Well I don't see how we have much of a choice, might as well have a little pow wow." He shrugged his shoulders noncommittally and joined the party in the small clearing of trees. The sun bore down on them making them warm and their eyes sparkle with an inner sense of drive and fulfillment.

* * * * *

Heather left Lady Mira's chambers carrying the chamber pot with her head swiveled to the side to avoid the smell. She didn't mind her job too much, for the most part the Lord and Lady were extremely nice to her and she would have to confess she had the best meals in her life while in their service. Carrying their smelly excrements out back and dumping it in the woods every morning, she had to say, was both gross and undignified to any individual on the planet.

She paused for a brief spell in the hallway where no one was around. We wiped her thin cheek and pushed her dirty blond hair behind her ear habitually. She straightened her long working gown and apron and hefted the bucket in her left arm to give her right arm a break from the weight and made for the back door. There was a burly elite guard standing post and he opened the door politely without a word and she swiftly darted through and staggered down the trail to the dumping hole where she had gone every day for the past two years.

The small dirt trail was rutted deeply by her years of weary steps. The branches of her familiar trees reached over her lovingly to shelter her from life's hardships and a bluebird chirped happily from a long hanging branch. She smiled to herself at such a boon from the goddess and made her way down the trail to the large pit that had been dug many years before. The stench assailed her senses, and she held her breathe as she quickly made her way to the edge of the pit and dumped the bucket into the pit and hastily retreated back to the edge of the trail.

From behind a nearby tree a cat purred lovingly and meowed softly. Heather noticed the cat with both curiosity and desire to hold and pet the dear creature. The pet made his way forward and the lovely maiden tentatively stretched forth her hand and stroked the brown and black feline. It purred happily and she readily picked him up and carried him back toward the castle. She didn't know how the rest of the castle would take to another animal, but she had dreamed all her life for such a pet and now was her chance. Green tendrils snaked around her arms, but the demon with his considerable power altered the curse and made the young maiden immune so she could more effectively spread the curse without falling under its deadly influence. Heather made her way back into the castle without incident and soon had the cat feeding out of a bowl at the foot of her bed while she stoked the cat. The cat just purred benignly, and the poor maiden was as happy as she had been in many a years. Little did she know that she had just brought the downfall of the castle within its very walls and she would go down in history as the killer of Grathmoor.

* * * * *

Sabbath finished viewing the goings on of the council hall and readily felt the tug of his corporeal body pull mightily at his spirit. He had been far too long out of his body and any longer could prove quite disastrous. Normally the resident beings of the astral plane would leave travelers alone, but once a person was weakened by travel or magical displacement, these beings would happily intervene to assume the vacant host. Sabbath had just reached his limit and he could feel many beings trying to slip into his body and push his spirit away into a relative purgatory until the expiration of the physical body. Some mages have lost such control, and Sabbath had seen the dire repercussions of such a faulty display of will. In fact he had even conversed with a displaced soul once of a friend to gather information on the resident mage of Pylreht to take over the small town. It was now that he suddenly raced back to the very same town to block such an action. Thankfully he made it with little room to spare, but enough to force himself into the body and slowly he sat up within his study. He rubbed his hair thoughtfully and grinned at the wonderful progression of his plan. He took out a map from his desk and as his plans grew, he considered the map of Thor's Hammer with more interest than he had since his apprenticeship under Lazareth the Wise.

* * * * *

With some trepidation and insistence by sword and bow albeit perhaps not openly, the party made their way around a creak bed and several small hills. It was surprising that before long they found themselves sitting around a fire circle that was still warm and several small lean-to shelters against the sturdy trees were evident around the tiny clearing. The lead elf took the initiative to talk and the rest of the elven troupe stayed well away but showed a force of inactive activity that any transgression would be met with immediate death.

"Let me make it easy for you since you seem somewhat confused." The lead elf leaned forward over the warm rocks, "I am Silverworm and the group I command is the Deadly Chimes." He said matter of factly. "We have known about this curse of yours for a good little while, what we are and do is of little concern to you, but what is important, is we are to lead you to the two horns. I know that your little human mind is configuring many questions, particularly why, why, why, but just stop your brain for two breaths. You will learn all of this Darkwolfe in the temple, but for now just believe what I am telling you. Something of the nature of the world has gone awry and there are many factors and groups at play now. For now, we are on your side, but if this curse gets a hold of you, trust me, I will kill you and all of your friends without a thought." He adjusted his clothing and leather armor to create what was obviously a meaningful pause. "What is important is that if you can prove yourself at this temple and do what the prophesies say, we shall all be the better for it; that is why the elves are helping you humans against our better judgement."

Darkwolfe was more than speechless at that moment. "What?" was generally all that he could muster. I don't know how elves are use to speaking he thought, but sense would be useful if they wanted him to respond in a meaningful manner.

"What part does your human mind not understand?" He said swaging a hip to the right and beaming forth a look that would typically call for warfare.

"Look elf, I know you have us outnumbered and have some advantage of who we are, but if you don't speak plainly, I'm gonna pull this sword of mine and hope your fellows give me a foot of honor while I stick three right through your chest!"

The elf seemed to consider the human language and terminology for a minute, and then began chuckling to himself. Darkwolfe was on the edge of drawing steel when the elf finally offered his hand in the human edict and smiled broadly. If Darkwolfe was half the man he considered himself to be he would have stuck the elf like a slaughtered pig and doomed his party, but he just smiled back as if just realizing some god-awful joke and shook hands with the wood elf.

* * * * *

Sabbath packed his bags including both spell books, cloths, and all his major magical items. It took a considerable amount of time, but as he stood at the threshold of his lair after most of the afternoon, he was ready to leave his lair for good.

Sometime later on the road north of Pylreht, he saw a rider racing down the road making from Grathmoor. He smiled softly to himself and as he came abreast to the rider on the road. A shot of magical fire beamed between them as they were about even. Sabbath quickly saw the rider expunge all his essence of livelihood and fall to the ground. Sabbath galloped forward on a mission that allowed no mistakes and no witnesses on a fine new steed.

* * * * *

Prophecy? Lead us…meant to do? The temple? These elves were obviously crazy that much was for sure. Darkwolfe and the party agreed to relax at the elf camp the rest of that day and night to gather their energy. Apparently the climb was long and dangerous, Silverworm had even suggested that a group of loathsome mountain giants were fond of crushing hapless adventurers and picking their bones clean for dinner.

Darkwolfe and Charlemette sat off together quietly away from the others.

"What do you make of that prophecy stuff?" she inquired. She was playing with an oak leaf, turning it between her fingers. She loved the woods and its wild calm usually, it brought great peace and stillness to the mind and soul. Especially this far from the familiar woods surrounding Grathmoor, there was a sense of peace and quietude beyond the reach of civilization and the markings of man. Now however there was something else apparent. Some lurking evil waiting to pounce upon the party and her dear Darkwolfe. It was something undefined, some presence that frightened her like she had never known. Char leaned over then and grasped his forearm in reassurance and love. She lifted her gaze to meet his trying to show confidence and to somewhat hide her inner trepidations.

"I can't be sure, he's just a mad elf for all I know. Maybe even worse because he leads this group of Deadly Chimes, pray-tell what in the hell that means." He clasped his hand over hers in a two-sided show of need and comfort, and scooted a little closer. "But don't we all have some pull of destiny? A month ago I only dreamed of going on some quest to an ancient temple, meeting elves, and fighting monsters. Now its really happening and its just like I jumped in a river and suddenly, albeit too late, found out that the current is a little too strong for my liking."

"This is true," she said, "but when we finally come ashore..."

"If we come to shore," he corrected.

"When we come ashore, we will be stronger, wiser from the experience, and perhaps in a new and exotic land of travel."

"I care not for my life overly much," Darkwolfe admitted humbly, "but I couldn't live with myself if anything ever happened to you because of my fantastic foolishness." The whole fool concept came to him suddenly and the man in the store so plain as day as if he were in a waking dream. The tarot deck, the deck of divination, seemed like a perfect solution to his present problem. Now seemed like a good time, and he reached into his pack and withdrew the deck.

Charlemette looked on curiously as he unfolded the lovely scarf; it sported a twisting pattern of black roses set on a blood-red background. Then he shifted back from her and crossed his legs to face her directly. She assumed a like position. She recognized the deck of divination. She made a slight finger movement and to her eyes the deck began to glow, illuminating its magical radiance. "What is that," she asked innocently, trying to reveal both her powers and her hand in the greater scheme that was now unfolding. The less he knew about what she knew and was doing, the better she felt about what she was actually doing in the name of all she believed.

"A strange jester-like man came into the Curio Shop the other day. He traded me this deck of divination cards for,...well, basically a bunch of junk. I wasn't about to argue with the man at the time, but now that all of this weird strangeness is about, I almost think that it was prearranged. In itself, I don't know its powers. The man did tell me to try and tap into its powers through use and familiarization."

Charlemette straightened her indigo robes and belt and sat up straight to correct her holy posture. "I don't know a great deal about the tarot, but I will depart what I have heard in passing and what I feel within." Her affect changed slightly and Darkwolfe could almost feel the energy start to exude form her being. From his limited experience, whenever he had heard a priestess or priest lecture or speak in a holy station, it was as if the person's personality was displaced and the patron god or goddess actually communicated through the host.

"Everything in the universe is energy. Over time, this energy began to group together into like forms. Each of the groups together became a sentient being or god-form. These groupings are what you humans now call upon as gods and goddesses. They are in principal nothing more than collections of energy. However they are much more than what they may at first appear. They are dynamic, and hold personal interests in the material world. This is where the deities have spawned. They are collections of certain prototypes. Love and hate, jealousy and trust, fortitude, honor, will, lust, desire, hate, and all other emotions and cognitive emanations are all created from this core. In the world there is balance, and balance is only achieved through a constant struggle between order and chaos. Only structure and we have stagnation; only turbulence, there is nothing to destroy. What good would life be if there was not death to make it precious? "

Darkwolfe stretched his legs and then quickly brought them in hoping he could appease the goddess and not upset her monologue with his undisciplined fidgeting.

"All of the universe resides within us, and if you can not find it there, it does not exist out here." She spread her arms wide as if to indicate the woods and sky above.

"What about the gods and goddesses?" He asked.

"Deities," she continued patiently, lovingly, "also exist within. Sure we also exist out here," she spread her arms again, "but how many men may walk through these woods and see nothing more than trees? Just because one can not perceive the spirit of the deities, does not mean they don't exist. Only when it is awakened within you can you see it all around you; then you will know us, then you may truly live up to the name you have chosen. Master Cheiron will train you at the temple. He has trained many young heroes in his time, you would do well to listen wisely and treat him with great respect." Then she fell silent for a moment of blissful silence, and the distant unfocused glare left Charlemette's eyes and then she glanced back down at the deck that sat between them on the ground.

She lifted her left hand and placed it over the deck. The cards started whirling in a blinding display before their eyes. Then two cards settled between them. One was a man and woman holding hands. They were naked in the woods; the card read *Lovers.* The next card was of a beautiful woman in a chartreuse colored robe. She sat within a cozy looking home and her belly was full with a baby ready to be born; the card read *Mother.*

Darkwolfe and Charlemette quickly grasped the meaning and smiled warmly yet timidly toward each other. As if suddenly blessed and bidden to do what they both had for so long desired, they came within each other's arms. And there in the woods they committed that sacred rite of union.

* * * * *

Sabbath was well on his way to Grathmoor when evening set in. His newly acquired steed had a sheen of sweet on its muscular body and a dry froth was evident around the mouth. It would live to ride another day, but Sabbath's mistreatment in riding and constant lashing would stay with it for the rest of its days. He reared the tired horse to a small clearing off to the side of the road and said a soft blessing to Fortuna for finding a ready made fire pit lined with stones and a large pine needle laid bed.

He tied the horse up to a tree and further examined the camp. It would do nicely he snickered to himself. He noticed that many of the trees around the clearing were missing lower limbs and a decent sized pile of wood was stacked by the fire pit. Sabbath realized that there was a good chance the inhabitants of the camp would be back. In fact the thought only made him too excited to sleep. He enjoyed the power of his magic and the lust for killing was only barely enticed earlier in the day with the killing of the rider.

Never the less he resigned the temptation to wait up and after casting a spell to amplify the noises around the camp to his ears he settled down and succumbed to his exhaustion.

It wasn't too long, and in fact Sabbath would have been better off staying awake. Crunching leaves and snapping twigs came to his ears clearly even though the men were still some distance off. He could hear them whispering to themselves and quickly discerned that three men were approaching and arguing about who was going to get to kill the stranger and how much the horse would bring at the thieves camp.

Sabbath chanted a few words softly to himself, causing an invisible barrier of protection to form. This particular spell was highly effective in deflecting projectile weapons like arrows and crossbow bolts. He quickly began casting again. When the spell was finished nothing appeared to happen, but with just a simple wave of his hand it would take effect. Because casting often took time, mages would often cast them but leave out a motion or word that would trigger the spell. This was very important in combat, and powerful mages could string several spells together and appear to destroy an entire army with nothing more than a little finger dance or a couple words.

Finch, Swallow, and Goose were a would-be group of thieves. They had not yet proven themselves to any of the wood's thieves' guilds and were set upon the road for a period of time to prove their worth. And while perhaps not fully indoctrinated into the order, they were far from harmless. Many travelers had met an awful fate by their gruesome hands.

The trio wore a mix-matched assortment of woodland clothing that had probably been pieced together from their victims. Many notches were etched into the hilts of their swords and daggers to show their kills. It was assumed to be a true reflection of their ability. Raven, the nearest thief guild master, had been known to have a man drawn and quartered for lying about his kill status, and marking his dagger in exaggeration of his skill. This was many seasons ago, but the limb splitting punishment was enough to deter most would-be status seekers.

Goose, the strong and burly type, had assumed leadership of the group after a sparring match. Finch and swallow hadn't yet figured out their pecking order, but were determined not to be the low man out. The lowest member of any group, no matter how small, always became the recipient of menial tasks and foreman for dangerous trap exploration. In short, the brevity of life would be miserable and once a trap was found that couldn't be disarmed, if the treasure was worth it to the group, this member would be used to trip the trap. If he was lucky he would die quickly. If not, well one thief was known to decay for two agonizing weeks in conscious death while bugs and carrion creatures picked his body clean. At which point, the skeletal remains became animated and sought to recover the treasure, but had been blasted apart by an ill tempered mage that happened to cross its path and became nothing more than dust in the wind. His soul is still rumored to haunt the treasure chambers of the thieves' guild.

The group split up as they came upon the camp and intended to surround the sleeping man from three sides to prevent him from fleeing. Goose had the most direct route and quickly came out from behind a tree. He saw Sabbath lying down in the prepared pine needle bed, with his arm up at an angle and his head resting lazily in his palm;

he smiled wickedly. As Goose approached, Finch and Swallow also began closing in. The thieves thought the man just a naïveté fool when he waved his hand as if in greeting.

The spell allowed Sabbath to take control of Goose's body against his will. He didn't do so just yet, but by releasing the spell he let a wedge open where all he had to do was slip in at any time he desired. Goose would be fully conscious of his own actions, but be unable to exercise his own will.

Sabbath went to sit up into a squatting position. Finch thought he was going to run and with blinding speed hurled his dagger at him. The dagger was deflected by the protective shield and fell harmlessly away. It was then that the trio realized how much danger they were now in. Sabbath assumed control of Goose then. Finch drew his sword. Swallow took a step forward cautiously. Then Goose turned and thrust his sword between Finch's ribs. The man gasped loudly and fell to the ground with the sword stuck straight through, protruding from both ends.

Swallow turned back to took, and met Goose's dagger. The tip drove through the notch in his neck and out the back. The second thief joined his companion in the forming red mud. Goose tried fighting the spell. For several seconds Sabbath and he had a battle of wills, but shortly Goose lost. The last thief ran across the clearing and impaled himself on one of the broken tree branches.

Before even the blood stopped draining from the corpses, Sabbath had fallen back to sleep.

* * * * *

Heather's small room was plain, but at least she didn't have to share it with any of the other servants. Catering to the Lady's needs did have some advantage she supposed. After bringing the cat back to the castle she had secreted it to her room and left some water and a bit of cheese to nibble on as she had finished her chores.

It was late now and both the cat and servant seemed pleased to see each other again. They played together with a piece of string, and after, the cat hungrily devoured a piece of chicken she had taken from the scrap bin in the kitchen. She finally settled into her bed and blew out the candle. After the cat was sure she was asleep, he jumped soundlessly to the floor and with magical ease slipped through the closed door into the hall.

No one was about and for a nice piece of intrigue, the cat/demon decided to slip down to the cook's room. Shortly, the cat returned to Heather's room and somewhere below the fat cook, Art by name, dreamed of poisoning the entire castle in the morning-draw meal.

* * * * *

Za'Varuk, the scheming demon, had been working on his plans for escape for many long years. He knew that certain alliances would have to be made, such as the one with the mage Sabbath, and other pacts with lesser creatures. Eventually he would gather forth many of the woodland goblins, and snake-beasts, but matters of a more immediate nature were with the mountain giants who resided in a large cave at the two horns. Over the years adventurers and pilgrims to the temple became somewhat of a regular tasty meal for these creatures, and they had long since taken up residence.

Long ago the Dragon Temple had a hand in the trapping of the demon horde, and Za'Varuk knew that ultimately it was here that his escape would be obtained. He had communicated with the chieftain of the group, Sheaglor, many weeks back and established a psychic link with him. It was through this now that the chieftain made contact.

{My Lord Za'Varuk}

[Yes it is I, speak mighty Sheaglor]. It really was not necessary for the demon to be so respectful and flattering, but until the demon's release he had to do some things quite against his nature. He knew quite well that loyal servants with good morale didn't need as much prodding to get a job done.

{There is a group coming up the mountain to the temple. What would you have me do with them?}

[Why kill them of course and pick their bones clean if it is your desire. Report back to me when the task is done. Have you made any progress in entering the temple?]

{Not yet. There seems to be a barrier preventing all that are not pure of heart from entering. Or at least not letting evil creatures like us in. We will find a way}

[Very well, carry on]

{What of the temple?}

[Don't worry, if all goes as planned, I should be there in a few fists, and you will have a new fortress to rule the mountains from great chief]

Both the demon and the giant Sheaglor, though many draws distance apart, felt the warm elation from the prospect of power and destruction. Za'Varuk waited patiently for the chaos that the morning would bring, and the giant prepared his clan for battle.

* * * * *

The elven party scouted ahead up the twisting rocky path. One of the horns appeared to have no ready way to ascend it, so the group had decided on taking the second horn, for after all, it did have a visible trail snaking around it as far as the eye could see. "This way," Silverworm insisted, and led the group forward.

"The air is so clear here." Charlemette breathed deeply to savor the crispness of the morning.

"Indeed," Sir Gedrick agreed. "What do you make of these elves?"

Darkwolfe piped in, "I'm sure we can trust them. Its obvious they aren't telling us everything about what is going on, but I doubt they would betray us and lead us into a trap or anything." He looked about the mountain anyway, wondering where danger would mostly spring. He noticed a large pine nestled into the cliff. It was lush and seemed so wonderfully free up here hugging the horn. Behind the needles roosting on a large bough sat a plump long-eared owl. Its wide yellow eyes blinked several times and looked on curiously.

"I accept your assessment of their character." Sir Gedrick responded in kind. "All the same though." He hefted his huge sword and continued up ahead of the two intently.

"Beware, paladins have an uncanny sense for evil. If he's jumpy, then there must be something amiss around here. Where did Cat run off too, I haven't seen him for quite some time?"

"Oh he's scouting with the elves. He apparently doesn't like being shown up, so he's trying to outdo their stealth. It's become somewhat of a game, and I believe I even say a few of those tight-lipped elves smile once or twice. Cat is good. He's, well, like a cat, but these elves in their own environment aren't much more than phantoms." He concluded, toying with the hilt of his sword. Sir Gedrick was up ahead looking even more agitated than before.

"How nice of them to take him under their wing." She chided. The continued curve of the trail up and around the mountain was like a goat's spiraled horn. It was almost hypnotic in its predictable twisting motion. Here and there were large loose boulders. There were many varieties of evergreen thriving in this isolated spot. The sky was an endless see of blue, set over another endless sea of green forests expanding in all directions. They were well above the tree line now and the view was both beautiful and spectacular in its array.

"I don't see any sign of a temple around these parts do you?" Darkwolfe queried with a hint of sarcasm and changing the subject. He couldn't get over his doubts about everything. The reality of the situation was settling in, and with it a sense of detachment. Like everything was surreal and he was just a kid who had magically been sucked into a storybook that he was reading. With each turning of the page he was carried forward into the tale and there was no escape or veering from the plot. Not that he really had any idea of what this plot might be, he suddenly felt like he had lost all control of his life. As if plunging into a cold mountain river he was now being pulled along by a vicious spring melt. It was both frightening and numbing.

Charlemette eyed him for a few breaths as they walked together side by side. She could see some of his inner struggles and knew how troubling this all must be for him. "Its up there, I can sense it." She said reassuringly.

"I thought you hadn't cast your location spell this morning," he inquired suspiciously.

"I didn't because we have the elves with us, but I still sense something. A great source of holy power. It must be the temple."

"Hmm," was all he managed and they continued walking in silence again. They curved around the continuing circular path.

Silverworm appeared then from behind a large rock outcropping and motioned for the pair to quietly join him. The two scuttled over like a couple of predatory spiders and huddled together with the elf conspiratorially.

"We've noticed some tracks and movement up ahead. We suspect it's a few mountain giants. I want you two to stay here out of harms way and we'll take care of them." As if that was the end of it, Silverworm started to turn and head up the path.

"We're not just gonna sit here and hide," Darkwolfe fumed. "I want to help. This is my quest as much as anybody else's. You're right that the woman should stay here though."

"What!!?" It was Charlemette's turn to explode in anger and indignation. She thrust her angry eyes forward in warning. "Just because we've shared a bed for a night, doesn't mean you own me!"

Silverworm was about to intervene and calm the two, when several loud guttural yells echoed around the cliffs. There was a crashing of rocks like deep thunder followed by more inhuman yells. "Do what you will," was all the lead elf offered. He drew his fine blade and agilely raced toward the action.

Darkwolfe and Charlemette looked at each other forgetting their anger and exuded their lust for adventure in their beaming glares and nervous stances. Then they too raced into the melee.

Cat and the elves had quit their stalking game and grown more serious as the tracks were discovered and fleeting shadows loomed around the bend. No matter how stealthily or quietly they tried to sneak a glimpse of these fleeting shadows, no solid information was ascertained. Never the less, it was a forgone conclusion that at least a pair of mountain giants were preparing to attack. Upon the motioning of the elven band, Cat slipped back to the rear of the group. He agreed that their particular skills and experience would be most effective in dealing with the threat, and he wasn't about to let his pride get him killed.

All at once there were many boulders flying at them and growls emitted from several giants who suddenly appeared from around the curve of the mountain. They stood abreast blocking the path, and their height loomed three times that of an average human. They sported shaggy hide clothing, huge muscles, grisly beards, and clubs the size of small trees hung from a wide leather belt at their waists.

Most of the boulders went wide, either sailing off the cliff or smashing into the cliff in a shower of rocks that stung the party with small cuts and scrapes. One unfortunate elf took one squarely in the chest. He was killed instantly and likewise flew off the cliff and plummeted to the forest below.

Without any words, the remaining scouts let loose their arrows. There emitted a strange sound out of nowhere that reminded Cat of wind chimes on a warm summer evening. It was hypnotizing and he merely lost all sense of himself and reality. He was in that enchanted summer and stood frozen to the spot. This spell was enacted by the

Deadly Chimes' longbows from which the band had so aptly named themselves. Unfortunately mountain giants had a natural resistance to such mind altering magic and only one of the giants stood frozen to meet the horrid onslaught of arrows. The others ducked back around the edge of the mountain, as their comrade fell smiling pleasantly even in death.

When Darkwolfe and Charlemette rounded the last curve, they were witness to total mayhem. A full score of giants had emerged from a hidden cave and were hurling a steady flow of boulders at the elven scouts. Several of the giants lay dead in a massive heap, but many more still lived to deliver the onslaught. The elves had also suffered casualties, and several were flattened or splattered unceremoniously against the cliff face.

"By the gods!" Darkwolfe protested, looking at the bloody carnage.

The companions huddled together, trying to keep their heads down from the continuing shower of fragments as stray boulders exploded into the mountain. Thus far the elves and giants had only exchanged missile fire, but as both finally expended their supply of arrows and throwing boulders, the elven scouts drew swords and charged, while the giants hefted their massive clubs and met them head on in nothing more than several giant leaping bounds. The monsters' size and relative slowness compared to the dexterous elves proved disastrous in close combat.

One elf cut a giant's hamstring, darted between his legs and drove the tip deep into its groin. Another attacked the sides of a giant's knees and quickly felled the foul creature. However the scouts couldn't totally maneuver unhindered in the close quarters. One giant simply kicked an elf over the ledge where he fell to his death in quiet contemplation. Another elf made leg cuts into a giant only to turn and meet a club head on; his head exploded like a ripe melon and bloody gore sprayed upward like a crimson geyser.

Cat decided to merely watch for now, but Silverworm and Sir Gedrick charged fearlessly into the fray. "We've got to do something!" offered Charlemette. Without thinking she took a step forward and began chanting a prayer-spell to her goddess. The spell came unleashed as she came to her conclusion, but the giant she had tried to put to sleep continued fighting apparently unaffected.

Darkwolfe drew his concentration and a flurry of energetic darts flew forth from his fingers and unerringly blasted into one of the giants. The giant groaned as if annoyed, not in any true pain, and summarily continued squashing his present foe.

"This calls for more powerful magic." Charlemette raised her voice and again resumed chanting. As if from the very air, a dual line of fire emerged, igniting two of the giants. They howled in true agony now. Several of the giants and elves shied from the scorching heat. In mere breaths the two giants were no more than bubbling fat and blackened bone and flesh.

Sheaglor, the mountain chieftain, watched this event from behind the combat. A potion had allowed him to become invisible, and now he examined the female cleric with interest. Of the two who wielded magic, the woman was obviously more of a threat. He only had one shot before his presence became known, and he now took aim and let fly the boulder.

Time appeared to stop then for Darkwolfe.

All at once he saw Sir Gedrick take off a giant's leg. The giant toppled and Silverworm instantly straddled the beast and drove his sword point into its throat. Above them out of thin air appeared a huge rock and launched directly toward Charlemette. He quickly thought to tackle her to the ground but he was to the side, and between her and the incoming missile. As if there were no other choice to take, he dove into the boulder's path and died instantly with a sickening splat. As he was consumed by eternal darkness, Charlemette's voice rang out to him across this abyss, "NOOOO!"

As if his death signaled the combat to begin in earnest for the companions and the elves, the tempo increased, and the sway of battle began to take a definitive side in their favor. One by one the giants fell in a river of blood and entrails. Out of pure rage Charlemette cast one final spell. Her hair flew out in a flurry, and her robes billowed about like a great sail. A huge vacuum appeared to suck the very air from the cliff, and in a fatal instant, the chieftain exploded.

The remaining two elven scouts, Silverworm, Cat, Sir Gedrick, and Charlemette stood around Darkwolfe's broken corpse. They all seemed dumbfounded by his loss and as if staring a moment longer would give them the answers they sought. They stood there and continued to stare.

The mountain felt so barren and devoid of life. Now there were just voiceless rocks, a mocking wind, and a trail that went both up to who knew where and down to a hostile world. What to do? Charlemette felt that it was right to continue the quest and bring his body to the temple, although even she was beginning to doubt that it truly existed. "Lets gather him up and continue on," she offered, "let his sacrifice not be for nothing."

"Sacrifice?" Sir Gedrick questioned, "You mean his honor."

Part II

The Visitor

The insistent beating of a heart, like the chorus of crickets,
In the infinite spellbound night.
A child weeping, wailing, for some primal fear, or the birth of its young soul's plight.
A darkened shadow, some weary shade, arisen from the seat of hell
With some warning or perchance some tale to tell.
But what great story, some knowledge must be known to grant thee insight?
Why so does he worry, hiding in that fury—of darkness beyond the reach of light?
I bid to grant him entry, to tell me of this thing,
And all so suddenly, almost beguiling, he started with a waving of his blood stone ring.
And then it seemed, as all at once, transported from my shell,
I was spirited instantly away.
There it stood, that darkened tower, the haunt of dreams;
Burning in my mind still to this day.
Enthralled I was, frozen within the icy talons called fear,
I saw man's destruction, coming fire, burning away the morning clear.
The host, the shade, with a wry smile playing upon his lips,
Licked them in a way that satisfies,

And spit upon the ground, he bled a tear, and dared me to question what he prophesized.
Although it hurt, it burnt my pride, as if helpless, I drew a rasping breath,
I said I'd try, to change our course, and bade farewell to death.

1

Master Cheiron

The remaining companions carried the corpse of their friend up the final portion of the mountain. They had no choice but to leave their fallen elven comrades laid out together in a line, Silverworm insisted that they return as soon as possible to get them and everyone readily agreed. The trail made one last twist inward and opened into a little clearing on the inside of the horn. Across from them was the other horn, and below them a gigantic saddle that curved between the two rocky sentinels. The party enjoyed the view momentarily for they could see many days ride in any given direction. The sky was a myriad of colors and swirling clouds, and here and there predatory birds drifted on air currents scanning for food scurrying about far below. They also couldn't help but notice a collection of vultures gathering as well, and morbid thoughts of what may befall their elven friends was better left unsaid.

Cat and Sir Gedrick looked at each other and shrugged their shoulders. As if saying, well here we are and there isn't anything here. Now what? Charlemette, priestess of Levanah who was dedicated to illusion among other things, held up her hand to her fellow travelers, "Wait." Then before them, like a desert mirage wavering in the heat, a structure began to appear.

It was a huge five story stone temple with crenellated towers and graceful parapets. It floated in mid-air and a long wooden rope bridge connected it to the two horns on both sides. Across the way in the other horn, a huge cave opening could be seen carved into the mountainside and they could only speculate as to where it led.

"Well I'll be a son of a snake-beast," Sir Gedrick proclaimed.

"How simply delightful," Cat added, and fearlessly started across the bridge beaming in his childhood delight. The bridge was very solid and wide enough for several men to walk abreast. Cat peaked over the edge and was slightly overcome with a sense of vertigo. It was many draws to the bottom. Draws? That term always made Cat chuckle. A draw was essentially an arbitrary measure of distance and referred to how far the Goddess Diana could shoot an arrow from her wondrous moonbow. It roughly equated to about a man of average height taking about 3,000 strides. But no men could actually agree on the exactness of it. In fact, in the more heavily populated and civilized areas of Alcyone, distance was measured with a standard called a kilometer.

A voice came into Charlemette's mind then; it was urgent but peaceful and calm. {Hurry priestess, bring Darkwolfe to the temple. There may still be time to save him. You must hurry; he is at death's door}.

"Come let us hurry, please," Charlemette insisted, and followed quickly after Cat across the bridge. "We may still save him, hurry." She turned and waved them on as they still just stood there dumbfounded wondering what she was babbling about, and if there was any truth to what she said.

"Alright," Silverworm put in and motioned his two scouts to bring the body. The entire party scuttled across the bridge like a bunch of crabs. They were soon before a great portcullis that yawned open and a pair of gigantic oaken double doors led into a central courtyard. A pair of monks in black robes greeted them and they silently motioned for the party to follow. The monks moved with haste and were so graceful that they appeared to float across the cobblestones. The air about the temple was cool and peaceful. After the recent battle it felt like a safe haven and they could sense that no harm would befall them while they were here.

The party was led through several doors and down many long hallways. There were several tapestries depicting the god and goddess and others that showed a great war with demons and dragons. After only a brief period of time they came into a large central chamber. The room was circular in shape and many colored tapestries hung on the stone walls here as well. Sizeable torches blazed from sconces around the perimeter of the room, and an intricate altar was raised on a dais at the far end. The most riveting spectacle was at the center of the chamber, where there was a circular pool and at its edge stood another priest. Charlemette concluded that this was the priest who had communicated with her, for her holy senses were going off as if she were standing in the presence of a god.

"Hurry, bring him here," Cheiron insisted again. "Take off his clothes."

The elves placed Darkwolfe at the edge of the pool and began peeling his clothes off though it was difficult because of the gore that clung tenaciously, as if conspiring against any attempt at saving the young man.

Charlemette was sickened and sad. This is not how I would like to remember his naked body she thought. Bones had broken upon impact of the boulder and were sticking out through the skin in many places. The body was already discolored, and an unnatural appearance of death's pallor was resident on his face. She turned away from the scene and went over and knelt before the altar. "Goddess hear my prayers. If there is any way to save my friend and lover, I beg that you can make it so." Her tears fell at the foot of the altar, and she put her head in her hands in grief.

Sir Gedrick and Cheiron took the corpse as the elves finally ripped and cut off the remaining clothes. Sir Gedrick looked into the other man's eyes. First they were brown, then green. They shifted to blue and violet, then gray. Cheiron nodded his ageless face and the two men placed the body into the swirling waters of the pool.

The pool was like a great lazy whirlpool and moved from right to left, widdershins. Sir Gedrick tried to look deeply into its murky depths, but could not penetrate beyond its surface. Darkwolfe's shell twirled in a couple awkward turns, bobbed twice, and then slowly sank beneath the mysterious water.

"What do we do now Master Cheiron?" Silverworm inquired.

"I beg that you continue to patrol the area, I am sorry for the deaths of your companions. While no loss of life is ever trite, there are greater things at play here than me or you, or even a thousand lives."

The three elves bowed respectfully and left the way they had come.

"And us," Sir Gedrick questioned? "I have a message for you from the Terra Paladins." He handed a rolled parchment to the man in black robes.

Master Cheiron nodded slightly as if he could perceive the essence of the message without actually reading it, and tucked the parchment into his leather belt. "Now we wait."

* * * * *

Heather awoke to the sound of a rooster announcing the birth of this day's sun as it broke over the woodlands and cast it's glare on the dull gray stone of Grathmoor castle. She quickly donned her work clothes, splashed her face in a wash basin, and tied her hair back in a bun. She stroked Furball absently and felt a wave of fear as his demonic glare penetrated her very being and she realized then how worthless and meaningless her little life really was. She shook it off as morning nonsense and dejectedly made her way to the lord and lady's chambers to begin her morning ritual of menial tasks and to wallow in an existence of unfulfilled desires.

This early in the morning the halls were empty and the only sound that kept her company was the rhythmic clapping of her sandals. She came to their chambers without incident where she was greeted by two of the elite guards bored with their duty. They opened the doors for her and watched lecherously as she swayed her way into the outer chambers.

"I'd like to get apiece o dat one I tell ya," one said snickering.

"Ya real prime bit a meat," the second one concluded swinging the doors shut after giving the girl one last look over.

Heather was quite use to such blatant comments by the guards and ignored them as best she could. I want to marry a lord some day she thought, definitely not some smelly guard. She began getting together clothes for the day and laying them out in an orderly fashion. She prepared several wash basins and gathered up towels and soaps and fine lotions and oils that the lady was so fond of. A lord would be nice she thought, or…

A wizard?

The thought had popped into her mind suddenly. A wizard? Well why not? A wizard usually didn't rule like a lord or king, but in some ways had just as much power didn't he?

Or a wizard king.

Yes, that was it, a wizard king. I could be a queen and rule. Maybe even I could learn magic too she considered. Really anything would be better than her present situation. She had seen many older women who had worked their whole lives in the castle as servants to the lord and lady. They were well cared for when they could not perform up to task, but they would never and had never been anything more than just a lowly servant. A servant who catered to the whims of another, and she felt, often lesser person. Why? Just because they were born noble. What in the hell did that mean any way? Yes, she thought, one day I will marry a wizard king and rule Grathmoor. Now I just have to find a way.

The smell of food cooking for this day's morning-draw wafted up from the kitchen below. The smell was intoxicating and Heather heard her stomach rumble in agony, begging to be noticed and catered to she concluded, just like everything and everyone else in this miserable life. Eggs and bacon, fresh bread and pastries, even a delicious new brew called coffee brought up from the south lands hung in the air, tempting and tantalizing the senses.

"Now I just have to find a way," she whispered conspiratorially to herself.

Art, Grathmoor's head cook, smiled and bellowed jovially as he went about preparing the morning meal. Many of his helpers shrugged at each other in a loss for words. This morning-draw meal was turning into a feast, and Art's attitude was far from his typical crankiness and unending tirade of insults and badgering of his staff. Never the less, the crew enjoyed this sudden change in character and let him make his special finishing touches without a word or hint of suspicion.

In fact all of the food had been sprinkled with a deadly mushroom powder. It was slow acting, but quite fatal. No one would really notice the effects until at least half way through the meal. By then everyone would be affected. Art was very thorough in his detail. The animal's food had been tainted albeit with a less exotic poison, and even helpers were enlisted to take food out to the guards at the precise time.

Art wasn't so much as being out of character, he was extremely happy and giddy that soon everyone in the castle would be dead.

Before the sun had risen even another span in the mornings beautiful cerulean sky, the lord and lady of Grathmoor took their places in the dining hall and all present gratefully began the morning-draw feast.

"Such a glorious display Art, what is the occasion?" Lord Noblin inquired, chomping into a greasy sausage. He gurgled it down with some fresh apple juice and indulged in a heap of flatcakes.

"Just thankful things are getting back in order around here my Lord, I thought everyone could use a little cheering up." He chuckled and hurriedly made certain that all of the guards had been delivered their meals and his servants had also taken a few bites of some of the delicacies. In some sickening way this was his magnum opus, his great work in life, to end the reign of the Noblin line and kill hundreds in one fell swoop of glorious assassination. I missed my calling; cook indeed.

Art continued beaming in his usual fashion, making sure no one was left out. Even the priests and priestesses were present he noted. He froze suddenly. Where was Javonavich he wondered? He didn't want the high priest to ruin everything. If Javonavich figured out what was happening, he would not only utterly destroy Art with his clerical powers, but he might even be able to save some or even all of his would be victims.

Just then Javonavich came into the dining hall. His face was a bit white and he looked ill. He made his way over to the table of priests and took a seat. High priest Javonavich was having a bout of stomach sickness. The last thing he wanted to do this morning was eat, but he felt at least somewhat inclined to show his face at morning-draw and demonstrate that he was still strong enough to handle any more problems that some mage or invading band may be conspiring.

High Priestess Amber reached out and took his hand reassuringly. "Are you all right?" She was as lovely as ever even with a somewhat pointed nose and eyes a bit too close together. Her smile and concern were genuine, and the unconditional love she exhibited to all was her true beauty and attraction to would be husbands, Javonavich included.

"Just fine," he replied. He didn't look fine. It took about all his effort just to restrain himself from running to get a chamber pot. Food poisoning perhaps? He had stuff flying out of both ends, forcefully and painfully, it was a wonder he was even still standing. It was too bad the high priest didn't take the warning signs for what they were, instead of attributing it to just a sickness. He had done his morning prayers, and did indeed feel better than he did the previous night. Clerics still got sick like everyone else. So be it. He would ride out the morning and then retire to his rooms to recuperate.

"Would you like anything High Priest Javonavich?" A young priest to his right asked.

Javonavich just shook his head and tried to look his best. His position was one of power and offered hope to the rest of the castle's inhabitants. Guards had wives and children. Cooks had family. Servants usually weren't alone. There were even some friends and their families who had chosen to live in the castle over the years. The dining hall was large, and even with its size it was still packed to capacity. Javonavich knew he had to be a figure of hope for these people, just as Lord Noblin and the High Priestess Amber were.

Young children were running around nibbling on fruit and powdered cakes. Some of Lord Noblin's dogs were under the great tables eating scraps. The canines may have noticed a presence or strange smell perhaps if they weren't so busy fighting for food. All in all it appeared to be a gay event, a feast befitting the lord of the land.

Sabbath had awoken early and made his way to the castle. After tying the stolen horse off to a tree, he had made himself invisible with his spell craft. Once accomplished, it was quite easy to stroll right into the castle and past the inept guards. Za'Varuk had filled him in on the cook's plan to poison the entire castle, in one fell swoop they would be gone. Sabbath could almost taste victory. He grinned sardonically as he watched many of the guards chewing on morning-draw foods.

He had made his way to the dining hall. There was a little alcove off to the side where he had a good view of the only mage and clerics; they were his only real threat. "Here I'll stay until the fun begins." The drone of conversation and scraping of plates and silverware was meditative and the ambitious mage used it to gather his strength and magical energies in case things didn't go quite as smoothly as he hoped. Of course they never did.

2

Death and Rebirth

There was only nothingness. Pure, irrevocable darkness. No sensations prevailed at all. No light or eyes to see with. No sound or ears to hear with. There were no things to feel against the skin or nerves to cry in pain or heat or cold. These things still lay someplace else in a broken shell that no longer drew breathe or pumped blood within its vessels. There was not even the scent of some dust or mold to assail his nostrils and thereby infer he was in the ground someplace or outdoors. There was not even the sensation of saliva or the metallic taste of hunger or its yearning, for if he were able, he must by famished by now.

Darkwolfe had consciousness though he suspected his brain no longer functioned. Somehow he still maintained his memories where he suspected the brain stored them, or to think and reason for surely they also were evident there as well. This unfortunately unleashed an ugly can of worms, which he concluded the saying should be altered for such cases to unleashing a nightmarish sea of monsters. If his brain was the seat of consciousness, then where was he without it? If not, where did it reside? He knew a man once who had taken a cudgel to the head and suffered substantial brain damage. This man was never again the same. So was his self and personality truly just some estranged construct of his brain? Were the whole ideas of soul and spirit just some way of making the prospect of death more manageable and therefore allowing the plethora of religions to evolve and influence the lives of millions. What if there was no continuation or afterlife and every theological debate was for naught. The fact that uncountable wars had been raged and lives taken in the name of religion seemed absurd.

Children obviously didn't think or function as adults until their development came to a certain point. He knew his thoughts came as language, a conversation with himself. What if he never learned language? Would he think pictorially? What then if he was blind, would he think through his other senses? What was this soul or spirit, and where did it come from if it truly existed at all? At what point did you become you? Perhaps more of a spiritual evolution, perhaps in complexity he thought. He remembered hearing High Priestess Amber talk about how time and all existence really persisted as a circle and not in a line like we thought about it. The goddess had taken this circle and straightened it out so the races could learn and know past, present, and future. However he also knew a man once who died for many minutes. When revived he was asked what death was like. He said, "I hate to disappoint you, but there was no light or tunnel as rumor has it. I just passed out and the next thing I knew you all were standing around looking at me."

And then even beyond Darkwolfe's thoughts and self-dialogue he began to know and understand things. He wasn't sure how they came to him, but he was just infused with knowledge. Beyond all real-world perceptions and explanations, things came into focus somehow.

Secrets I can tell you, the mysteries you must experience for yourself.

He could think and speculate, but he had no idea of where he was. He remembered the boulder and diving in front of it to save Charlemette's life. Then everything ceased to exist. He supposed this was what death might be like. However he wasn't particularly happy about it. Great, how fun would eternity of consciousness be like if there weren't any stimuli to break the abysmal monotony. He figured he probably wouldn't last long before he started hallucinating and became totally insane, and yet he didn't even have ears or eyes to hallucinate with, and then he supposed that somehow psychically he could through thought forms and a distortion of his inner will.

Then he became angry. Nothing ever was like a great story or myth. The hero saves the day, kills the evil knight or dragon, marries the girl and lives happily ever after. No, he goes out on his first adventure and gets splatted by a boulder saving Charlemette.

Then he was happy and sad at the same time. It was worth it. To sacrifice himself for Charlemette and for her to even have one precious breath more of life was worth any pain and agony that he may suffer. He was sad at the prospect that he would never see her again. He hoped she found someone someday to care for her and have children. Though he had no tear ducts to cry with, he wept.

Then out of nothing there was a study of sorts with a figure in midnight robes. The cowl was drawn tight around his face and no features could be discerned. There were several plush chairs, an intricately carved mahogany table with chairs, and the walls held bookshelves from end to end. There were far too many books to approximate their number, but it was more than Darkwolfe could ever imagine. How much knowledge could be held within their covers? Warmth emitted from a deep fireplace where burned several thick logs brightly and a carved statuette of a majestic salmon sat on the mantle.

The figure then waved his hand, and a blinding red light flashed from a ring on his third finger. The walls of the study disappeared, and the two of them found themselves amidst a raging battle. In the distance could be seen ruined, burning cities. Demonic beasts fought man, elves, and dwarves. The humanoids were caught up in a whole scale slaughter, and the demons drank of their blood. The world burned with fire and magic and with this came the annihilation of all the Pleides, not just Alcyone. Then there was only death, chaos, and the hordes of demons ruled for all eternity.

"What is all this?" Darkwolfe asked.

"The end of all life, peace, and balance." A deep resonant voice spoke.

"But why?"

"The demons are a very old and powerful race. They feed on fear and hatred, anger, anarchy, and destruction. They care not for the delicate balance that is life. Even a tree or human or fish must be in perfect harmony to continue to exist, the demons live only to upset the balance and end all life in the universe."

"Like death?" Darkwolfe offered meekly.

The creature chuckled lightly in amusement. "Oh no, not at all. Creators and figures of death seek balance. Building up and breaking down. It is balance and union through opposites; a circle with no beginning, never ending. These demons only want destruction and nothing more. They don't kill and destroy because it is their nature, say like the goblin race. These demons are highly intelligent. They have the capacity for good and to make favorable choices. Instead they allow themselves to be ruled by power hunger, jealousy, and anger. They are a bitter race. In fact they could even represent all of the negative aspects of humanity. Such humanoids do exist and are truly evil, because like the demonic race they do not strike out against balance because of their nature, but through choices of free will. You can not blame a snake for biting you or a scorpion for stinging you because it is their nature, but this destruction you see is out of choice, bitter, unadulterated, and viciously conceived. This vision can be reality."

Darkwolfe looked around at the killing going on all around him. Endless fire, destruction, death, suffering, and wretched strife. "Why are you telling me this? I'm dead. How am I supposed to do anything about all this? Gods know I would never wish any harm to come to anyone, but dead is dead. I don't even have a body anymore. What am I suppose to do float around and scare the demons into submission?"

"Death is only change not the end. If I give you the chance to return to life, now, not in a future incarnation as would inevitably happen, will you move to stop this horde and save the balance?" The screams of the dying were all around them. Several bodies were ripped in half and became a meal for a small host of creatures. Acrid smoke clung to the air. There was the unbearable stench of death and decay, even without his senses Darkwolfe was aware of these things and both sickened and appalled by their presence. He felt so helpless, but earnestly wished he could make a difference even if it saved one helpless child.

"I'm nobody! I can use a handful of weapons and one or two spells, how am I gonna fight a demon, let alone a whole bunch of them?" Darkwolfe stated emphatically, and held up his hands as if there the power might be found. He saw only a wispy image of his former self.

"In time your powers will grow. The council of Pleides has foreseen this. As well, you will gather together the Dragon Band like was done the last time the demons were a threat. Don't worry about the intricacies of this now, there will be guidance along the way. Also, you should be able to find help from the Terra Paladins. It is their mission to protect Alcyone and all of the Pleides. Be warned however, there will be many who will stand against you. I won't lie, it will be a hard path and you and all your friends and loved ones will most likely die before all of this is through. So, what do you say?" Death's hand was extended as if to close a deal. It was human and strong looking. It was warm and friendly to Darkwolfe's ethereal hand.

"An offer I can't refuse. Not only do I get to get myself killed again, but everyone else I know as well. However, seeing how I can't do anything in my present condition, and the alternative would be total destruction of everything the humanoid races hold dear, I accept!"

It was morning now, and the companions' vigil was complete as rays of colored light beamed in through the intricate stained glass windows set high in the central chamber of the Dragon Temple. The group all looked weary, but no one, including master Cheiron, was willing to leave the swirling pool. There was some mounting power and energy building within the chamber and everyone was becoming antsy and nervous by its presence.

Cat started suddenly in a defensive movement and drew his short sword. At first nothing was apparent and they all thought Cat was just a little jumpy after being up all night in the spooky esoteric place of worship. "Look," he said pointing with his sword.

Then where before there was nothing, a wispy image of a man in brownish robes appeared; a ghost. Simultaneously the group uttered, "Darkwolfe?" Soon it became evident however that it wasn't their dead friend, but a scarecrow-like figure of a priestly nature and devoid of any malevolent intent.

"Its Tucker, a cleric of the Great Mother from Grathmoor," Charlemette stated, coming nearer to the apparition. She was a friend with Tucker to some extent. Over the years she had spent in Grathmoor they had had several discussions about theology and magic. While he wasn't a close friend, Char was a little saddened that he had passed on. That and for some reason he was trapped between the worlds, for now being prevented from going to the other side where he would contemplate his last incarnation and eventually be reborn to continue his spiritual evolution.

The ghost's voice was audible to everyone present, but very faint. "I must warn you. Warn you about Grathmoor," he stated hesitantly in a haunting tone.

"What about it?" Sir Gedrick boomed, and then seemed embarrassed by the reverberations the volume brought forth within the chapel. Thankfully no one seemed to notice and the companions waited for the ghost's reply.

"The curse was created by a powerful mage. He's now trying to take the castle. Most of the town is already dead." The ghost's form wavered as if it were standing in a strong breeze, its robes swirling in a hypnotic and rhythmic pattern.

"What does he want?" Charlemette asked this time. She was now within arms reach of Tucker's incorporeal form.

"He is in league with a demon now who is trying to gain its freedom through the gate."

"A demon?" Cheiron blurted out and also moved closer. He appeared worried and a mask of contemplation settled over his facial features. His stride was graceful and purposeful. Beneath his loose robes the party could tell there was a solid mass of muscles and though he was a priest he could strike any warrior as a formidable opponent.

"Yes, a demon. The core is weakened and this demon, Za'Varuk, is close to escape. The demon is helping this mage take Grathmoor in turn for his freedom."

"Aaah, so the time has finally come." Master Cheiron chimed. "Very well, you have leave to go spirit, your task is complete. May the Great Mother welcome you into her fold."

"Blessed be," Charlemette added and bowed respectfully.

Tucker smiled in ghostly glee. He then drifted from sight and was no more.

A loud bubbling noise erupted from the pool. The companions spun about. Another ghost? The pool had reversed direction and now spun from left to right, deosil. Huge air bubbles rose to the surface and burst. Small wafts of tendril white smoke drifted up toward the ceiling with each miniature explosion.

The pool became even more turbulent and the group looked on in curiosity and anticipation of what was to come. A great scaly head of black plates and barbs broke through the surface of the black-azure liquid. Cat and Sir Gedrick jumped back brandishing their weapons, ready to slay the unexpected beast.

"Hold," Cheiron yelled over the sacred pool's din. He held both arms out to the sides to prevent the paladin and assassin from attacking the creature. A human-sized dragon came out of the pool. Its sharp claws scraped on the mosaic floor setting all of the companions' nerves on edge and a chill quivering through their bodies. The dragon landed on the floor with a great exhaustive thud and sighed in bestial relief. It shifted as though but an illusion, and in one blink of an eye there lay a dragon, and the next, a naked man.

Darkwolfe was reborn.

* * * * *

Eversleep mushrooms were an interesting poison. They were slow acting, and when they did actually take effect the person just became overly sleepy and fell into a deep sleep from which there was no waking. If the individual was extremely lucky and a competent cleric was handy, the poison could be nullified, but timing was critical and few who had digested the shrooms ever lived to brag about their brush with death.

This is how the fall of the Noblin reign began. In the midst of the meal, and much to Sabbath's delight, dogs grew quiet, children lay down to sleep on the floor, and several people plopped face first in their plates. One rather obese lady bubbled loudly in her bowl of porridge before drowning in the stuff. The great commotion in the hall began to wane, and Javonavich in his ill state didn't notice anything was awry until Amber let out a sigh at his side and crashed to the stone floor with a thud.

"By the gods," he began and gathered a sense of clarity about him. He scanned the room briefly and instantly took in all the falling bodies, like wilting flowers in a blazing sun, so fast to change from their vibrancy and color to fetid remains. "Poison," he whispered and instantly stooped to try and counteract it by calling on his priestly powers.

"Silence priest," Sabbath intoned as he became visible, his dark robes swirling about him, the floor littered with dying bodies at his booted feet. He stepped from the alcove like a vampire rising for his evening meal, teeth bared and murder in his hate-filled eyes. His words held the power of a spell, and Javonavich in his weakened state could not counteract the effect and therefore was helpless to invoke the power of his god Sin through speech. He tried by will alone, but in his weakened state he was just not strong enough to fight this powerful unknown mage who stood before him.

Sabbath smirked in satisfaction as he continued to survey the great hall, momentarily ignoring the helpless high priest. Every second another castle dweller fell into eternal sleep. Soon the room became deathly still. All who were presently alive, were the cook, Sabbath, and the soon to be extinguished priest. Sabbath brought his gaze back around to the helpless priest.

Javonavich knew things were far out of control, but he was not one to give up. If this wretched mage took over Grathmoor, all of the surrounding area would soon fall into his control. Could he somehow gain the Noblin's power to control the dead of the land? This right had seldom been invoked by the good Lords of Grathmoor over the centuries, and even then only in defense of the region. If somehow this mage could control them, he would possess an army of undead to terrorize all of the surrounding communities and perhaps beyond. Javonavich knew however that the reign was bound by election, and only proper residents could elect their new lords. The priest quickly scanned the room and set eyes upon the foul cook who had undoubtedly poisoned the entire castle. He could pass the lordship!

With all the priests willful power he could not attack the mage, but the cook was another matter. He felt the power of Sin flow through him and reached out across the room with a magical claw, grasping Art's heart and crushing it within his chest.

"Aahrg..," Art issued forth in the throws of death, clutching his chest with both hands. The traitorous cook fell to his knees, shattering a kneecap on the stone floor. Oblivious to such trivial pain compared to a rendered heart, Art continued to clutch at his chest, as if he could reach within and hold the magical claw at bay.

"Ralweeth gnan-ta," Sabbath commanded. Javonavich felt as if he were suddenly plunged into an icy stream. He quickly solidified into a block of ice, perched on his chair with an arm reaching out toward the cook. But all too late, for just then Art crumbled to the floor beyond repair, dead as dead can be.

"Raaagh!" Sabbath bellowed and swept his arm out to the side toward the block of priestly ice. Like a resounding crack of mighty stones the block exploded and icy fragments rained down upon the slaughtered, sleeping field of corpses, like some diamond glitter dust to speed their souls quickly on their way. But this was not to be so, for this would be his army. These would be the beginning of his conquest. They must obey, Sabbath thought to himself. He strove his whole life even from a lowly mage to always seek more power, to conquer that next tier, and dominate with his art and his wits. When this all began he had a limited vision of taking Grathmoor and maybe some of the surrounding areas, to be a Lord Mage. Now, with the demon at his side, all the world could be his. Total victory. Releasing the demon Za'Varuk didn't sound like a terribly great idea, Sabbath knew he could not hope to win over the demon, but in his conquests certain items and spells could be obtained to ensure that he had the upper hand when the unavoidable confrontation came to fruition. And yet he still thought somehow, by will alone he could deny the rules of ascension here at Grathmoor and defeat the ancient magic.

"Arise my soldiers. Come and serve me, your lord." There was only stillness. "Obey me you worthless dogs. Wake and fight you things of death!" Nothing stirred; none would hearken to his call to undeath.

{Oh so close my mage friend, and yet so terribly far away. Close only counts in firestorms and beheadings you know, as of course in both cases the end result is still the same; annihilation and bloodletting. Never the less we appear to be at some quandary do we not? }

[Is this some kind of trickery fiend. You promised me the castle. We had a deal!]

{And so we did. But even I can not bypass the laws of rule. The magic of this land is too great for only a portion of my spiritual self to overcome. The undead will not bow to your command until you are appointed. Call it a minor detail, but it is quite explicit. Never fear for I have made some arrangements that will assure that both of us get what we want.}

It was then that Sabbath was made aware of the maiden Heather as she approached him from across the room, weaving through the littered bodies as if it were a boulder-strewn field, and she sported a pleasant smile as though it were nothing but a spring time stroll. She quickly came before the mage and they looked deeply into each other's eyes; there was hunger there. He wanted conquest. She wanted power. They came from very different lives, but they were in many ways quite the same. Sabbath had nurtured this desire his entire life, and while the demon had awakened it in the servant girl, it was there all the same, hungry, dominating, and all pervasive.

Year after year living in poverty had created a repressed anger and hatred toward her betters. Every morning cleaning chamber pots, and fussing with the Lady and Lord. Lewd comments delivered by the guards, condescending priests and mages, even the newly expired cook had treated her as no better than a child or dog over the years. This fostered a great void of anguish and yearning for something better.

"I am your new Lord, bow before me woman." Sabbath sought to force Heather into doing his whim, but the girl would have none of it.

"I shall be your queen and rule by your side, nothing less." Heather was more scared than at any other time in her life. In fact she could picture the mage turning her into a big block of ice too, but the demon was in her mind and soothed her, giving her strength and determination to see this through that she never thought possible. She had always cowered before her betters and for once she felt equal to this mage and would strike a bargain at all costs.

Sabbath's face contorted in rage and he nearly incinerated the servant there and then had the demon not entered his mind.

{Hold mage! This is how it shall be Sabbath. You will get what you want, but the woman will be your only link to your hold on your army. If you betray me in any way, I will destroy the girl and your link to the castle's title. Agree to the woman's terms, and the castle's honor and magic shall bind you both in marriage and in title to the land. We shall all get what we desire. Don't be a fool, you are too smart for that. The mere cunning of your curse and assault on the town, while not nearly close to perfection, certainly admirable. We can rule all the lands of Alcyone for a time, more years than a human life before I blast it all away into dust. Agree to her terms and let us find conquest together.}

Sabbath cold not discern any better way of dealing with the present situation. As powerful as he was, he could not forcefully take control of the powers of ascension. The ancient mages and clerics of this region had created this defensive magic to prevent this very thing from happening. A willing resident had to grant lordship. On second glance the woman wasn't ugly by any means, what difference if he took her as his wife to get total power. Later he could always find a way to dispose of her.

"Fine my sweet lamb, let us be wed in spirit and rule together over all the lands." Sabbath placed his hand on her thin shoulder and put forth his best smile though his eyes belied betrayal and ungodly tortures for the lass as soon as he found a way to do so.

She knelt before him and bowed her head. Tears trickled down her cheeks and she quivered with joy and anticipation. Just this morning she was a lowly peasant girl, and now she was about to become a lady, a queen.

"As you wish my Lord."

3

Preparing for War

Breath. Life. These things never felt so good. Darkwolfe sat up on the wet tiled floor, and looked into the faces of all his curious companions. Not until scanning the crew, gazing longer at Master Cheiron, and then settling fondly on Charlemette's glorious features, did he realize that he was naked and modestly covered his groin area with the tattered and bloody clothes that lay near him. All appeared joyful, but mystery and even fear of sorts exuded from the spectators, and the newly revived man did not entirely know how to react, so he waited in silence pondering the meeting with the robed man in quiet.

"Thank the Goddess your alive," Charlemette quickly ran over and embraced him, smothering him in kisses. She felt his arms and chest and looked for any signs of blood or broken bones and found none. She was truly amazed, but so happy with relief that any magic that could heal her beloved must be good and she invoked praises and prayers to her goddess in thanks.

"Yes, it is truly wonderful that you are okay," Sir Gedrick added, patting him on the back like welcoming an old friend home from a long and arduous journey.

Cat stood back along with Silverworm and watched intently at the spectacle not really sure that what they were seeing was real.

"Time is of the essence I'm afraid," Master Cheiron came over shooing the companions away as if they were children in a kitchen vying for sweets. Charlemette gave him a dirty look and reluctantly retreated to the side. "We must attend to a few things, the lad and I, but I would like you all to make yourselves comfortable and get some sleep. My attendants will show you to some quarters, and Darkwolfe and I will join you later for mid-draw." With that said, Master Cheiron helped Darkwolfe to his feet, and thankfully so, for the newly resurrected (as one might imagine) are a little unsteady on their feet. "Come, we have much to do." He led the young man toward a darkened alcove and the pair instantly vanished from sight in a blink of magical light.

The two found themselves in a large circular chamber with the walls curving up toward the ceiling forming a great dome. The floor was polished hardwood and shined eerily in the unnatural lighting. There weren't any torches or even magical globes present that were apparent. No shadows were even cast to discern the source. The chamber was just lit. Along the walls were racks of various weapons: swords great and small, short and long, axes, daggers, maces, flails, spears, halberds, longbows, crossbows, and many other esoteric weapons that Darkwolfe had never seen or heard of in his limited existence.

"Where are we," he asked.

Master Cheiron didn't respond right away, but rather seemed to be meditating, taking in the beauty and peace of the place. "This is a training chamber that was created very, very long ago. It has been quite some time since I have come her with a pupil to train. I am merely enjoying the familiarity of the place like one would a wife after a troublesome war."

"So I'm here to train," the impetuous lad concluded, heading over to pick up a sword.

"Patience. You are here for more than just sword training. Patience is one of the things you must learn. Come over here and have a seat."

Darkwolfe sauntered over and sat down on the floor with his legs sprawled out lazily.

"Not like that," Cheiron stated in a loud flat voice. He bent both legs at the knees and sat back on his heels. "This is the dragon position, and any time I ask you to sit or meditate you will assume this position unless stated otherwise."

"But.."

"Silence! You will now give me push-ups. Move! You will not speak unless I give you leave to do so."

Darkwolfe rolled over and started cranking out some push-ups. So this is going to be like warrior training. A little discipline, a few push-ups, a pain in the rear but totally doable.

Cheiron began again, "We are here so that you might have a tiny chance of living longer than two seconds when you face a demon in battle. We will train with weapons, but more importantly we need to train your body so that it is a weapon itself. If you make it that far, then we may consider your magical abilities, and then finally blending the two so that they are in harmony. I have a feeling we may not make it to this last, blending part, but we shall see as things progress we may not need to do so. Time does not exist here for us. We can do our training in a week or ten years, it matters not to me at all, but know that when we finally leave this hall that resides outside of reality, we will be just in time for lunch with your companions. It would be a trifle embarrassing to great your lover as an old man, for rest assured you will indeed age in here, but your friends will not."

Darkwolfe kept pumping out the push-ups and decided to take a look at his newfound teacher in speculation.

"NEVER, look at me unless I give you leave to do so. You must learn to sense me without your eyes." He let Darkwolfe continue to near exhaustion to where the lad could not lift himself off the ground at all. "On your feet!"

Darkwolfe weakly rolled over and struggled to his feet pathetically.

"When you move, you will move quickly at all times. What do you think this is a stroll through the woods with your girlfriend?! Down on your back, give me sit-ups!"

He fell to the floor as quickly as he was able and instantly began doing sit-ups as fast as he was able to, hopefully appeasing his teacher. Again when he had slowed, and each movement felt like a snake-beast feasting on his stomach, his teacher yelled for him to get to his feet. He didn't feel as though he had actually moved very fast regardless of his greatest intent to do so, but much to his surprise Master Cheiron didn't tell him to drop and do sit-ups or push-ups, but merely stood there motionless. Darkwolfe did his best not to look in his direction, but time went on and on and still he did not respond and finally he looked over at his teacher.

"Do not look at me!!! Run around the outer edge of this chamber until I say that you may stop. Move!"

Darkwolfe began running, his bare feet slapping on the wooden floor and his breath coming in a rasp even though he had only just begun. Out of boredom he began counting laps around the structure and even came to memorize all the weapons in fine detail with each passing. He came to realize there were two very thin bedding mats laid out along one section of the wall, but as far as he could tell there was no evidence of food or water. If he stayed here for any length of time he figured he would die long before he even got a glimpse of a demon. Somewhere around lap 600, Cheiron bid him to come over to him.

"Here," he offered holding out a small black pair of leggings, "we can't have you flopping about for the next 10 years now can we?"

Darkwolfe tried to offer a faint smile, all the while looking toward the floor or off to the side. He took the pants, and struggled for several moments trying to get his fatigued legs through them, but finally was covered and standing, albeit unsteadily in front of his master, panting heavily.

"Now, attack me."

Darkwolfe turned to retrieve a sword from one of the weapons racks.

"Not with a sword boy, with your bare hands."

He was perplexed for a moment, but then remembered some of his warrior training and then in a rage raced toward his teacher in an effort to tackle him. Just as he was about to grab him, Darkwolfe grabbed empty air as Cheiron sidestepped at the last instant and the lad crashed to the floor and tumbled several times before screeching to a halt. The floor had left several burns on his upper torso and arms. His rage grew even more and once again he charged his teacher. Again he grabbed empty air and crashed to the ground. The third try at least he didn't fall, and by the fourth he was on to the game.

"When engaged in combat you may look at the chest or waist of your opponent, but never his eyes. You may do so when we battle, but at no other time."

The fourth pass turned into more of a dance, or chase as would be a more appropriate description, for when Darkwolfe finally collapsed and could go no more he had still failed to lay a finger on his teacher several hours later.

Master Cheiron let him sleep where he lay and settled himself down on one of the bedding mats for a quick nap. Training here would be continuous. He would allow himself a quick break and then magically revive the lad and begin again. Darkwolfe would be sore for sure, but would feel as though he had eaten and had a good night's sleep. No sleep or food or even water would be had here, only these magical infusions. Darkwolfe's new *blood* would eventually take hold from the resurrection pool and then allow him to learn more quickly and go for great periods of time without rest and before the end of training no infusions would be needed at all. It was this bond with the pool that would ultimately allow him to face the demons with conviction, without worry for personal loss of life and limb. The trouble was in instilling the flow without burning out the host. The nectar of the gods could be both sweet and deadly.

He was awake. He was sore in muscles he couldn't fathom even existed. As the days wore on, if he could call them days because they were really just periods of training and periods of rest, his empty hand techniques improved greatly. He would often still have to do push-ups or some other meaningless and strenuous exercise for moving too slow or because Cheiron didn't like the way he smelled or some such thing, but he was impressed with his progress even though his teacher wouldn't say so. He learned how to block all manner of strikes, how to strike back with his fist or open hand, how to grapple and throw, and even how to break legs and arms and necks. He learned how to jump, tumble, roll, fall, and to use an opponent's energy and force against him.

"I think we are done with playing around, let us do a little sparring and see how you fare." Before Cheiron even finished with his last word he lashed forward with a kick and followed up with a series of punches and strikes. High, low, middle, and side, but each time Darkwolfe blocked methodically and entered into the rhythm of the offense and defense. He then began counter attacking and lashing out with spinning kicks and then driving in with blinding hand attacks that the master miraculously fended off with quiet calm. The two men raged with beauty, muscle, sweat, and passion. Finally the two separated, facing each other in a sudden stillness that defied the previous storm. Then the two bowed respectfully.

"Now that your body has become somewhat useful we shall begin to tackle the use of weapons. Remember humility in all that you do, there is always someone better no matter how great you may think you are. You must always use your wits and know when to fight and when to run; when to attack straightforward, and when to use deception. A weapon is merely an extension of it's wielder, if you allow your body to atrophy because of reliance on a weapon, then your swordsmanship will only be a shallow reflection of what true skill you may exhibit if all is within harmony."

"I believe I understand, but I must meditate upon it to truly understand further."

"Perhaps you are beginning to understand after all little one." Cheiron retreated to his bed mat and let Darkwolfe go about his meditation. Training was always as important as reflection and this lesson just as valuable.

Darkwolfe settled into the dragon position as was his custom and even though Cheiron had taught and allowed less painful positions for meditation in the months they must have been holed up in the training hall. He quieted his mind. When he at first began the meditative practices, it was almost impossible to cease the endless banter of his internal monologue that seemed to incessantly plague his mind. In fact until Cheiron had pointed out the difficulty of actually finding a moment of total silence, Darkwolfe had not realized the plaguing cacophony of sound that resided within his own mind. Cheiron said when you find that moment in time of total silence beyond thought, space, and even time, then you will know bliss.

Of course Darkwolfe couldn't really figure how his feet going numb and the inevitable agony of the later pins and needles figured into this whole bliss paradigm. In fact most of the time bliss came when he fell asleep. Sure, sure he thought, I have made some progress. He found the position more comfortable over time and even glimpsed pieces of oblivion as his teacher often referred to it as, but in truth it was extremely frustrating. Even the lessons on astral projection seemed all for naught. As much as he tried, as much as he didn't try, as much as anything he did and didn't do, he still couldn't lift out of his physical shell. Yes, frustration and pain and agony was all he knew. It wasn't the same excruciating weight of his physical training, but in some ways it was worse. He could see a punch, and hold a sword, but all this spiritual stuff was just so intangible; the more he scrutinized it, the more elusive it was. When he thought he was smarter than it and tried to ignore it and draw it to him, it was if he created a loop and still ended up pushing it away by some reverse idiomatic scheme of irony.

"Stop that brain of yours, you're giving me a headache," Cheiron uttered, breaking the illusory silence of the training hall. "Let your true self guide you. Your spirit, your higher self, your divine will or whatever term makes the most sense to you, let it do what it needs to do, not what you think it should do or what you want it to do. If nothing happens, well, then nothing happens. All that means is you're not quite ready. Sometimes people use plants or magical charms and spells to reach that bliss or to project their ethereal self, but what good is that? Just like not honing your body and relying on your weapon, if you can't reach these states on your own, then in a sense you're stealing the experience and pushing the ability even further away from your grasp. Like I said before, we may be here a very long time and it will not effect when we return. Don't fret about Charlemette or worry about the threat to the land, what you need to do is remember why you were given a second chance. Not to be with your girlfriend as much fun as that might be, but you are here as a chosen warrior to fight for the balance of the Pleides and nothing more. Feel like a puppet if you will, but you are not here to have fun, you are not on some vacation or holiday, and the quicker you get a grasp of this the sooner we can have that long awaited lunch." Master Cheiron glided around the room in thought, internally debating if he had said all that needed to be said.

"Master, can I ask you a question?" Darkwolfe still didn't eye his teacher but stared at the polished wood floor that had become so familiar over the last several months. His feet were heavily callused from going barefoot the whole time, and he suspected his barefoot kick would do as much damage as a hard leather boot.

"Ask away." Cheiron said softly, exhibiting more kindness and emotion than the student had ever heard.

Darkwolfe actually had many questions and hadn't really expected a favorable reply, so he did some quick mental formulations of hierarchical importance and then still didn't know how to ask until he finally blurted out, "who are you."

"A humble priest, a teacher, a student of life," he replied mildly.

"No, I mean really, who are you."

"I knew what you meant, but I'm not sure what parts to tell you. Not that I don't want to mind you, but there is just so much to purvey that only pieces would not give a clear meaning, and the whole life story would take more time than any mortal could rationally stand, myself included. I suppose it wouldn't hurt to give you a little piece and let you mull over it for a while if you promise not to ask any more questions about me until I decide you may be ready to learn or know more. Agreed?"

"Agreed." He wasn't entirely sure just why, but Darkwolfe was actually excited that he was about to get some piece of information about this mysterious teacher of his. He was just so,...perfect. It couldn't be described as anything else, and now he was about to glimpse that perfection.

"As I'm sure you are aware of, there are other worlds out there. Big? Vast? You have no idea. In fact a mere glimpse of creation by a mortal would drive you totally insane, thank the gods that our conscious perceptions of reality are limited and within scope of our comprehension." Cheiron came across from his student and assumed the dragon position also so they could talk face to face and on the same level.

Darkwolfe had lost all feeling in his legs now, but he knew that if he moved or tried to change his position Master Cheiron might see it as a sign of weakness and not continue the story he so dearly, and now had to know. Somehow he felt that their fates were somehow connected and for his teacher not to finish would be like losing a part of his soul that was finally so close to fusing with his.

Cheiron could see both the anguish and yearning in his pupils eyes. He had seen it many, many times before in the faces of his students who would one day become heroes and legends in the archives and psyches of mankind across the Pleides.

"The Pleides are a string of eight stars and eight habitable planets." He waved his hand and a real-life image of what he spoke appeared in the air above them filling the dome of the training hall. He pointed to one end of the spiral string, "This here is Alcyone where you are from. Each star as you can see has a similar blue world orbiting it. I was born here." He pointed to a planet at the opposite end of the spiral model. "Earth."

"But.."

Cheiron eyed him warningly to be still. "Absorb what I am saying, think later." He waited to make sure Darkwolfe both understand and quieted his mind to receive the information. People had to open themselves up to new thoughts and new experiences otherwise they could never learn and grow. As a teacher, Master Cheiron knew this to be a critical point. He continued to wait until he was sure his student was ready.

"Very long ago, the gods and goddesses were often found to walk amongst the mortals of the various worlds. As well, sometimes they would mate with them and created many new races and even humans of mixed blood. I was one such creature. I was even a teacher back then. One of great reputation and many young aspiring warriors would come to me for training. Let's just say that I eventually died and was brought back to life in the same manner that you were, and thankfully I have been able to continue training young sprouts like yourself ever since." He waved his hand again and the magical illusion dissipated.

From the look in Cheiron's eyes, Darkwolfe could tell that he wouldn't be allowed to pursue any more questions about his teacher, so he changed his line of thought. "What about me? I feel much different than before I died. It's hard to describe, but almost like I have raw energy buzzing around inside of me. And why haven't I eaten or drank anything the entire time I have been here? I should be dead by now or extremely thin and sick. I'm huge now, rippling with muscles, and I've never imagined I could feel so great or be in such excellent condition."

"The pool of resurrection can do strange things to those who enter. It takes the body of the deceased and the true spirit of the person, not just their present incarnation. We are the sum of all of our incarnations. Every time we reincarnate we forget our previous lives and experiences, but they are still a part of our composite existence. The pool blends our spirit with the magical energy of the pool and recreates the person in a more balanced self. You might consider yourself still you, as Darkwolfe from Grathmoor, but you are much more than that now. When you emerged from the pool we all saw you as a dragon."

"A dragon?"

"Not just in name only. Dragons are magical beings and as such you are akin to them now by being infused with the energy of the pool. Over time you will come to understand and utilize these new powers. That is your true intent now, to lead the Dragon Band against the demon horde. You are the Capit Draconis, the head of the dragon.

* * * * *

After the morning festivities and mushroom death, Grathmoor castle took on an eerie gloom and silence. One by one the dead arose and picked up sword and shield to guard the battlements. Ever so slowly the longer dead began to arrive from the streets of the town and from nearby graves. The influence of the Lord's control over the undead in the region stretched out for many draws in any direction. As the morning wore on Sabbath's army of skeletons and zombies grew into the several hundreds and the stench of rotting flesh became unbearable.

"It will be okay," Sabbath chided as Heather once again vomited into a basin. "It was careless of me not to think of this sooner." He quickly waved his hands and spoke an unintelligible incantation and suddenly the ungodsly smell was gone. "The protection from the smell should be permanent, but I'm afraid I can't do much about they way they look, there are just too many of them to hide their true form with an illusion."

"I'll manage," she said defiantly and straightened her back and wiped her mouth with the back of the sleeve of one of the former Lady's dresses. "I will be strong and make my lord proud. I vow not to be a nuisance and in time you will see my usefulness."

"I see it now quite plainly," he smirked fondling her sizeable breasts. She smiled coyly as he carried her to the bed tearing her dress open on the way.

* * * * *

As much as she tried, and as tired as she was, Charlemette could not drift off to sleep. After Master Cheiron and Darkwolfe disappeared through some kind of magical portal, several priests appeared and led the companions to separate sleeping quarters. They were told that they were free to explore the temple if they wished, but otherwise they would be wakened in time for the mid-draw meal.

"Everyone else is probably sleeping by now, what's my problem?" She questioned herself. Char lay spread out on a small cot with an olive green wool blanket. It was a little scratchy, but comfortable enough she reasoned. She had been up all night worrying about her friend and lover, and after the long hike to the temple and the battle with the mountain giants, she found it a veritable miracle that she still hung on to some semblance of consciousness at all.

She pulled an amulet of silver and garnets from beneath her robes. The magic of the artifact had been depleted by its many uses, but she was thankful for High Priest Javonavich giving it to her before the journey began. "How is Javonavich," she wondered. Many of the spells and great magical feats she had performed during the trip had made her appear to be some awesome priestess, but in truth she was really just a novice. She could never have destroyed the giant chieftain without the help of the amulet. What would happen in the future to her or her companions if she could not help or cast such powerful and useful spells?

Javonavich had revealed to her much of what he suspected about what was transpiring and of her friend's destiny. She had been the one under Javonavich's direction to leave the texts in the Curio shop for Darkwolfe. It seemed a little cloak and dagger for her, but he did benefit from the books and his learning abilities far exceeded the expectations of the priest. She was suppose to stay close to him and watch him for the temple, but friendship became much more than that over time and now she truly loved him. She couldn't imagine life without him. Now that he had been revived by the pool, would he still have time for her in his heart? She knew that he was not here out of some fantastic whim, and that his greater mission would have to override any feelings the two had for each other. But she loved him totally and completely, and that, she could not deny.

She prayed to her Goddess.

The room was sizeable for sleeping quarters in a holy temple. Cat and Sir Gedrick, not unlike Charlemette across the hall, could not sleep for the life of them. Sir Gedrick had gotten out of his heavy plate armor and now lay comfortably on one of the cots wearing a borrowed tan robe that the priests had so happily supplied. Cat sat across from him, but he still wore his leather armor, more out of laziness as opposed to thinking a battle was eminent.

"What do you make of all this," Sir Gedrick asked.

"Which part," Cat replied sarcastically, "the fact that Darkwolfe was brought back to life, that they disappeared, or that we're sitting here having a casual conversation in a floating temple in the middle of the mountains?"

"Well, I was referring to the dragon."

"Oh, well we had all been up all night and were talking to a ghost of all things, I imagine it was just the lighting or us being tired or something to that effect."

Sir Gedrick smiled, he could tell by the look on Cat's face that he didn't really believe a word that he was saying.

"When are we heading back to Thor's Hammer?" Cat asked slowly. "The deal was just to get here with you and back, nothing else. So we're here, now lets go. I like this Darkwolfe fellow and all but none of what's going on around here involves me or is any of my concern. I just want to get back to my life."

"Back to stealing and killing for a living, is that what you want to get back to?" His look was accusing, and he sat up in bed to face the thief/assassin.

"It's a liven ain't it?"

"Didn't ever do anything in your life because you knew it was the right thing to do, or for some greater purpose than putting gold in your pockets and food in you stomach?"

"Sure, sometimes, but to tell you the truth most people don't care. Most people do whatever they can get away with, take whatever they can get their hands on, and say what will help them accomplish their goals. They don't care whom they step on, cheat, or destroy in the process. Its harsh but reality baby, and as much as I agree with what the Terra Paladins stand for and do, you guys live in some fantasy land where honor and ideals are some sort of tangible thing." Cat was frustrated and torn between his horrible childhood on the streets and the direction his heart told him to go in. He wanted to be good, felt their was some kind of righteousness in his heart that told him he should do certain things, but he had been around and seen what the world was like.

His parents had been murdered when he was seven and he had only escaped by hiding under the floorboards in their little shack. He had to vomit quietly so they wouldn't hear his cries as the murderous dogs cut up his parents and ate them raw. Blood and other bodily fluids dripped down on him in their feeding frenzy. He would never forget the atrocities of a *civilized* city.

"Here, I was suppose to give you this when we reached the temple." The paladin pulled out a sealed letter he had in his pack and tossed it to Cat. It bore the seal of the holy order, a crescent moon within a circle and an equal armed cross of four pointed arrows.

Cat eyed it suspiciously and looked at the paladin. "What is it?"

"I honestly don't know, I was just told to give it to you when we got to the temple. So much has been going on that I forgot to hand it over sooner."

Cat broke the seal and began reading.

Mr. Cat, the order appreciates your efforts in accompanying Sir Gedrick on his journey to the temple. At this time you are free to go. We apologize for the little ruse in forcing you to go along, but you did try and steal from us after all. (Lord Dorn, High General of the Terra Paladins)

"Aaaagh…rrrrrr," Cat started groaning and emitting various sounds as he crumpled up the letter and threw it at Sir Gedrick. He jumped to his feet, grabbed his weapons and stormed out of the room, slamming the door behind him.

Sir Gedrick read the letter curiously after he left, and laughed himself to sleep.

* * * * *

Anteas, the Black Paladin, sat quietly in meditation at his woodland shrine to the god of entropy, Anu. He was amused with people and their superstitious ways. In fact it made him quite agitated and more often than not he would rather kill them than look at them. As it was this morning as he traveled to the secluded shrine and safe house for travelers of his kind. A woodcutter came across him on the trail and upon seeing his blackened plate armor and shield, babbled for the paladin not to kill him. If the woodcutter had shown some spine he would have let him go, but his annoying chatter practically begged for the paladin to ram his broadsword through his chest, which of course he happily did with joy and utter elation. He left the corpse where it fell on the little dear trail. After all, carrion creatures deserved to eat too did they not?

It was somewhat ironic that Anteas too was bidden to travel from Thor's Hammer toward the two horns as Sir Gedrick and Cat had been. But of course they essentially represented different sides of the coin. The Terra Paladins tried to preserve order, whereas The Black Paladins strove to destroy it. Who was right or wrong? Such an age-old question of perspectives, but one could not live without the other in a universe of duality and opposites. It was through their union and eternal struggle that relative balance was achieved.

The safe house was magically undetectable and concealed except for by those faithful to Anu. Much like the barrier that prevented the mountain giants from entering the dragon temple, but to a much lesser degree. It was merely a wooden shack with a modest altar resting near a subterranean tunnel. Anu was a reptilian god and often appeared as a snake or a muscular human with a cobra head. As Anteas lit some oil lamps and threw aromatic incense on some burning coals, this was how the deity appeared.

{Greetings Anteas my faithful servant.}

[May the terror of Anu lay waste to all the land.] The paladin knelt before the god and bowed his head submissively. This was always a critical test for a Black Paladin, for many servants who had failed their liege were stricken down at this point in the greeting. In fact Anteas truly wondered if this was the god Anu, or some servant of his, but he had no doubts that this being spoke for his god if it was not the god himself, and by all means had the power to end his meager life in a heartbeat.

{I have a special mission for you that is delicate and a little beyond our normal scope of operations, but in the end will favor our goals.}

Anteas raised his head and looked upon the ethereal image of his god. [Of course I will do whatever you ask without question.]

{As I knew you would. There is a mage who has just taken over Grathmoor and annihilated the entire town. As well, he has invoked the power of lordship and called upon the undead army. It is my understanding that he has done so with the aid of the demon Za'Varuk.}

[A demon? I didn't realize that any have figured out how to escape the inner core yet.]

{He has not escaped in any real corporeal sense of the word, but he can project enough of his will to influence things here. The mage and the demon made a deal. The demon helped win Grathmoor, and now the mage is suppose to help release the demon. The demon and/or the mage may be able to read what you are up to, so for now I will not reveal your true mission. For now, I want you to go to Grathmoor and help the mage in any capacity to release the demon. That is all you need to know for now. We will communicate later at the appropriate time.} With that the image disappeared.

[As you wish.] Anteas was familiar with such vague orders and didn't mull them over too much. He liked things simple; Grathmoor, mage, release the demon, that's all he needed to know.

With that he left the small shack to get his warhorse and be on his way with all speed. He was surprised to see five other horses with riders outside. All were identical black stallions, and the riders were exact duplicates of the image of Anu. He knew they were called Shaithen, or snake-men, and were apparently enlisted to accompany the paladin on his mission. He looked to the cave entrance suspecting that they lived and had come from there. They were heavily muscled men who wore only a white wrap around their waists. They all sported golden belts and scabbards where hung scimitars and curved daggers. Their scaly heads were frightening and swayed unnaturally as they looked about with their vertical pupils and forked tongues flickering. Silently the Black Paladin mounted and headed for Grathmoor at a trot with the Shaithen following directly behind.

* * * * *

Weapons, weapons, and more weapons. His hands were blistered and taped and still Cheiron insisted that they continue. "I'm thinking about lunch lad, do you want to give up so soon? At this rate you'll be 80 by the time we finish with your preliminary training."

With that Darkwolfe charged in with his two short swords flailing, each in a wicked display of double cuts and thrusts, but Master Cheiron easily deflected them with his 6-foot staff. Finally the student thought he got an edge and lunged, but the teacher spun about, hooking his lead leg and twisted, causing Darkwolfe to fall into the splits. Cheiron spun again quickly and struck the back of his head with the staff.

Darkwolfe lay unconscious for a very long time, but began to come around with a few groans. He rubbed the knot on the back of his head painfully.

"You should not overreach or commit yourself like that even when you *think* for sure you will land your attack, for as you can see you may be wrong."

"Choose your weapon or weapons of choice," Cheiron stated sitting off to the side against the wall. Darkwolfe eyed him suspiciously and went over and picked up a fine straight sword and a short sword for his off-hand. He would never have thought to use this combination before, but his strength and dexterity over the last year had greatly improved and he felt confident with nearly all the weapons present, alone or in combination.

Darkwolfe came on guard in the center of the training hall waiting for his teacher to attack, or at least get off his feet. Cheiron just smiled mischievously and loudly clapped his hands. Instantly Darkwolfe was surrounded by six goblins. They were brown and green creatures a little shorter than an average human. Their skin was tough and was probably as resilient as the studded leather armor that they all wore. They had big evil-yellow eyes and drool dripped constantly from their gaping toothy grins. Some held short swords, others wickedly spiked clubs, and they danced around him in a circle ready to attack.

Darkwolfe spread out his vision and knew that to focus on one would readily get him killed. He paced back and forth measuring their attack and movements constantly turning and moving. Out of the corner of his eye he saw one with a short sword lunge in. He twisted and rolled along the creature's arm. At the same time one of the goblins from the other side stepped in and swung with a club. The momentum of the stabbing goblin with the sword impaled the club wielder. Darkwolfe snapped his wrist down ward taking off the goblin's hand at the wrist, and the club wielder fell back with the sword sticking out of his chest with the severed hand still clinging on.

Darkwolfe continued to spin along the goblin and ducked behind him. The unfortunate goblin not only lost his hand, but also suffered a barrage of slices and hits from his comrades. The injured assailant was finished after that and fell weakly to the floor in a pool of gore.

Wasting no time for the creatures to rethink their plan of attack, Darkwolfe reversed direction and with his long sword took off his nearest assailant's leg at the knee. He quickly reversed again, catching the other goblin by surprise and drove his short sword through it's throat. He lost the weapon as the goblin fell away in a pumping spray of red, and he retreated several steps to face the remaining two with his long sword alone.

It was several frantic moments fending off the two creatures with his blade, but he was able to circle around in a fleeting moment and scored a gash along one creature's side, exposing several ribs. This was enough to break the rhythm of their attack, and Darkwolfe viciously drove in on the uninjured creature and overwhelmed him by brute strength and speed, finally thrusting into the creature's chest triumphantly.

One creature was left, but badly injured. He was undecided whether to finish it off or let it live. It was questionable if it would live at all, but if he let it live, would this creature go on and kill at a later date? Hadn't this thing just a moment before been trying to kill him? He lowered his sword in indecision and turned toward his master. With a feral scream the goblin ran at him. He dodged to the side, slapping the blade across it's mid-section, he spun up and around on the ball of his foot and came down in a fluid motion behind the creatures neck, taking off it's head.

He was a little sad at having to kill the creature, but things had come to their logical conclusion and he wasn't about to wallow in pity and despair at defending himself.

"Well done," Master Cheiron said, coming over to face his pupil. I didn't think you would pass that last test of character. If you had simply killed the defenseless goblin outright, then it would have demonstrated your propensity for evil and destruction. Even though he had tried to kill you, you offered peace in return, and that is the way of life and light. If we continue on schedule we may just make it in time for lunch.

* * * * *

Anteas and his snake-men guard sat atop their steeds in front of Grathmoor castle. The sides of the road leading into the place were lined with undead holding weapons from pitchforks to boards with nails to kitchen knives; the stench was sickening. The day was overcast and a light drizzle was coming down which only added to the dank gloom of the place and the old gray stones almost dripped dark and foul evilness. Anteas felt right at home.

The party of six walked their steeds into the open courtyard and dismounted. A pair of newly dead guardsmen appeared to be waiting for him and motioned for him to follow. The snake-men stood rooted to the spot and obviously meant to wait with the horses, so Anteas followed the undead guards.

They wound through several halls, where other undead wandered about spreading their malodor, oblivious to their trespass upon visiting nostrils. Soon the trio came into a council chamber where stood many more undead, and a mage in dark robes.

"Greetings Anteas oh most noble paladin of black. I am Lord Sabbath, the new ruler of these lands. A Shaithen priest communicated with me telepathically from their temple deep in the woods. It was said that you and several of their warriors are willing to aid in my quest. Is this so?" Sabbath eyed the paladin and tried to pry into his mind carefully so that Anteas would not be aware he was doing so.

"Quite so. It appears that your quest to free the demon, and the wishes of Anu are the same, and so I am at your bidding. What is it that you wish of me? I will be plain is saying that I don't know you or care about your personal ambitions, but I certainly welcome some bloodshed and destruction, and in viewing the way you run business around here I can assume I will have my hands full in the near future."

"Yes indeed. We are not so different you and I. I work for myself and you work for your god, but the outcomes are the same. Come and sit," he motioned to a large chair by his side, "and let us drink and talk."

Anteas came around the table and took a seat in the fine throne-like seat. An undead servant poured the two men red wine in gold fashioned goblets. They toasted with a dull clink. "Yes, let us drink and talk; let us prepare for war."

4

Laws of Magic

"As you are probably aware of, magic is a very intricate and delicate thing. All things in the universe are made up of energy. Things appear to our eyes to be solid, but even wood, rocks, metal, and other such objects are really just collections of energy. Magic is simply the bending or altering of energy to conform with our will. There are different aspects of energy and magic as you might imagine.

An illusion for instance, doesn't act directly on the observer's eyes, but alters light radiance to distort what appears to be present and indirectly affects the observer's interpretation of what is there.

A common spell like attack darts, which you know, is no more than an extension of your will. After many, many castings the magician must rest to recuperate his innate energies.

More powerful spells like working with the elements or combinations thereof, works both on will and by drawing this energy from nature. Such examples would include lightning, fire, ice, windstorms, etc. I can teach you the elements and their dynamics, and over time you will develop a relationship with them and to utilize them by their consistency and by the extent of your imagination.

As well..."

Darkwolfe didn't think it was possible for anyone to talk for so long non-stop. Eventually his brain was full and just shut down, that was when he slept. When he happened to wake, some indeterminable time later, Cheiron continued right along as if he merely stopped to take a breath.

Eventually Cheiron seemed pleased with his thorough elaboration on the arcane arts and stopped. The silence was deafening.

"Alrighty then, now lets get down to business."

It was the first time Darkwolfe had actually taken a look around his surroundings in some time, and he then realized that the weapons were all gone, and several man-sized dummies lined many of the walls. Some were made of what appeared to be some kind of fleshy substance. Some were wood, others stone, and even others were all of metal.

"Well what are you waiting for lad have at it."

Darkwolfe took a hesitant step forward and released a few attack darts at the flesh dummy. It went *thump-thump-thump*, and several charred marks appeared on its surface. He turned toward the wooden dummy and released a spiraling cone of wicked flames. The dummy was blackened and left smoldering in the cone's wake. He turned toward the stone dummy and released a bolt of lightning. It misfired and began ricocheting around the hall. Both Cheiron and Darkwolfe dove and rolled to stay out of its deadly path.

When the bolt finally ended its rage, Cheiron yelled, "Damn boy, concentrate, are you trying to get us both killed?"

He jumped up into a crouch, "like this," he blasted the stone dummy into oblivion and then sent forth such a frigid wave of cold that the metal dummy turned blinding white and then crumbled into a pile of distorted pieces. He rubbed his hands together in satisfaction, smiling broadly. "Errr, not to show off or anything mind you, I just wanted to show you how it could be done."

Darkwolfe didn't think Master Cheiron could ever be embarrassed, but if it were possible, he was now. He could almost see a little pinkish tint to his complexion, and yet with the weird lighting like it was, he couldn't be totally sure.

"Now that just covers some of the basic attacking techniques, but just like fighting empty handed or with weapons, defense is invaluable. In many senses, it's like inverting the energy that you would use to attack and picture it surrounding you or repelling an attack. It is a bit tricky, but with time and practice you will get the hang of it. Let's give it a shot. I'll minimize the energy of my attacks so that if something slips through your shield it won't kill you. However I must warn you that you may wish you were dead again, so concentrate and don't let anything slip through."

The two men squared off like they were about to duel, and in fact they were, but they were much further than any sword or spear could reach. Darkwolfe calmed himself and pulled a barrier of energy about him that he likened to the energy of the attack darts. Cheiron raised his hand, fingers extended and unleashed a flurry of attack darts. They swarmed toward the student like hungry red hornets, when they met the shield they winked out like candle flames and were no more.

"Very good. Now lightning." Cheiron raised his hand. Darkwolfe quickly erected another shield. As the bolt met the shield, the shield absorbed the energy and even seemed to be strengthened by it. "Fire," Cheiron yelled as a cone of flames raced toward Darkwolfe. He tried to alter the shield to ward off fire, but he was too slow. He felt as though his flesh was melting and his eyes popping out. He smelled burning flesh and hair, and then he passed out.

* * * * *

The morning was growing longer and mid-draw was quickly approaching. The two men would think it was a late night tavern or something the way they kept chatting, laughing about their wicked plans, and draining their wine goblets one after another. Anteas could have countered the alcohol's effects with his paladin powers, but Sabbath would have been sure to notice his lucidity and hence forth not trust the man. Trust was the key to playing this dangerous game, and Anteas always played to win.

Similarly, Sabbath could have countered the effects but wanted to foster some kind of relationship with the paladin to understand better his personality and later his motives. Anu didn't usually lend out his most prized warriors out of the goodness of his godly heart, and Sabbath knew at some level there was an ulterior motive to his plans. Never the less, the mage would take full advantage of this powerful fighter and his consort of snake-men to further his plans. He felt that the morning had been productive enough and it was now time to get on with business.

"Come my friend I must show you something of what we are to be about," Sabbath said rising to his feet a little unsteadily, "and let us be done with this drunkenness." He pulled a small vial from a pocket deep within his robes and took a small sip, no more than a drop really. Instantly the effects of the alcohol were gone and the mage was clear headed and alert once again.

The paladin smiled and whispered a silent prayer to his god. A light cerulean aura flashed briefly around the warrior and he stood strong and sturdy at the mage's side. "Yes, let us get down to business. My sword hungers for the taste of blood."

At the far corner of the council chamber there sat a lovely sculpture of Aphrodite, goddess of love and beauty. Sabbath winked slyly at the Black Paladin and pushed in on one of her nipples with his index finger. There came a grinding of stone and mechanical gears, and a secret passage was revealed in the wall.

"Illuminati," Sabbath spoke, creating a globe of light that surrounded the two men and radiated out for a sizeable distance in all directions. "Let's go."

The two entered the secret passage and immediately came to a spiral staircase leading down into the earth. There were many cobwebs and dust on the floor, which indicated that either Lord Noblin hadn't known the place was here, or had no need to enter the secreted place. Za'Varuk had indicated that down here was where the treasure hunt would begin.

The stairwell was deep and finely crafted. Anteas had seen dwarven workmanship and suspected the hardy little fellows were responsible for their construction. He suspected that this place may have existed before the present surface structure of Grathmoor castle. Soon the stairs ended and opened into a large hall. There were many alcoves lining the halls, and huge double doors at the far end, opposite the stairwell. The doors were finely carved with magical wards. A huge circle was inscribed in the doors with empty sockets where one could place gems or stones of some sort.

"Greetings Sabbath, Anteas." A voice rasped, and a figure stepped out from one of the darkened alcoves. Anteas drew his broadsword, and Sabbath quickly brought a spell to mind, ready to incinerate the creature. "It is I, Za'Varuk." The creature came into the circle of light. "Do not let the shell of Lord Noblin bring you any distress, I was so tired of running around as a cat. This newly dead body is much more appropriate don't you think?"

Sabbath took in the spectacle. It was certainly the old Noblin fellow in his black tights and leather boots, white frilly shirt, and dark green vest. His dark hair and beard were sharply contrasted against the stark white skin of undeath, and glazed over eyes. However, the flickering of red beneath this glaze belied something more ominous and wicked than that of a zombie. Even the more fluid gate and gestures of the creature, sharply contrasted to the disjointed movements of most undead, told a more interesting tale to the careful observer.

"So Za'Varuk, demon of the inner core, what is it that we must do. I am a man of fulfilling my word, especially when I'm the one to profit by it." He snickered at his own humor, pausing for a moment. "You said something of a treasure hunt." Sabbath looked over to Anteas, who made no motion to comment, so the mage figured he would be the spokesman of the two.

"Indeed. What you see before you, is the gate to the inner core," he motioned to the huge double doors, more comparable to a giant than any man-sized creature. "During the last battle of my kind, we were being beaten back by Darkwolfe and his Dragon Band. A host of wizards and priests came together and with the help of the dwarves and Thor's Hammer, they were able to construct this gate. One by one we were tracked down and captured, at the cost of tens of thousands of pitiful souls, but caught none the less. One by one my kind was banished behind the gate, trapped within the fiery core of inner Alcyone. For each demon banished however, a mage and cleric had to sacrifice their life force to bind us by their magic. This magic was concentrated within various gems and stones, and thus the *spirit keys* were created. As is apparent from the empty sockets in the doors, these keys have been scattered to the fore winds and hidden. There is no way of locating them magically or otherwise except one; Thor's Hammer. The hammer, which created the gate and the keys themselves, can act like a divining rod of sorts and lead one to the keys. So that is the treasure hunt. Get the hammer, and then find my stone. That is all I ask in return for me winning Grathmoor for you. Don't think to betray me, for I can easily take Lady Heather and sever your tie to your powers. Understood?" The demon's eyes flickered dangerously with their inner fires.

"Absolutely." Sabbath rested his chin in the palm of his hand and scratched his cheeks lazily with his fingers in thought. "The hammer on display in Thor's Hammer proper seems too easy."

Anteas then took the opportunity to contribute to the conversation. "By all accounts the hammer on display at the king's palace certainly is magical in its own right, but I agree with Sabbath in concluding that it would be idiotic to leave the means of unleashing the demon horde out in plain view." The Black Paladin took a moment of consideration, flexing his left hand and examining the heavy gauntlet. After several moments of thought he seemed to come to a resolution. "So we can't locate the keys through magic, but I'd bet we could however divine the location of the hammer, or at least its general whereabouts with the aid of all three of our magics; arcane, clerical, and demonic. Most shielding spells are specific, such as preventing scrying by a wizard or a priest, but we could weave our magic into a single spell and slip through any shields that have been put in place."

"You're smarter than you look," Sabbath said jokingly.

"I agree with the paladin," the demon concluded. "Let's go to the spell chamber above and make preparations."

* * * * *

Like taking a bath in magma, that's what it felt like. Total all-consuming pain. Dying was actually pleasant compared to being consumed by magical fire. However when Darkwolfe came around a good time later he noticed no burns or ill effects of his failed shield spell.

"Just an added effect to your new blood. Given enough time you can regenerate just about any injury." Cheiron came over and gave him a hand to his feet. "I know it may seem a bit cruel, but I thought it would be better to taste a bit of fire while we are training as opposed to out there with a demon or some vicious mage. The only difference is you would really be dead instead of waking from some gruesome nightmare. Let's give it another try. You seemed to have the first couple down, but lost it at fire. I want to continue, and make you deal with cold and acid as well."

"Lovely," was his only reply and he took a stance some distance away from his teacher. Darkwolfe created his shield, and mentally prepared for the subsequent shieldings.

Instantly a mighty swarm of attack darts came flying in, there must have been 50 or more. Darkwolfe had never seen someone cast more than five at a time, this display was more than a little unsettling. The mere awe of it almost made him lose his willful control over his shield, but then the prospect of those things tearing into his flesh was more than enough incentive for him to focus his defenses. He could feel the jarring vibrations as they slammed into his shield, and thankfully they held. He didn't have time to congratulate himself however. Cheiron was already chanting and preparing his next spell.

On a whim, Darkwolfe tried something different. He honestly couldn't say whether his teacher was going to cast the spells at him in the order he had described. What if he prepared for lightning, and Cheiron cast fire. What if he shielded for fire, and his teacher spit forth ice, or a stream of acid? It seemed logical suddenly. In battle one couldn't tell what his opponent was going to cast. He suddenly threw a protective barrier around him in a myriad of colors that he presumed would protect against all four. When Cheiron's wave of frost billowed forth, Darkwolfe mentally strengthened that aspect of his defenses, and the cold was absorbed or forced away. Lightning came and was diffused. A huge glob of greenish acid was hurled his way and deflected by the shield. Fire flared down from out of the very air. It billowed and swirled around his protective shell, but did not do any harm to the lad. When the assault finally ended, Cheiron stood some distance away with his hands on his hips nodding his head in satisfaction.

"I'm truly impressed this time," Cheiron piped, "I didn't think you'd figure out how to create a greater shield of warding until I blasted you into oblivion half a dozen more times. Come, let us talk."

The two men made their way to a portion of the wall that seemed no more remarkable than any other, but as they came closer, a portal appeared and beyond was evident some kind of altar with armor and fine weapons lining the wall. They entered the chamber, and before Darkwolfe could get a look at the fabulous chamber, Master Cheiron ushered him into a side room where there were two benches, some towels, and a wooden door.

"The greater skill of blending both your fighting and magical abilities will come with time, and I'm not sure wasting any more time here would be for the greater good. We can simulate many things here with illusions, such as the goblins, but out there," he pointed in some random direction, "is where you will truly learn to master your abilities. Your fighting abilities are as they will be in Alcyone beyond this created dimensional construct, but your magical abilities were enhanced by the chamber itself. Your magical abilities must be fostered for a while before you can regain the measure of proficiency that you now wield. Be patient, and in time it will come.

Remember your mind and your wits are your greatest weapon, so never let it atrophy. As well, remember the lesson of the goblin always. If we kill creatures that are simply evil to our ways of thinking, then we become just that which we abhor. We live in light and liberty and love. As soon as we fall prey to vengeance, and hatred, as soon as we hunt down goblins or other creatures and kill them just because they may or probably will commit heinous acts some day, then we become nothing more than murderers. Not only of these creatures, whom the gods have seen fit to create for whatever reason, but of the ideals and beliefs that we hold so dear. Without our greater purpose, and devoid of any substance of righteousness, we become slayers of good, not protectors of it."

With that Cheiron pointed to the door, "now go wash yourself, I imagine Charlemette would faint right away if she got a whiff of you now." With that he left the little room and went back into the other chamber with the altar.

Darkwolfe didn't have to be told twice. How long had he been here he wondered. A year, maybe two? Who could really tell? He stripped off his black trousers, opened the door, and went inside. The room was nothing more than a circular structure with a deep-set pool in the middle. It was dark and soothing and bubbles periodically broke the surface. Along the rim of the pool were various soaps, oils, lotions, and scrub brushes. He hesitantly tested the water. It was wonderfully warm, bordering on hot. He instantly stepped in and realized it wasn't deeper than the bottom of his rib cage, and he luxuriously sank beneath the water's surface and drifted around for a while in bliss.

He felt at great peace as he methodically washed and scrubbed his body. He was still sore from all his training, but in a way he had become use to the constant ache in his muscles. He looked down at his bulging muscles and slim physique and smiled admiringly. The heat of the water drained away his pain and aches and even seemed to clear his mind of all concerns and worries about his training and the future trials he knew lay ahead. As he finished, he noticed a small vial of oil set back away from the rest of the washing paraphernalia. He picked it up tentatively and uncorked the stopper. Instantly a beautiful wafting aroma assailed him and bid him how to use the oil to finish the ritual bath. He nodded his head in understanding and satisfaction, and dabbed some of the eucalyptus oil on his index finger. He slowly scribed a pentagram on his forward with the oil while whispering, "blessed be the goddess and the god." He instantly felt a wave of light wash over and through him. For a brief instant he was glowing from all his energy points, or chakras, and then he was done, feeling more alive than ever before.

Darkwolfe was naked as he walked into the temple and found Master Cheiron standing before the altar in flowing red satin robes. His face was set in a mask of concentration. Candles were dispersed around the room in no apparent order. Some were on the floor, some on little pedestals, but on the altar itself burned a huge candle of gold and another of silver. Darkwolfe knew enough about the mysteries to know these represented the male and female aspects of all things in creation, —the goddess and god, men and women, force and form.

"Choose your weapons and armor," Cheiron said flatly.

Darkwolfe looked about the room. There were many fine weapons and armor. There were spears, swords, maces, plate armor, leather armor, and even armor and weapons he did not readily recognize. He saw a pile of black under-clothing, long pants, and a padded shirt, so he put these on first. He then went back to survey the armor. One piece in particular stood out to him. It was a short sleeved scale shirt with pieces to go over the thighs. He quickly put these on.

"He has chosen dragon scale," Cheiron boomed, seeming to speak to no one in particular.

The young aspirant then found an assortment of footwear, and donned a pair of high leather boots. After doing so, he felt incredibly light on his feet. He even snapped out a few kicks to test them, and his speed was blinding, hard and deadly. He nodded his head in satisfaction. The boots seemed to sense his will of action and helped to initiate and guide the movements of his feet. He even suspected that they aided his muscles somehow and would help prevent against fatigue.

Next he worked his way around to an assortment of arm bracers. There were many of leather and gold and silver. Some were plain; others intricately carved and etched with designs. He chose a pair of sliver ones baring fine interlocking weaving patterns, and in the center of the forearm was the symbol of a snake twisted in a circle biting its own tail; a powerful magical symbol. As he went to fashion them to his arms, the silver automatically molded themselves around his forearms. They were light and extremely comfortable. He could sense their imbued magic, but could not discern their exact function.

Darkwolfe eyed a pile of helmets and decided against them. He then wound back around to a line of swords and picked a simple straight sword and strapped it on his side with its accompanying belt. He then found a short sword with crossbars of the head of ravens and instantly grabbed for it and strapped it on also.

{Welcome young warrior.} The voice echoed in his mind; a sweet feminine sound both peaceful and strong. Darkwolfe jerked his head in surprise.

"He has chosen the sentient sword Kiriana," Cheiron bellowed again from his perch on the stairs by the altar. The candle light sent scintillating sparkles across his robe. "Come," he said.

Darkwolfe came over before the priest and kneeled before the altar.

Music started suddenly. Drums, little tinkling bells, a lute, a pan pipe, even a melodic and haunting feminine voice came in, filling the room, weighing down on the neophyte. Darkwolfe's eyes were down on the floor, but out of the corner of his eyes he could see ghostly figures dancing around the chamber. The music built up to a crescendo, and stopped abruptly sending his consciousness into the void. There was an intense feeling of vertigo and he thought he might vomit for a moment as he fought it, but upon surrendering himself to the sensation the sickness passed.

He found his consciousness, his sense of self displaced. He assumed this was something like astral projection, for he suddenly found himself drifting amongst the stars. He saw a likeness to the illusory model of the Pleides that Master Cheiron had shown him, but this time it was real. All so real. He saw many wonderful worlds spinning around burning balls of fire. He drifted further away from Alcyone, and further still to that one world Cheiron called Earth. It was beautiful. He came closer and puzzled at the array of metal objects floating around the planet. Deep down upon the ground he could witness lights like never imagined, and people in strange clothing too numerous to count, buildings as tall as mountains, and noises both grating and wondrous. What a strange place...

He found himself once again before his teacher, but Master Cheiron was once again wearing his plain dark robes. "Rise Darkwolfe." Darkwolfe rose to his feet and found himself still decked out in his new garb. "And so a glimpse of the workings of the universe is yours." With that the teacher clapped his hands loudly and all the candles winked out. "So mote it be."

"So mote it be," he replied in response to his master.

"Now, how about some lunch."

* * * * *

Anteas, Sabbath, and the walking corpse of Lord Noblin, where a portion of the soul of Za'Varuk the demon now resided, entered the casting chamber of the late mage Starsender. The chamber itself was circular in shape of darkened stone and worn smooth by wayward energies over the years. In some places even the surface was baked to resemble glass and it was here that the light reflected back casting eerie shadows upon the trespassers. A squat wooden table was in the center of the room that functioned as a worktable of sorts. It was littered with a variety of arcane objects and powders, and a wide shallow basin filled with water. Sabbath picked the bowl up while Anteas summarily swept the other objects to the floor. Sabbath then returned the bowl to the table.

The scrying bowl was golden on the outside, but blackened on the inside. This created a sense of being drawn into the bowl and reflected light in such a way as to maximize the magical spells of vision and location. The three viewers formed a triangle around the bowl and pushed forth their energies while maintaining a mental fixation on Thor's Hammer. Almost indiscernible to the naked eye, three slightly different threads projected forth from their foreheads. Anteas and Sabbath wore looks of concentration and effort, while the undead creature showed no change at all except for perhaps a greater flickering of heated flames behind its pupils.

The energies of the three wove themselves into a braided rope and encompassed the scrying bowl completely. "To the north," Sabbath concluded. Then there was more silence, and all so slowly an image began to form on the water's surface. It was as if they had a first person's view, and that person was a bird moving at incredible speed. The road north of Grathmoor swept by in a blur. Many trees zoomed in and out of focus, and soon the hills and ranges further to the north came into view. "Rockshome. The dwarves must have kept a hold on the hammer after they were done using it to seal the gate. Which is certainly characteristic of them, they never want to let go of their greatest works of art."

The bird's eye view came to ground entering the great dwarven mining complex. Down halls and stairs, deeper and deeper into the darkened earth where other creatures dwelled of a less goodly nature than that of the dwarves. They quickly flashed by hundreds of the short, stocky humanoids going about their daily tasks and chores. They passed a large quarry area where ore was harvested. Several smiths were hard at work in dug out alcoves near huge burning furnaces. Workers in dirty overalls fed coal into the hungry maw of these metal beasts, their repetitive shoveling created a perfect yet unbearable heat.

Their magical vision passed walls and walls of quality armor and weapons that would eventually be loaded onto huge wagons and taken for sale in Sanctuary, Thor's Hammer, and other areas further south. Dwarven metalworking was the best in all Alcyone, and though they worked incessantly at their production, there was never enough to go around and thus, prices for these items were astronomical and usually entered into bidding wars at market.

Down more halls, past a dining hall, barracks, and smaller rows of sleeping quarters, more weapon rooms were found. They came upon other craftsmen at work making astonishing jewelry and goblets and other more elaborate items. Nobles and kings usually contracted these items. Elves were also known for their great detail in crafting, but they were not as approachable as the dwarves, nor were they as greedy. The elves created such items for their inherent beauty, not for what price they might fetch to some human incarnation of greed, or a miserly king who would just horde it with the rest of his treasure like a renegade dragon or playful faerie-kin.

At last the scrying eye came to a huge locked door that was magically barred and so, the end of their journey. There were several guards milling about, pacing back and forth out of apparent boredom, obviously diligent in their duties regardless of the implicit tedium of the task. No one had probably ever tried to steal the hammer since it was placed here some 2000 years ago, Sabbath concluded the guards were more routine, and judging by the ages of most of the dwarves present, a rite of passage.

"This is it," Sabbath affirmed. "The hammer must be inside. The problem is, its going to be near to impossible sneaking in and taking it from under their noses. Dwarves have an uncanny way of detecting invisibility, so my spells won't do us any good."

Anteas spoke up then, but with equal pessimism. "I am impressed with your undead army Lord Sabbath, but I'm afraid the dwarves would make short order of them on their home ground. Even if we could some how muster a force of goblin and giant mercenaries, we still would have a low probability of success. Frankly I'm at a loss for any feasible plan of retrieval."

Sabbath and the paladin looked to the undead creature, for after all it was the demon's freedom in question. Neither of the two had any great desire to go on a suicide mission, and the demon had been quite resourceful up to this point. If there were a way into the complex that was not apparent, he would have figured it out or soon would.

Za'Varuk merely cracked a ghastly smile as if he was privy to some private joke. He reached his hand into a deep vest pocket and pulled out a gold medallion. He tossed it the mage. Anteas's hand shot out and snatched it out of the air like a striking viper. He held it up before their eyes and inspected it curiously.

"This will get you there and back. I believe that there is enough magic left in the thing for two group teleportations.

"You believe," Anteas questioned angrily? "What if we get in and can't get out? I'd rather take my chances rushing the front gates."

"Where did this come from?" Sabbath wondered, inquiring with true interest and taking the amulet from the paladin's outstretched hand for closer examination.

"Oh dear Sabbath, you really should take a closer inventory of this castle's treasury. Those alcoves below are stacked with little goodies. I'm afraid I won't be coming with you I must, ah, attend to finding a new host. This one is failing; live ones tend to last a bit longer. I suggest you take a few of those snake friends of yours with you, dwarves can be such a surly lot. Pop in, grab the hammer, pop out, no problem. There appears to only be a few guards, young ones at that. You might even be back by mid-draw. I hear the prime rib is delicious, and the service is simply to die for." The demon burst out in rasping laughter, and in his giddiness began losing whatever hold on the corpse he had left holding it together. His presence in the lifeless shell was burning it out quickly, and the late Lord Noblin's features began melting and blurring in running fatty rivulets. They splatted on the floor grotesquely. Like an avalanche, once the process started it was unstoppable, and soon the entire host was nothing more than a giant puddle spreading across the room.

{Don't fail me Sabbath. I'll meet you in the dining chamber upon your return.}

"Well that was interesting," Anteas said sarcastically, not particularly amused at dealing with the demon in the first place or excited about *popping* in and out of Rockshome for a robbery.

Sabbath shook his head in agreement. He wasn't too excited about the way things were going either. He couldn't help but wonder at how he might maximize the situation and his position, by keeping the hammer for himself. Hell, so he lost his hold on Grathmoor's undead if Heather broke the lordship bond, but so what. If he could somehow indenture the demons into his service, who cared about a bunch of zombies?

"Go get your *snake friends,* we'll be leaving shortly."

* * * * *

Loreena McDermott commonly called Little Sunflower by her friends and family, puffed loudly in boredom and exasperation and stormed away from her fellow guards. "Just one song, that's all I want, one song." She ambled down an adjacent corridor to the one leading to the Hall of the Hammer and sat down against the wall.

While average in height for a young dwarf of 60 years, Little Sunflower was slight of build, had smooth skin, a fair complexion, and a wild mane of gorgeous blond hair. "Guard duty? What kind of assignment is that for a bard," she asked herself in her usual nasal high-pitched voice?

Bards weren't particularly common for dwarves, especially for the daughter of one of the leading clan's chiefs, but after spending her entire youth singing, dancing, and playing her flute, everyone had pretty much given up on trying to change her mind in vocational choosing. Even bards however had to take their turn guarding the hammer, and singing and dancing were definitely not allowed while on duty. If she were exceedingly excellent, the guard leader probably would have let her have that one song. It wasn't that she was terribly poor at being a bard, but it was more in that no dwarf was ever a good one. In fact the dwarves often paid great amounts of money to lure human and elven bards into the dwarven complex for performances. The dwarves were a very stubborn, loud, and outright obnoxious race, which only made the prices of visiting bards that much higher. If only Little Sunflower didn't have such a grating voice the community would accept her more readily, but as it was they fled in all directions when she broke out in song and dance.

Little Sunflower had heard tales of great bards traveling with heroes, writing music and lyrics to memorialize their deeds. In fact it was a way of historically recording actual events first hand and orally passing them on through the years, from generation to generation. Most people, dwarves included, didn't read much if at all, and books were essentially non-existent. However, everyone would catch a bardic performance from time to time. In a town square, a festival, or more often in a tavern a bard would grab a corner and sing the night away often for nothing more than a meal and a place to stay. Loreena thought it was her duty to follow her heart of the muses. She knew she wasn't all that great, but it was her calling and so she followed it unwaveringly. In time she thought, I could only get better.

Anteas, Sabbath, and two of the snake-men stood within the casting chamber. The amulet would have worked from any location really, but the clear scrying bowl still evoked images of their location and holding this in mind while teleporting is what would bring them to their destination. Being unfocused, or having wandering thoughts of some other place would likely send them to some random locale, and while not harmful necessarily, it would destroy their only chance of getting the ancient artifact.

Sabbath wore his usual dark robes and held several spells readily in mind to cast at a moment's notice. Anteas had his broadsword out and eagerly anticipated splitting a few young dwarves before this little jaunt was through. The two snake-men had scimitars and daggers in hand, and no one could figure out what they thought or felt as their heads swayed about in their usual scanning mode, tongue flicking rapidly.

Sabbath held the amulet in hand and mentally unleashed the power, instantly teleporting them directly outside the door to the Hall of the Hammer.

"Can you believe the nerve of that one," Dirk said snidely, "Think'n she can just start singing while were here on guard duty." The burly young dwarf tested the weight of his large battle-axe.

"Especially with that shrew voice of hers no doubt," another put in.

There were five of them total, including Sergeant Bilger, and he took the opportunity to defend his friend's daughter. "Alright boys, sur'n she ain't no soldier so lets just leave it at that. Stay focused on the job at hand. Just because no one has ever attacked Rockshome, doesn't mean they won't."

"Twelve draw under the daylight soil? Sur'n we would hear something long before they got this low in the city." Dirk said.

"True enough lads, but this is a guard duty of honor no less. This is the hammer that banished the demon horde, and prophecies say it will also one day unleash them," Sergeant Bilger said with some conviction.

"Those are just stories to scare little ones, we don't believe that stuff," Roger added as if it were all just common knowledge.

One second they were in the middle of a conversation, and the next chaos erupted in their midst. Sabbath instantly blasted one of the dwarves with a lightning bolt and sent him bouncing off the cavern wall.

Anteas took the head of another of the dwarves.

"Back lads," Sergeant Bilger yelled, and he, Dirk, and Roger retreated several steps away from the oncoming blades of the snake-men. Roger didn't get his weapon up in time and was impaled by a thick thrusting scimitar. Bilger grabbed Dirk and threw him back around the corner of the corridor, and then engaged both of the snake-men with his battle-axe.

Little Sunflower was rather lost in her own thoughts when all the ruckus and screaming commenced. A moment later Dirk came tumbling around the corner with sheer terror in his eyes. Unfortunately she didn't have time to ask many questions.

Bilger got a meaty hack into one of the snake-men's side, downing the creature for good. Sabbath instantly released a number of attack darts, which slammed into the sergeant painfully, but not killing him. The snake-man did however take the opportunity to parry the axe to the side and bury his curved dagger into his unprotected chest. Sabbath waved him on, meaning for him to track down the last dwarf while he and Anteas worried about getting the hammer.

Dirk was barely getting to his feet when the snake-man rushed around the corner. Sunflower had never seen someone die before, and she knew the moment it happened that it was something that would haunt her for the rest of her life. Time seemed to slow, and reality to twist into some kind of surreal alternate dimension. This was her home, this place was safe, this is where dwarves were born, raised with love and joy, and died at a ripe old age (barring any mining accidents). This was a haven of safety, and any problems where always handled by men like her father or the clan shamans.

But no, this had all changed in a moment of fear and blood.

The snake-man was instantly upon the young dwarven warrior. He was no match for it, and in just two moves the beast had chopped into his neck with a splurting hack and followed up with an eviscerating dagger slash. It was over before it even began in a pile of entrails and a fountain of blood. Immediately the snake-man set its gaze on Sunflower.

She knew to freeze now, or to turn and run would mean just as grotesque a fate as Dirk. However the only weapon she had was a couple of blow darts concealed in her flute. They were more for fun, and purely experimental, not to be relied upon in a life or death situation. Then again she really had no other alternative, and slowly brought the flute up to her lips. The snake-man eyed her curiously, blood dripping from both his blades.

Granted she had to admit that she couldn't sing very well, but she also had to say she could play the hell out of her little flute. She immediately went into a soothing melody like she had read once about snake charmers doing in a place called Ashra. The snake-man's vertical pupils seemed to widen and then to sharply narrow dangerously as if it was on to what her intent was. It's cobra hood flared out wide as it prepared to strike. Sunflower quickly pressed a little button on her flute and blew as hard as she could, once, then again.

The first dart stuck in the cobra's hood, but the second pierced the left eye and the snake-man hissed shrilly and retreated several steps. In that fleeting moment, the young female dwarf ran as fast as she could down the hall, turned, turned again, and went through a secret door leading to the upper levels.

Sabbath and Anteas heard the flute music while they were in the midst of examining the door for traps, but wanted to waste no time in investigating, and went about their own work. The door didn't appear to be trapped, but it also gave off a high aura of magic that concerned Sabbath more than just a little. He could blast it all day and possibly have no effect. They had precious little time to fool around, so he opted for a less direct approach.

"Stand back," Sabbath said, waving Anteas off to the side. The Black Paladin eagerly complied, for what fool would stand in the way of a mage's casting, particularly one with the feral determination that Sabbath presently wore on his face.

Sabbath chanted for an exhaustively long time, but slowly a rainbow colored dust began flowing out from his fingers in a fan shape. He aimed it not at the door, but toward the rocky wall just to the right of it. Slowly the rocks lightened and turned into a clear gelatinous substance. He aimed the fan just at the correct angle, as to wedge around the door and access the room or hallway beyond. As the magical field penetrated deeper and deeper into the stone and turned into gelatin, a hallway appeared through the translucent stuff and with a sigh Sabbath concluded his spell.

The mage's face appeared pallid and sweat dripped steadily from his temples and matted hair. He slumped from his normally perfect posture and leaned heavily against the far wall for support.

"You overstepped your magical limits mage," Anteas stated matter of factly, as opposed to questioning in concern or sympathy.

"I'll live," Sabbath rasped, "please do the honors of hacking your way through will you." With that he could stand no more and heavily thumped to the floor and closed his eyes to rest.

Anteas shrugged his shoulders and went over to the weird wall of unknown substance. He pressed his hand against it. It was spongy and gave way easily to his hand. He was able to push his arm in and scoop out a big clump of the stuff. He smiled to himself seeing the obvious opportunity for fun here. He hefted is large broadsword and readily began hacking his way through to the other side. It was quick, slimy work, but he soon stood at the end of the unnatural tunnel at the backside of the door.

The Black paladin whispered a prayer and then scanned the hall. The only traps that became known to him, were a cluster on the back side of the door. He assumed that if someone were able to open the door somehow, they would be assailed by a sequence of spells that would easily wipe out a small army. His gaze fell to the back of the short hallway where rested the hammer in an ornate cradle atop a marble pedestal. He easily retrieved it and was back by Sabbath's side where the wounded snake-man was now patiently waiting. It appeared unharmed, and Anteas would not have been surprised for the Shaithen were known for their clerical abilities. In the blink of an eye the three of them were gone.

* * * * *

The dining hall at the Dragon Temple was relatively plain and humble befitting the orders of Levanah and Sin. The walls were lined with pillars and many open archways led off to other areas of the sacred place. Half a dozen monks in plain brown robes were seated along the huge rectangular table. Another six were gliding about with trays of fresh fruit, cold pitchers of water and birch beer, roasted garlic chicken, various salads, and warm bread.

Sir Gedrick, Silver worm, and Charlemette sat clustered together, straining to make small talk. "I don't see any women around here, are these priests celibate do you think," the paladin wondered breaking the silence.

"Actually," Silverworm dictated, "there are very few orders that I have ever heard of to force their priests into such actions. These priests in service to Sin do abstain from sexual interactions while they are here in training for periods at a time, but only because the priestesses of Levanah aren't presently about. I can assure you when they next make their appearance you'll see these priests in a frenzy vying for their attention. Its all a game and just for fun. Long lasting relationships are almost never formed here in a mundane marriage sense, but the sacred union of male and female principles are highly honored here and so both priests and priestesses find release here from the trials of the outside world."

"Really?" Sir Gedrick questioned eyeing Charlemette curiously.

"For your information I never trained here paladin," she was quick to state, but she was curious that while the priests had been perfectly courteous to her, not a one had looked at her in more than friendship. She looked around the table at some of the priests and they merely smiled or bowed their heads respectfully.

"Of course the priests know the lady here is with Darkwolfe, and none would dare even look at her with sexual interest. Not out of fear or possessiveness mind you, but simple courtesy for the love you two share. Souls bound by love have a spiritual link, and that special trust should never be broken." Silverworm's voice was very melodic and his speech was lulling like a song, making the talk of love more imbued with mystery and magic.

"Have your elven friends been taken care of," Charlemette asked.

"Yes, more of the Deadly Chimes were still here in the temple. I sent them out after the bodies before we rested this morning. The bodies had not been terribly molested by the carrion birds, and are being prepared for a ceremonial funeral pyre even as we speak." Silverworm showed no pain on his face, but everyone could hear it in his voice, and the closeness of the members of the elite band became evident.

"My condolences proud elven lord, may Hermes the messenger of the gods swiftly spread their heroic deeds. May they find rest in the great forest in the sky." Sir Gedrick spoke an elven saying in honor of the deceased.

"So, where's Cat? Did he sleep in or what?" Charlemette put in trying to divert the conversation away from her and Darkwolfe's apparently public love life as well as their fallen companions.

The Terra Paladin fiddled with his fork for a second or so under their scrutiny, "he decided to head back home after he was released by the order."

"Is that so," Silverworm remarked, "I would have thought him to be more of the adventuring type. I imagine the fun is about to begin in earnest now, it seems unlike him to run away at the first signs of any real danger." Elves, particularly the Deadly Chimes, were the best at stealth and tracking in all the lands. Their uncanny senses were heightened beyond any human comprehension. Upon taking his seat earlier at the table, Silverworm had detected Cat hiding behind one of the pillars eavesdropping on their conversation. Now he was just baiting him, waiting to see what the rogue would do.

"I agree," the priestess countered, "I thought Cat would be happy to come along after being released from his bond, at the very least to train longer with the elves."

"If there ever was such a bond," Cat said loudly and sternly, stepping out from behind the pillar into plain view. One monk passing nearby was startled and dropped his pitcher, in a crashing of pottery and water.

Cat, unaffected by the mess, stepped around and glided over to the table with his feline grace.

"This wonderful holy and righteous order lied! There was no bond in the first place. What kind of sick torture is it to make a man think he is going to die at any moment if he does something perceived to be wrong by the parameters of a stupid spell? One minute I could have been munching on a turkey leg, and then next, poof, exploding all over the place like a dew melon being smashed by a mace or something. Well I'll tell you, its very unnerving. Just look at my nerves," he held out his hands for the companions to see, and they were rock steady. "See, I'm in shambles. How am I ever going to pick a lock or disarm a trap ever again?" He eyed a newly placed plate of fruit, looking like a robin about to snag a bug, and popped a grape into his mouth.

The trio looked at each other amusingly and smiled at Cat's histrionic display.

"Not that I truly believed there was any danger or anything, but if I did,...well, a lesser man would have gone out of his mind by now." Cat popped another grape into his mouth and looked around. All of the companions, and even the monks were smiling at him and chuckling by now. "What," he said innocently?

A deep resonant gong sounded from somewhere within the temple. The monks darted about finding their places at the table and standing erect behind their chairs at attention. The four companions took the hint and also stood up, Cat last, reluctantly, grabbing another grape for good measure. The group noticed for the first time that there were two large chairs at the head of the table, not one. From a side hall walked in Master Cheiron and Darkwolfe.

Charlemette gazed at her friend and lover, hardly recognizing the man. He looked like a prince. The scales of his dragon armor glistened in the lamplight. He floated and stood tall in his rich boots that could have only been crafted by elven kind. His arm bracers spoke the powers of the arcane and of the temple, but none could mistake that this was a deadly warrior standing before them. His muscles bulged solidly, not in exaggerated form, like some of the body builders she had seen once on a trip to Sweetwater. He wore two finely crafted swords, one with the cross guards of raven's heads. He wore them well, and it would be a good guess that he knew how to use them. He hair was cropped short like many of the professional soldiers, and a strange mixture of wisdom and intensity were set in his hazel eyes. Darkwolfe had gone through a radical transformation, even putting on considerable weight in just the few hours since this morning. Charlemette was truly baffled.

Master Cheiron looked like a peasant in comparison, but the way he carried himself told a different story. Here was perhaps the most powerful being on all of Alcyone, but he knew humility, and needed not to stray from the path by a darkened ego. The two men stood behind their chairs at the head of the table also at attention. They made a fist with their right hands, placing it in front of their chest and then cupped their open left hand over the top. This was a sacred way of honoring the spirit. The open hand on top meant that peace and love, giving and nurturing should be dominant and rule the heart. However the closed fist meant that it was ones right and duty to preserve this, even with force if warranted by the situation. One would exercise the least amount of force necessary to end a confrontation, but be not mistaken, if the life or liberty of innocence were threatened, these priests would sacrifice themselves and kill in the name of truth and justice. Individuality and free will were the edicts of the elder gods and servants in their name were the benefactors of freedom.

Another gong sounded from somewhere deep within the temple and all of the monks and Silverworm bowed. A split second later Darkwolfe and Master Cheiron bowed in response and everyone took their seats.

Seeing Charlemette about to burst with a thousand questions, Cheiron calmly set the group at ease by briefly explaining the events of the morning. "We had entered a training hall in a place outside of time when you had last seen us. There, time and space do not exist, so while you all were busy for the last several hours, Darkwolfe and I have been training for just over three years." Darkwolfe blanched slightly at hearing how long he had really been gone, but quickly maintained his composure. In the future he would have to be strong and most likely lead many people in a war against the demons and their minions. Emotional reflexes would likely get him or people he was responsible for killed. Master Cheiron seemed to witness this inner struggle and decision somehow, and gave Darkwolfe a slight smile and almost imperceptible not of his head.

Cheiron continued. "He has passed some of the preliminary milestones expected of him." Darkwolfe was really starting to feel uncomfortable up here on display like some horse up for auction. "The other tests will not be given by me, but by the spirits of the land, for the land is the dragon, and he the head. Capit Draconis. We have much to discuss, but first I must ask who would join him in his trials."

"I Silverworm Vialtryneari lend my sword and bow in this good cause."

"I Charlemette of Sanctuary, priestess of Levanah shall aid you on this quest."

"I Sir Gedrick of the Terra Paladins call you brother and friend. I will die protecting the head of the dragon."

"Certainly I'll not miss all the excitement, count me in," Cat said exuberantly.

"Good and by your own words and free wills you enter into this quest together, I ask that we eat in silence to honor all the lives that may be lost in our battle for balance, and those lost over the millennia." Cheiron filled a plate and set it off to the side. "This offering is to the dead, may they bless our mute supper. Following the meal I will fill you all in on what I think would be the best plan for you to take. Now lets have some lunch."

The meal was not extravagant but good and filling. The sensation of eating and drinking felt weird to Darkwolfe after going so long without, but he was thankful for the sensation and savored every bite. Every time Char cast her eyes his way she almost lost control of her willpower and started blurting out a comment or question, but in the end she managed to maintain the silence of the sacred meal and their dining passed without event.

5

The Quest Begins

Since the fatal breakfast, the undead servants of castle Grathmoor had been busy cleaning and getting rid of any and all of the poisoned foods. While the cook Art was certainly dead, Za'Varuk put him back to work doing what he did best. The newly deceased could function in the capacity of kitchen help, but the more decrepit creatures would only slough off into the preparations and were maintained outside for other duties. At the time Anteas and Sabbath were returning with the hammer, the servants had put together a glorious lunch and set it about the table in anticipation of their success.

Za'Varuk's essence seemed to grow stronger with each hour with the prospect of freedom coming within his grasp. Thousands of years of banishment within the magma core had helped foster a bitter taste for revenge. If Thor's Hammer was acquired, then by all probabilities the stone would not be far behind. Anteas and Sabbath were useful to the demon, but in truth nothing more than pawns in a greater game. Heather looked at herself in the huge full-length mirror, flames burned behind her pupils, "we all have our masters."

Za'Varuk had entered the girl for no other reason than because she was the only living creature in Grathmoor, and assuming control of an undead creature would only whittle down their forces. The demon would have to change bodies every few hours, and in only a fists time he would have lost 60 zombies. Not a route he wished to take with the prospect of war on the horizon. He could stay in the girl for a similar amount of time without doing any permanent damage. Besides, she could be useful in many other ways.

Heather's will was sublimated, but present and conscious of all that was transpiring to her and around her. The demon was in complete control, but the girl didn't have any objections, not that it would have done any good if she had. This was what true power was like. She could feel the raw magic and chaos burning within her arteries with each pumping of the heart. She would watch and wait and learn.

Heather took great satisfaction as the former ladies of Grathmoor waited on her and dressed her in luxurious gowns and bedecked her in the castle's most precious jewels. The demon allowed her these simple pleasures, baiting her, tempting her with wealth and power. When the right time came, Za'Varuk knew what choice the girl would make, and it almost made him cry out in glee.

While the hammer and stone were critically important to the demon's release, Za'Varuk knew what other agendas were in play. The wizard and paladin would most likely succeed at the dwarven stronghold and that would inevitably lead to a small army racing down from the mountains to protect the gate. Long ago the dwarves were honored with the construction of the hammer and gate, and after the great conflict was ended, they took the liberty of preventing their release. They could never have thought their precious hammer would ever disappear, and so with it missing, it only made sense that they would block any approach to the gate. The only favorable aspect that Sabbath and the demon had going for them was that the dwarves didn't know that Grathmoor had already fallen. Their small contingent, if wiped out, would prevent any further intervention in the near future, and by the time a larger force marched down from Rockshome, of course it would be too late.

Heather was still a carrier for the curse and with the demon's help in further tailoring it to his needs, the undead were also now able to spread it through contact. Upon his command, many of the undead, including some of the horses and dogs, were now scouring the surrounding woods. Every living creature for many draws in all directions would soon be brought into Grathmoor's dark fold. Every peasant, every deer, every bird and mouse, boar and squirrel would become an ally. Soon even the hidden thieves' guild would be found and rooted out. Not even their great defenses could prevent a mouse from sneaking in and spreading the curse. Very soon they would all serve Za'Varuk the Conqueror.

"More, much more," Heather said with a demonic twang. She left the Lord and Lady's chambers and scaled the stairs to one of the castle's towers. At the top of the cold stone steps she came to an open turret with a crenellated edge. The light from Ra's eye burned down brightly from its zenith in the cerulean sky and a welcoming breeze drifted over the swaying treetops. At first glance the scene could be thought as beautiful, a utopia in visual aesthetics, but this concept waned quite quickly upon further examination.

The town of Grathmoor was mostly abandoned and several buildings had burned down during the curse's rampage. A few undead patrolled the streets. They were in a spectrum of decay. Some were no more than skeletal remains, others hardly discernable as these horrific monstrosities at such heights, and yet others grotesquely in-between. They all wielded weapons of sorts: clubs, pitchforks, daggers, axes, and swords.

The demon looked back around to the castle and examined the many undead manning the walls. There were many, but zombies weren't necessarily the smartest servants. They only followed basic instructions, and the dwarves were very resourceful and resilient fighters. They would do he reasoned, for now. Eventually he would need to put word out and enlist the aid of the goblins and giants of the area. He didn't have the time now, but in time they would be helpful. He smiled contentedly and then turned his gaze back to the turret around him, his real reason for coming up here.

There were several birdcages full of courier pigeons. The cages were labeled: Thor's Hammer, Rockshome, and Sanctuary. The demon doubted that the curse would have much if any effect on the dwarves to the north, or elves to the southeast that had natural magical immunities. In fact it would probably only alert them to some kind of foul play. Thor's Hammer however was primarily a human city, and these creatures were weak of will and prime candidates for targeting. In a day or two the entire city would be in a chaotic frenzy of murder and intrigue. The soldiers and Terra Paladins would have their hands full for a long time, and their forces would inevitably become depleted when Sabbath and the demon expanded their vision for conquest.

Za'Varuk reached into the cage labeled Thor's Hammer and brushed his hand over a pair of birds, rustling their feathers with green misty tendrils. With that the birds darted out of their cages and were soon flying far to the south.

The demon made his way back down to the dining hall, passing musty corpses on his way. When he reached the hall he found that Sabbath and Anteas had already returned and were seated at the table drinking wine and eating bread. The mage looked drained, but alive, and he sipped his glass quietly eyeing Heather as she came into sight. Anteas was ripping into a loaf of bread, but whispered a prayer to protect against poison before taking a bite. Apparently he wasn't taking any chances after the mornings deadly meal. Resting on the table between them was the artifact, Thor's Hammer.

The hammer hadn't really belonged to the god Thor, but it was one of the deities that the dwarves worshipped and was crafted in his honor. It was as long as a human's forearm and the twin heads half as wide. Its thick handle was wrapped in plush red leather, and a silver radiance magically emanated from the metal.

"I hope you don't mind Sabbath, I'm borrowing your wife's body for a few days. Just until you get me the stone and release me of course. I think of it as a little incentive. Her body can only deal with my demonic powers for, say a couple days, a fist at most. Once she goes, so does your Lordship. However, I have taken measures to protect your precious town and further your ambitions. I will serve you as faithfully as you do me; have no doubts we need each other. Besides I can better fight the dwarves while in possession of a living host."

"How so?" The mage asked weakly, seeming too tired to really show interest, but still held that greedy gleam in his eyes that Anteas was quickly becoming accustomed to.

Heather straightened her dress and thrust her breasts out for emphasis, quite ill fitting a demon, and walked across the room taking a seat near the two men. Sabbath vowed to himself never to touch that girl again. The thought of having sex with a woman with the spirit of a male demon looking you in the eye was enough to make any man balk.

"I have your undead gathering an even greater army from the surrounding woods for one, who else do you think will fight the dwarves when they arrive?"

"Dwarves," Anteas remarked blankly.

"Yes of course," Sabbath chimed in, seeming to regain more of his composure and strength with each passing moment. The bitter potion he had mixed in with his wine was starting to take effect and he began hungering for more conflict and killing.

"You appear to be recuperating nicely," Za'Varuk commented. "The wonderful world of magic, elixirs, and sacred artifacts, what no world would be complete without." The demon smirked at his obviously inside joke, while Sabbath and Anteas looked on curiously, wondering if the demon was going to share.

After several moments it seemed he was not, and Sabbath came back in, "and for two."

"In addition to building your army here and dealing with the dwarves," he waved his hands outward, nonchalantly like shooing away a gnat, "I have also taken the liberty of spreading your wonderful little curse down to the city of Thor's Hammer. After I am released, I thought we could destroy the place as well. If you do not wish to maintain our allied union, then I leave it to you and commence my revenge on those blasted elves in Sanctuary, and that meddling priest Cheiron. Rest assured the Dragon Temple will stand no more." The demon put his fingers to Heather's lips and pondered momentarily. "And you Anteas, I confess I do not know what ulterior motives are driving your god into allowing us your services, but we welcome you amongst us as long as your loyalties remain true."

Anteas the Black Paladin leaned forward, looking directly and unwaveringly into the flickering fiery pupils of the demon's host. "Have no misconception that I serve the will of Anu and no other. As long as you continue killing, stealing, and generally destroying everything in sight I don't see why he would want me to leave this merry band, but if he does, I will certainly let you know before I destroy you."

"Good, now that we all understand each other, lets get started." The demon reached out and grabbed the hammer, instantly feeling the power of the thing surging through him. Even Heather, hidden within the recesses of her own brain was jolted by the mere touch of the ancient artifact. Za'Varuk thought of his stone even though the location of all the gems were assailing his senses all at once, and was able to pinpoint his singular object from among the others. "Its somewhere in the Foothills of Fellowship north of Sanctuary. As you get closer to it, the hammer will further guide you like a divining rod."

Anteas took the hammer from the demon and tucked it into his sword belt. Sabbath steadily rose to his feet with a mixture of aloofness and grim determination. Without another word the two made their way out of the dining hall leaving the demon Za'Varuk in the guise of a peasant girl wearing the guise of a lady. When they reached their horses, the snake-men were already mounted and ready to move out. The group was on the trail heading east a moment later through a slalom of meandering undead.

* * * * *

The clan chiefs McDermit, McConnor, and McCloud stood before the Hall of the Hammer with no less than 500 warriors, mages, and clerics crammed in front of the door and adjacent hallways. Little Sunflower stood before the mob trembling all alone. She tried to explain what had happened, albeit precious little from around the corner, through tears and incoherent sobs. The chiefs, including her father, only shook their heads in a mixture of anger and disappointment. For a guard to flee and not protect the hammer even in the face of certain death was not only shameful, but also sacrilegious.

The fighters shifted noisily about in their heavy plate and chain armor, restless and anxious they were to seek revenge and retrieve the hammer. Many were already grumbling about protecting the gate and heading for Grathmoor. Chief McDermit was always kind, generous, and loving to all of his clan, especially is only daughter, but his face was stern and torn now as he spoke softly with the other chiefs. Such failure would be met with a dishonorable execution or at least banishment if mercy were given.

Ironoak, a kindly old mage who had befriended Little Sunflower long ago, came to her side and patted her shoulder reassuringly. He would have tripped on his tremendously long beard had it not been wrapped around his neck like a scarf. "Silence everyone," he boomed with his magically enhanced voice so all could hear. "This is a grievous act of violence here today." He toed the snake-man's corpse for emphasis. "But the responsibility of protecting the world of Alcyone from the demon horde is not through. We must protect the gate." Cheers rose up in a wild din, weapons were thrust up toward the cavern ceiling over and over again. It took quite a while for Ironoak to calm them back down from their frenzy.

"I ask the chiefs mercy for the only surviving guard, we all know that she is a bard and not a warrior." Protests were voiced, but only a few. Not many had the courage to openly go against the wise and powerful sage, even in such a large crowd. "If amenable to the chiefs present, I ask that she be banished until which time she returns Thor's Hammer to Rockshome and restores her honor." The chorus rose up again and the three chiefs nodded their heads in mute consent.

Ironoak didn't want to waste a second for the chiefs to change their mind or for some young vigilante to hurl a dagger her way, so he grabbed Little Sunflower's hand and they were instantly teleported away.

When the bard regained her baring and adjusted her eyes to the intense sunlight, she saw that her and the mage were standing outside the gates to Rockshome. Ironoak took out a small pewter figurine of a bird and with a blur and flash of light there stood before them a gigantic hawk with red tail feathers. It looked from the mage to the bard and back again as if being given instructions and then stooped down so Little Sunflower could climb into the comfortable leather saddle. She did so, silently and emotionally withdrawn from the recent events and then looked to the old mage for some kind of answers as to why her world had suddenly been tipped upside down.

Ironoak was the only one who she felt ever listened to her or cared to know who she was and who she wanted to be. He had encouraged her to follow her dreams and to become a bard regardless of what everyone else said and whether or not she had the greatest singing voice. He had said that the right path was always the hardest to follow.

"Here," the friendly mage said and handed her a beautifully hand-carved flute and slipped a silver ring with intertwining vines onto her finger. She let him, and tucked the flute into a saddlebag. "Just a few gifts to help you on your way, I know I'll see you soon so don't fret.

Everything will be okay. Freesia here will take you to a safe place, now sleep." He waved his hand across her face and she instantly fell asleep. He magically bound her to the saddle, so even if the bird flew upside down the whole way she would never fall out. With that the hawk launched into the skies, sending the wizard's beard spinning about in a flurry of wind, and was soon out of sight.

"Gods-speed," he offered at last, standing alone before the mountain's gates. He then teleported back down to the chiefs and the army, preparing for war.

* * * * *

The mute meal in honor of the dead was over and the companions looked to Master Cheiron for direction and to some degree explanations about what was going on. Darkwolfe also waited and watched with curiosity. For three years he had trained with the master and never once did he really explain the greater picture in detail, other than some vague *stop the demon horde* kind of comment. Darkwolfe didn't have a clue what the plan might be or to go about saving anyone let alone the entire planet.

Cheiron collected his thoughts and ordered his words in the most concise way before beginning. He didn't want to go into a lengthy history lesson just to get the young heroes out the door, but leaving too much out might not give them enough understanding or motivation to continue when the quest truly became difficult or sadly, one of them died.

"During the last conflict, or demon wars as they are often called, the gods and goddesses decided not to kill the creatures, but rather to capture them. They were after all created for some purpose, the deity of deities may only know, but it was felt that by eradicating the loathsome species there might come about some unforeseeable repercussion and imbalance in the universe.

A way was discerned, but it was costly in lives, both in their capture and in the sacrifices needed to be made for the making of the *spirit keys*. Thor's Hammer was used to construct a magical gate and to be able to locate the keys, for once the keys were fashioned, they were scattered throughout the region. If a time came where it was decided to finish the demons off for good, one could locate the keys with the hammer and use it to also destroy the keys and demons for good. Unless one knew what they were looking for, they could not tell the difference from any other gem or stone. Only the hammer could locate and identify the keys. If the hammer came into the wrong hands, one could locate the keys and by going to the gate release the demons.

I believe Za'Varuk, a very nasty demon even amongst his peers, is working with some mage to gain his physical freedom. I suspect they will be going after the hammer and then to hunt down his stone. Thankfully I...," Cheiron stopped in mid-sentence as a lovely young dwarven woman walked into the dining hall escorted by a monk.

She was wearing a white blouse tucked into baggy brown leggings with a leather vest over the top pushing the white curves of her breasts out the front on display. Cat rose slightly in his chair to get a better view. She wore frilly brown, soft leather boots that came to the knee and made no sound as she made her way toward the table. Her features were radiant and exquisite despite her red puffy eyes from obviously haven recently been crying, and her golden hair was fitting her name. "Master Cheiron, hello I'm Little Sunflower."

"Please do come in and make yourself comfortable," he motioned to a monk with a pitcher, "and some cold water might be refreshing."

"Yes thank you," she took a seat near Charlemette, finding comfort in being near a priestess of the good goddess. "Thor's Hammer has been stolen from Rockshome. I was on guard duty, but..."

"I see," Cheiron instantly caught on to the dilemma and the nature of her visit. The priest figured the dwarf was lucky to still be alive, and the fact that she was must mean that she had been banished, a fate worse than death for a dwarf. This young lady would do well to join Darkwolfe's quest for they were inextricably intertwined. "Ironoak was always a very wise man. It is good that you came, however it doesn't change our plans." He directed this last bit to the companions already gathered here.

Sir Gedrick came into the conversation, "how are we going to stop them from getting Za'Varuk's stone when they have the hammer and you said yourself there was no other way of finding where the stones were hidden?"

Cheiron replied naively, "oh, did I fail to mention that it was I who hid his stone in the first place?"

Part III:

Images

Filtered through the fern and dense canopy of wizened trees
The light of purple dawn awakes
The stoic earth and faeiry ones alike
Honey suckle, rose, and new fallen hay march upon the senses
Spilling memories so freely as though
It were the blood of last falls slaughter calling across the
Wake of winter's death;
Sending to flight the swallows as though the mere thought
Of predation could kill
More so than that of a cat
Behind the pane of a windowsill.
Tapestries in ancient stone stirred by the breeze of change;
Intertwining snakes as in love and the mysteries beneath
The dark bottomed surface lake that spoke of things to come—
A foreshadowing of a dawning age and one gasping on its death bed,
Soon it would lay still, soon the fear would dissipate,
Soon we would all be free.

1

The Foothills of Fellowship

The dining hall of the dragon temple lay in total silence. All of the companions were shocked into a mute stupor by Master Cheiron's last statement. The priests sitting at the table were not overly surprised, but took note of their visitors difficulty in comprehension and they quietly took their leave. The same question kept going through everyone's minds all at once; *how could he have been the one to hide the stone, that was over 2000 years ago; how could he have been the one to hide the stone, that was over 2000 years ago?* This question kept circling in their minds over and over again. The concept was just so inconceivable, that with time they thought they could make some sense of it, but none came.

Cheiron was amused and was enjoying every minute of the companions' mental struggle. He took a sip of water and ate a few slivers of chicken waiting for the inevitable questions to come. Finally the silence was broken.

"But how is that possible," Charlemette asked? "No magic that I ever heard of could sustain someone for so long, and you don't look a day over 40."'

"I age like a good wine," he mused. "No seriously, I guess it wouldn't hurt to tell you a little about myself, but I will try to be brief. Every second that you are not on your way towards your destination, a second more the mage and demon have to get to the stone ahead of you."

The adventurers settled more comfortably into their chairs, feeling the contentment of the good meal and the lethargy it produced. "You may think me immortal now, but I am not. However very long ago I was, a child of the gods no less. However a friend of mine sacrificed himself for the sake of mankind and was punished horribly. He suffered in torture, day after day. And so I sacrificed myself, my very immortal self to save him. Before I died, I was a teacher of martial arts, weapons, magic, and music. I taught many heroes and demi-gods, offspring of the mating of the deities with mortals. These heroes and their deeds went down in history, in poems, and in song. The council of the Pleides did not want to lose such an awesome teacher and trainer of young heroes, for in times of trouble these heroes would always be needed. And so I was brought here to Alcyone and resurrected in the pool much like Darkwolfe was. I have remained here ever since, and am forbidden to leave the temple. It was I who trained the original Darkwolfe, the Capit Draconis."

"Well if you were forbidden to leave the temple, then how did you hide the stone unless it was hidden within the temple?" Cat deduced.

"You don't miss a trick do you my young cutpurse?" Cheiron smiled, taking another sip of his cool water. "An exception was granted during the demon wars and I was allowed to leave the temple to supervise the construction of the gate and spirit keys. The demon Za'Varuk as I've said before is particularly nasty and strong among his peers, so I took personal interest in hiding his stone. Before his banishment he vowed to hunt me down and destroy the Dragon Temple if he ever escaped. If he retrieves the stone, I'm sure this will be at the top of his places to visit on his tour of destruction.

Za'Varuk's stone is in the Foothills of Fellowship north of Sanctuary. I am bound to the temple as you know, so I can not go with you. I will show you the way." He reached into his robes, producing a rolled parchment and handed it to Darkwolfe. "If you ride now, today, you can beat them to the stone. We can not destroy it without the hammer, but without it they can not release the demon. This stone is crucial, the pivotal point to what is happening around us now."

Darkwolfe unrolled the parchment and gazed at the map intricately drawn there. The path seemed fairly straight forward, but at one point they went out of their way to pass near a little lake. "Why are we going out of our way to pass this lake if we're suppose to be in such a hurry," he questioned his teacher.

"Like I said before, there are others who must test you before you can officially become the Capit Draconis and begin assembling the Dragon Band. Be swift and follow the path I have laid out for you. If you remain true to your spirit, you will be fine. The guardians of the elemental watchtowers will either bless you or fight you, so beware. Now go! Follow the priest, Morning Glory," a priest stepped out from one of the hallways making his presence known to the companions, "he will show you the quickest way out of the Dragon Temple."

Master Cheiron suddenly embraced Darkwolfe like a father would his son. Darkwolfe thought it might be the last time he saw his teacher. They had grown close and developed a respect for each other in the three years they had spent together in the training hall.

Without another word Darkwolfe rose from the table and followed the priest out of the dining hall and down a long hall. Charlemette, the priestess of Levanah, followed close behind. Then came Silverworm, the elven Lord and leader of the Deadly Chimes. Behind him came Sir Gedrick from the holy order of Terra Paladins. The dwarven bard, Little Sunflower came behind the paladin with Cat near her side trying to get a look down her top, "so are you really a bard," he asked conversationally?

The party wound through the hallways on the other side of the temple from where they had initially entered. They emerged into a sunlit courtyard and found the open air refreshing. The sun was making its daily descent though it was still relatively high in the sky, and dusk far away. A large archway led out of the courtyard and onto a long rope bridge. Huge thick double wooden doors were tied open and a raised portcullis was evident within the archway. Darkwolfe had never imagined that any one would have the gall to invade the Dragon Temple, but with the prospect of the demon attacking if it were released, he was thankful for the defenses. He felt bonded now to the temple in a way he could not readily describe, but he knew when this whole thing was over, and if he was still alive, he would like to spend some time here in this quiet and beautiful place.

They exited the temple's outer courtyard and walked directly onto the wide rope bridge. The mountainside of the horn loomed a long ways off and the bridge entered directly into a large cave opening. Charlemette remembered being able to see this cave from the beginning of the other bridge when the temple had at first appeared. Half way across the bridge Cat got the urge to look over the edge again.

It was a little embarrassing for the great thief, and assassin for hire, from the regions biggest city, Thor's Hammer, to be afraid of heights. Every chance he got, Cat would try and face his fears, but that inevitable terror and loss of balance and control came. He crept over to the edge and looked over, wham, it hit him like some paralyzing fear. Vertigo set in and he felt like he was going to vomit.

The bard watched him with interest and curiosity as Cat slowly backed away from the side railing. This is when she decided to look over the edge as well, and use his fear to play with him. "Wow, we're pretty high up aren't we," she said teasingly.

Cat saw that she showed no fear as she leaned dangerously over the edge. He respected her courage, in doing something that he himself could not, but he was growing fond of the cute little dwarf and would hate for her to accidentally fall over. He grabbed her arm and gently pulled her away from the edge. "Come on, we're falling behind," he said. Little Sunflower let him lead her, she giggled with a batting of her eyelashes, and the two quickly made to catch up.

Darkwolfe and his friends gave one last look of awe back at the Dragon Temple, floating high between the horns. It wavered like a sheet in the wind and then became invisible once again.

The cave was gloomy but lit well enough from the infiltrating outside light for movement and sight to be unhampered. The cave narrowed a short way in, forming a huge circular room with a joint or groove apparent about a step away from the wall. The huge circle was large enough for 50 people or more to fit within its boundaries. Morning glory went to the center of the circle and stood next to a huge intricately carved staff that was set in a hole in the smooth stone floor. The staff was capped with a fist-sized chunk of purple crystal, an amethyst.

"Come along everyone. Get within the circle. Stay away from the edges. If your balance isn't so good, you might want to sit down." The old priest rattled off these statements as if he had been doing them his entire life like the dull monotone of a museum's curator. He quickly looked about in an exaggerated sweep of the chamber, leading with his big pockmarked nose. Once satisfied, he lightly tapped the top of the crystal staff and it began to glow, slowly at first, and then more brightly. The huge circle of stone began descending into the very mountain itself.

The companions were a little startled, and a vision of the bridge crept into Cat's mind. The descent was relatively slow, but steady. After only just a short while with the group speaking softly about their need for swiftness in their race for the stone, the magical rock elevator slowed its descent altogether and entered into a lower chamber.

The round stone stopped all together. The chamber was a gigantic dome carved out of the base of the mountain horn. There were several small wooden structures sprawled around the chamber. The circle where they were standing appeared to be the central location of the chamber and everything else was fanned out from it. There were little sleeping cabins where through open windows cots could be seen. There were other storage shacks, a small open bar where drinks could be served to weary travelers, and a sizeable stable where many horses were corralled. Darkwolfe thought it more than just a coincidence that six saddled horses with full saddlebags were being led in their direction by an equal number of priests.

"We have packed provisions and water for you. These horses are very strong and good, they will get you where you need to go and fast." One of the priests said offering the reigns to Darkwolfe.

"We thank you for your kindness," Charlemette replied, eyeing Darkwolfe as though he was rude in not responding first.

"Yes thank you, thank you very much," he offered.

Everyone mounted up rather quickly, but Little Sunflower had a bit of trouble, and Cat was more than eager to help. "I've never ridden a horse before," she said apologetically.

"That's okay, I've ridden millions of times. Just do what I do and follow my lead and you'll be fine." Cat gave her that mischievous smile of his as he fumbled into his own saddle. He had actually only ridden twice before, but he sure wasn't about to tell her that. Once he was situated he reassured her again, "see, piece of cake."

They were then all sitting high, yet no exit was readily apparent. Sir Gedrick continued to scan the base of the mountain, but still could not discern a way out. "Hey, how do we get out of here?"

"Don't worry," another priest said, "the horses know the way out."

As if on cue, all of the horses started walking over toward one of the mountain walls. It didn't look any different than any of the other walls. Darkwolfe was in the lead, and as the horse was about to walk straight into the wall, he yanked back hard on the reigns to stop the stupid beast. The next thing he knew, he was squinting in the sunlight on a dusty trail. He heard other shrieks and complaints as the others passed through the illusion, but they were all soon standing outside.

"What a truly remarkable illusion," Charlemette said in awe. "I couldn't even detect a hint of magic that would have alerted me to its presence, but it would take incredible power to create such an illusion, let alone maintain it for any length of time.

"Well if that floating temple up there is any indication of this places power, I'm not surprised." This time the bard spoke up trying to become part of the group, casting char a friendly smile.

A breeze continued to kick up dust and the Eye of Ra beat down on their brows. Darkwolfe thought that maybe he should have picked a piece of headgear, at least it would keep the glare out of his eyes and the sun off his head.

"This way," Silverworm said. "If Darkwolfe does not mind, I know this area well and my scouting abilities may detect many of the dangers that lie ahead. I ask for the honor of being point."

"So be it," Darkwolfe said.

The companions followed the elf down the path toward the forest and onward toward the Foothills of Fellowship.

* * * * *

Dusk was falling on the wondrous city of Thor's Hammer, the great goddess Nuit, preparing to stretch her magnificent starry body across the heavens. The view the courier pigeon saw was one of countless spires and awesome sentinel towers, as if the city itself wished to impale the blessed night. It would seem impossible for one to think this little-brained bird would find his roost amongst a plethora of such structures, but with unerring flight it came to it's familiar coop where it would be fed and once again rest with its own kind. The cages were lined on the outer balcony of one of the gigantic towers.

Clive, or as people were often fond of calling him *the pigeon boy*, was in the process of cleaning up the cages and feeding the birds for the evening when a lone courier fluttered in and landed on one of the roosts. He wiped his dirty hands on his pants and flicked the straggling mop of blond hair out of his eyes with a twist of his head. Clive was always told never to open a message and to alert his master when a new arrival came. As much as he would have liked to peek at it and see what sorts of things were sent to kings, he decided against it with great conviction. For one, he knew of a boy who had opened a letter concerning many of the king's lecherous affairs, and the ensuing scandal had gotten the boy's head separated from his body. And for two, well, he couldn't even read so what would be the point other than putting his life in danger. Just because he wasn't educated, didn't mean that he was a complete idiot.

So without further speculation the pigeon boy unfastened the little sealed tube from the strap at the bird's leg. He turned in a flurry of swirling green smoke and headed for the door. He entered one of Lord Bastion's studies. It was immaculately well kept and decorated with rich woods, statues of nymphs and satyrs, and tables piled with documents, maps, and letters. Lord Bastion was one of the king's advisors and mostly took care of communication and relations with the peoples in the areas surrounding Thor's Hammer. Clive saw that the Lord was not about and headed toward the central stairwell.

The climb down was long, and Clive often wondered why the Lord would ferret himself away so far removed from the rest of the castle. He found that counting the steps as he went often made the climb go more quickly. He didn't realize that someone was coming up until the two painfully crashed into each other and he bit his lip painfully, drawing blood.

"Watch where you're going you stupid oaf!" The Scorpion yelled amidst a fog of sickening green. The pigeon boy was the worse off of the two, for the Scorpion was a large-built man who was trying to make a name for himself by doing deeds and favors for the king. Fighting, thieving, assassination, it didn't matter to him as long as it improved his status. He had long black raven hair with eyes to match. His face belied charisma and intelligence but not compassion, and he eyed the boy like one would a bug, deciding whether it was worth one's time to squash the miserable thing.

"I..I, was just trying to deliver this message to the king," Clive offered, showing the little message tube. "It just came, but Lord Bastion isn't about, so I thought I'd…"

"Deliver it yourself boy?" The curse was grabbing a hold of the Scorpion's already volatile nature. "Give me that," he snatched it out of the boy's hand too quickly for the pigeon boy to react.

Now it was the boy who was becoming angry. "Give that back you big ox," he yelled, baring teeth and nails as if he were some badger protecting it's little ones.

The Scorpion was truly enraged by this little worm's display of aggression. The powerful fighter thrust his right hand out grabbing the boy by the neck. With one incredible display of strength he crushed the boy's throat and tossed him against the stairwell wall like a rag doll.

While the curse did have a hold of the Scorpion, his better sense warned him against bringing the message to the king. The boy's body would be linked to him and the message. He quickly tore the little container open to read the small rolled note inside. It was blank.

The large fighter picked up the boy's body after tucking the tube and note into one of the pouches at his belt. He then continued his way up the stairwell and into Lord Bastion's chambers. He dumped the body off in one corner and quickly tossed the room, sending papers flying and stealing a few gems and precious items. He found a small box with several small crystal vials within. The labels described them as magical potions. He drank one down that said invisibility on it, tucked the box under his arm, and hastily made his way out of the tower. Anyone who came upon the scene now would think it was a robbery and the pigeon boy fatally happened to have gotten in the way.

* * * * *

Sabbath, Anteas, and the snake-men rode hard that afternoon and came to the Black Paladin's hideout. It was also near the lair of the

Shaithen, and as they approached they saw many of the priests waiting for them. There were a dozen of the snake-men with steeds, and they had provided fresh mounts for the incoming party. It was a fearsome crew with a power hungry mage, a Black Paladin, and no less than 16 of the snake-headed men sitting astride their huge black stallions. After a quick exchange they were riding hard again toward the stone. A lone priest gathered the tired mounts and led them into the cave entrance.

* * * * *

The forest was quiet and easily negotiated by the knowledgeable elven Lord. They soon broke out of the shaded canopy and stood at the edge of the forest line. Before them were rolling foothills of golden grasslands as far as the eye could see. Darkwolfe checked the map to establish the desired route and showed it to Silverworm. The elf merely nodded as though disinterested. He knew the way to the guardians well and wondered if their newfound leader would be able to pass their tests. If not, he would continue the quest without him. Many have tried to claim dominance over the elements and seek their blessing, but most have failed. None since the last Darkwolfe had claimed the pagan crown and led the Dragon Band. Silverworm had some confidence in the young warrior, but he still had his doubts.

"Come, I don't think we should rest at all. If we ride through the night we will reach our first destination at dawn." The elf didn't wait for an answer, but merely prodded his horse forward and took a meandering route through the troughs and valleys that the sizeable hills created.

Darkwolfe tucked the map away and rode on with Charlemette quietly at his side. Sir Gedrick scanned the area as they rode looking for unexpected trouble despite his faith in the elf's competence. Cat and Little Sunflower rode together talking, giggling, and exchanging flirtatious looks.

The night was long, tiring, and uneventful, but finally the sky began to lighten and as dawn began to break Silverworm held his hand up motioning the party to halt.

{Hail to thee who salutes the sun at first light, for with sword in hand the night is not so dismal, nor the day quite as bright.} The voice was male and stern, echoing in Darkwolfe's mind. He tried not to show his excitement and trepidations to his fellow companions, but he was slightly disturbed. He himself was afraid of not passing the coming tests, and the entire fate of the Pleides not just his friends rested on the outcome and his success.

Just as the sun broke the crest of one of the large hills on the horizon, Darkwolfe drew his long sword and held it aloft vertically in front of his face in salute to the rising orb of fire. The companions witnessed the event, and Silverworm, and Sir Gedrick thought it appropriate to follow suit. Darkwolfe didn't know but he listened to the voices in his mind, not sure if they were real or not and began to follow a side trail up and around the nearest hill. He was rather oblivious to his companions. Part way up he left his horse and proceeded on foot.

Silverworm motioned the rest of the party to stay put. "There is nothing we can do to help him now. He must face the elemental guardians by himself. All we can do is wait and get some rest." Reluctantly they dismounted and made an impromptu campsite that they could pack up and be back on the trail at a moment's notice. They were all very tired and laid down, but it was a long morning before any of them found that bliss of restful, deep sleep that only has the power to banish the onset of fatigue and dullness of the mind.

The whole time Darkwolfe climbed the hill and left the sight of his companions on further trails and hills he was assailed by the incessant drone of the voice in his head.

{Your mind is all-powerful. Your mind is what matters, your capability to reason. Emotions are nothing, they are weak. If you can not logically understand something, then it doesn't matter, it doesn't exist. I am called science. Science can answer all your questions. There is no such thing as the gods and goddesses. There is not magic and the spirit or some all-pervasive force running through the universe. I analyze and define and categorize all things. I am the brain, all-powerful over all the elements.}

Darkwolfe was being lulled into the logic of the words. They made sense to his rational self. Yet a part of him begged for love and compassion and the esoteric less tangible things of his existence. What would the world be like with no emotion or joy? A dull land without music and art, dance and comedy would prevail unless it was fashioned in some mechanically rational way. Too much thought can annihilate the very beauty of spontaneity and love spurious actions. So what he thought, can't I just giggle and laugh and tickle and play for the sake of it without some goal or reason behind it beyond simple and pure fun? He began to discern what was happening even as he rationalized the very thing itself. "No, the mind is useful, but only a tool. I will not be swayed by the guardian of air." All at once the voices stopped and he continued along the trail.

He curled around another hillside and walked between two large rocky outcroppings where there sat a large fluffy bush. He examined it thoroughly and though very knowledgeable about the area's flora he could not identify it. Suddenly it burst into flames.

{How dare you awaken me it bellowed.} The bush became the roaring form of a great lion's head growling in defiance. {Do you challenge me?}

This is just some bush, a lion head, I can defeat it Darkwolfe thought. My will can defeat anything. I am the Capit Draconis! Nothing can stand before my might. And yet, he reconsidered. An image of Master Cheiron came to mind. A child of the gods; an immortal. His teacher was quite possibly the greatest force on all of Alcyone, and still he wore humble robes and spoke plainly and considered the thoughts of such young humans as him and his friends. What was this thing called humility? Was it not necessary for those at peace not to exercise their power unless situations warranted it? How could such a great immortal being such as Master Cheiron be so nice and respectful and caring. He could rule anything and anyone, do whatever he wanted and conquer any kingdom with a mere candle flame of his will. And still Darkwolfe knew down in his very being that this was the way, the true way; not to dominate but to be a part of everything; to live in harmony not oppression.

The fiery bush of a lion smiled its great rows of teeth. {You must be like a father, showing both severity and compassion.} Then the bush became a bush again and the fire and the image of the lion were gone.

Darkwolfe came over the crest and saw before him a great depression between a ring of earth. It was like he remembered once throwing a large rock into a patch of thick mud. The rock sank deeply into the mud, creating a depression surrounded by firmer mud, and over time water filled the depression forming a pool surrounded by higher ground. This was what he saw here on a much larger scale. The pool before him was a lake of such captivating beauty and the color blue he might liken to royal but with a hint of green, and yet not aqua either. It sparkled brightly as the light of the rising sun struck it's surface and seemed to call to him evoking emotions he never knew he had, and some he had hoped to forget.

Like a zombie from Grathmoor's castle, Darkwolfe rigidly walked down the trail to the edge of the water and plopped to his knees in agonizing and overwhelming sadness and depression.

Images of his mother, his great love for her and all of their memories flooded his mind. He saw his birth and his first few years suckling at her breasts. Being washed and fed, and even taught how to talk and later how to read. She was always there and encouraged him in all that he did even though he was always much different than all the other kids. She congratulated him on his successes and encouraged him when he failed.

She always mended his wounds and fed him hot broth when he was sick and sat by his bedside. She wasn't gorgeous as one might describe a lady or a fine maiden, but she had the loving qualities of all women; perhaps a model of the goddess herself.

Then he saw her deathbed and the pain and tears of her loss for both he and his father. He recalled all the good times with his father. He forgot all about the bad things that had occured after his mother was dead. All he saw was the good times of his father showing him how to fish and hunt, and how to use a sword and dagger. Letting him run the store for the first time and helping him like some hero when he got into trouble, as foolish as he might have been in getting into the trouble in the first place. He was his idol back then, and his love for him was all that mattered.

Then he saw his decapitated head, hanging from Ben's outstretched hand; blood dripping eerily to the dry floorboards and being sucked up hungrily by their dry, thirsty splinters. And now all was lost. His parents gone. He had died, but was most likely to die again with all his friends. The town of Grathmoor was destroyed. He had nothing, no future, and even his love for Charlemette would eventually be all for naught. He could even see his newfound death, and wondered why he should even continue living in the first place.

The lake beckoned him to just dive in, swallow its precious waters and drown into nothingness. It would be so easy to forget everything and just dive in. Do it! Dive in! You have nothing to live for! All is lost! The voices, the emotions were intoxicating, it was total all consuming black depression. Then through these wicked black dream clouds came the rays of light and with it reason. Yes his mind was just a tool, but it was also there to balance his emotions.

What would one be if they lived in perfect boxes of reason and analytical networks of thought? What would one be if they were nothing but a downpour of uncontrolled masses of emotions? He realized these two were compliments and it was through their balance and use that one could understand the seen and unseen, the rational and ethereal things in life. As with any other tool, they could be used, or if let out of control, became the wielder themselves.

"I recognize you lady, in your beauty and terror. Isis veiled and unveiled, I see you! I welcome you but you shall not dominate me." On a whim he unsheathed his long sword and end over end sent it spinning out over the waters. It hit point first, and with nothing but a tiny splash sank beneath the waters.

In opposition to the pain and fear and loss came a great fulfillment and contentment of total bliss that he thought could only be spoken of in poems. His love for all the races, and his fellow man, and particularly Charlemette came to him and filled him until he thought he could hold no more.

The waters appeared almost indigo now. Several herons and other wildlife became apparent at the lake. There were deer and elk, raccoons and skunk, trout and bass and bluegill could be seen swimming, and out of the lake's center rose a lady in veiled white. She was ethereal and even her skin was pale, and flowing golden hair billowed out behind her as if it were a windy day, but none blew. She carried a magnificent sword and beckoned the young warrior to come to her across the lake.

Darkwolfe had heard of great mages walking on water. During his training with Master Cheiron, his teacher had even spoke of another great teacher back on Earth who had done such a feat and had spread the word of the creator. Apparently this was what the guardian of water and emotion now expected and he was not sure if he was up to it. Yet he also knew that it was his rational mind that would betray him. He had to let go and believe in the miraculous. Slowly and tentatively he took the first step. He didn't sink or fall beneath the surface, and took the confidence from it. Step after step he became more sure of himself and soon he was walking briskly across the water's surface and then was before the guardian standing on the water in the middle of the lake within some fantastic crater.

The wondrous female entity smiled her ghostly radiance and handed him the sword. It was magnificently crafted. He had seen no sword its equal. In appearance it was almost as plain as the one he had cast into the lake in the fist place, but he could now feel the overpowering magic of the weapon and knew that it was a gift from the gods themselves.

In his head he heard the sound of Master Cheiron's voice, "he has chosen the Demon Slayer Blade."

Darkwolfe couldn't help but smile and sheathed the sword. The maiden creature of water dissolved into the watery lake, and instead of returning, Darkwolfe continued across the lake to the other side. There was another trail there awaiting him, beckoning him to climb the steep hill to his final test, his final glory.

The rough dirt trail ended abruptly at a sharply angled staircase. It was fashioned of green marble and inlaid with ancient symbols of which he could only guess their meanings. They must have been old indeed. He had seen and witnessed many writings from across the lands, both present and from ages past and he was at a loss to even identify one. Yet in some vague way they suggested things to him in their archaic hieroglyphs and he steadily strode ever forward with faith and thought, will and emotion, hoping and desiring lamentations to end his trial and be on to Za'Varuk's stone. However he knew that no matter how far he may have come, only one mistake could be the end of him, so while confident and trusting he also stepped with care, humility, and prudence.

The top of the mound was truly nothing of which he could have ever suspected. It was a ring of giant stones with a rocky altar at its center. Like a wavering illusion, suddenly the entire hilltop was covered with gold coins and precious jewels, rock-sized diamonds, sapphires, and rubies. There were rare and precious magical items and a horde of faithful servants and a harem of women to heed to his beckoned call. He was suddenly the king of all Alcyone and everyone would obey his command. No one would defy him. He was as powerful as a god was or even stronger. There was an image of him nonchalantly crushing the body of his teacher Cheiron. Who needed him anyway? He was now the Capit Draconis, who needed teachers now. His word was law. He had all the wealth, magic, and power, any woman, desire, and conquest instantly fulfilled.

Like before, he started to figure out the temptation and fought it with all his being. What would be the use of all this wealth and power without his friends? What would be the greatness in having followers who did so out of fear and not respect? Why bed women when they did so out of fear or personal gain? Wasn't the lot of man to act out of free will, and any way of destroying that inherent right contrary to what the Pleides represented and believed. Wasn't he the spokesman of the Pleides? He had no personal agenda any more, he was a messenger and a warrior for the greater good.

"No, I want no wealth, power, or material things. I am here for the good of the Pleides and for no other reason. I am a vessel of good and balance, I represent the collective unconscious and no other. Do with me what you will, but I work in your name. I bow before no elemental watchtower and work for no single deity." With that the illusions vanished and the mount was clear.

Darkwolfe took a moment to collective himself and slowly walked over to the altar. The only item thereon was a truly awesome crown. It was platinum. The circlet was of intricately carved intertwining ropes. Some were like knots and others snakes, but as hard as he looked and tried to find, there was no beginning of the pattern and no ending. It was a fabulous network of art, describing the wheel of life and death and rebirth. Coming out of the circle crown itself were two stag-like horns of six on one side and seven on the other. They were miniature in size and he thought it wouldn't be terribly difficult to wear, or that it would impede fighting or spellcasting in any way.

Slowly, tentatively, and with utmost love and respect he accepted the blessing of the elemental watchtowers and donned the pagan crown. In the air above the great hilltop came a symbol of a great pentagram. At first it was inverted, and once again a voice came to him, but it was very majestic and surpassed any of the elemental voices he had heard thus far.

{I am spirit, and I must rule over the elements or all is lost. Any symbol inverted is perverse.} There were suddenly other symbols in the air, a long armed cross, a cross with a rounded head, a peace symbol, a six pointed star consisting of an upward and downward pointing triangle (one solid and one ethereal), and many others. They were then flipped upside down. {As you can see, any good can become evil to our nature if reversed. Love becomes hatred,} the cross disappeared, {eternal life becomes, infinite death,} the ankh disappeared, {peace becomes war,} the peace sign disappeared, {the old magical saying, "as above, so below," becomes ruled by earthy desires,} the hexagram disappeared. Suddenly the upside down pentagram turned right side up. {Only when spirit rules over the elements is balance achieved, and truth found.}

And thus was the new king crowned, and the full burden of the Capit Draconis placed upon his shoulders.

2

Lava Falls

The ride was long and hard, but on the following evening Sabbath and his deadly escort finally made the overlook of the Lava Falls. Upon consulting Thor's Hammer it was concluded that Za'Varuk's stone lay somewhere far below. The trip was wearing on all of the companions and if the stories about this place were true, they would need all of their strength for their upcoming quest for the stone.

"As much as I would like to go on, I think it best that we at least have a short rest and prepare for the network of caves that inevitably lay below," Anteas warned.

"I agree," Sabbath said with some finality and summarily dismounted and began gathering his things.

The snake-men were a mute and mysterious lot and collected off by themselves for the minor stop. As the two small camps became settled into the evening, the snake-men could be seen going about some ritual to their god Anu. Eventually both camps grew still and an unnatural silence fell over the lava rocks that bespoke of some long forgotten volcano where many myths had been born, and legends perhaps were still to be brought to life.

* * * * *

The Scorpion had made his way out of the castle and to an out of the way tavern on the riverfront before his invisibility spell had finally worn off. He paid for a room without much conversation, but eyed a few of the topless dancers on his way up the stairs telling himself that he would hook up with one them before the night was through.

His room was small and sparse of furnishings, but more than adequate for his present needs. Soon the pigeon boy would be found and he kept going over things in his mind, trying to think of anything that might link him to the murderous crime. He couldn't rationalize why he had killed the lad, as much as he mulled over the confrontation, other than the fact that the poor boy had pissed him off, and he inevitably snapped (no pun intended) the little guy's neck.

The Scorpion sat on the thin padding of the bed and looked at himself in the oval mirror. Its surface was marred and dirty, but he could still make out his features and mildly cursed himself for his indiscretions.

{It's not really your fault you know.} The voice came into his mind suddenly.

The man whipped his head about looking for the voice's source, but found none. He was not totally virgin to such mind intrusions. He had often worked for one of the city's less reputable mages, Cobalt Hue, but he was still unsettled by the telepathic way of communicating. There were several seconds of silence, and so he just waited to see what would transpire. He knew that something was amiss, or that he had been the object of some spell or curse. Often doing nothing was the best course of action, though paradoxical as it sounded.

{As you might imagine, you have been infected with a curse.}

[And who might you be?] The Scorpion thought wryly.

{Just a player in the game as things may be. I can help you if you are willing to play.}

[Why would I want to play?] He asked, but his tone showed greed and deception of which the demon was extremely use to dealing with.

In fact Za'Varuk was more than thankful for the luck he had in the curse infecting such a useful host.

{Let's just say that I think that we can help each other. What would your price be? Hmmm?}

There was only silence as the Scorpion thought frantically how to better his situation. Money, power, women,—what? He knew what he wanted, but he didn't want it to be wasted like some lamp wish. Words just couldn't describe his feelings, and his *ruthless* feelings and his stifled will where what ruled him and though he never spoke them, the demon understood. In an infusion of magical thought forms the demon showed the Scorpion what could be his if he worked with him. It didn't take much for the human to agree whole-heartedly and begged for his mission to begin.

{There are two things that I ask of you. First, I want you to spread the curse to as many of the poor, common people of this city as possible before mid-draw tomorrow. Second, if real power is what you desire, I want you to go below St. Thagle's Cathedral to the catacombs and find Sciloren's tomb.}

[There?] The Scorpion asked in morbid fear. His response told the demon that he knew of the failed priest.

{Yes, precisely there. Don't let old myths deter you, I trust you will see with time that my information is favorable to our,...kindred hearts.}

With sincerity, but much awe and hesitation the Scorpion agreed to the demon Za'Varuk's terms. Chances were what made men great, and by running from a little ghost story, no matter how real, would surely end his ever-aspiring career to be king of Thor's Hammer. Without delay, the assassin made for the bar-level of the tavern to begin spreading the curse. Then it came as an organized plan: the whores, the beggars, and the merchants. He had to touch those who touched many, and exponentially the curse would spread and thus make his task most efficient, and less timely.

* * * * *

Darkwolfe finally came down the path from which he had first left his friends. Some were still sleeping, but Charlemette was wide-awake and came running up to him with her purple robes swishing and swaying as she ran. Her long blonde hair frothed like a golden sea and the look in her eyes was of great relief that he was still alive. The rest of the camp quickly came alive.

Wordlessly they embraced with kisses and strong hugs, and finally she pulled back to look at him in full. It was then that she saw his stag-crown and awe-struck knelt before him. "My king I vow allegiance in your name, Capit Draconis."

"Rise my love, we are wed in my heart if not in name, and I can not abide you kneeling before me." He brought her up to his level and then kneeled himself. "It is I that should kneel to the goddess that lives in you and every woman that is the true creator of all life. For too long man has oppressed the real creator of life, and it is my will that the new age shall herald your name." Darkwolfe hugged her legs strongly and kissed the sides of her thighs, bowing deeply and humbly.

It was then that he stood again, just as the rest of the companions came up the rise and caught a glimpse of his stag-crown.

"Hail the Pagan King," Silverworm bellowed, dropping to his knees and prostrating himself.

"Hail," Sir Gedrick also said with reverence, assuming a similar position.

Cat wasn't sure about the whole bowing thing, but upon seeing Little Sunflower assuming the position, he did likewise, hoping to please her rather than doing it out of any real dedication to the head of the dragon.

"Rise please my friends," Darkwolfe quickly said. "For all I know, we'll get killed before the day is through, so I would rather we all be alert as opposed to you all bowing and scraping and all that stuff.'

Silverworm looked on him now with hope and allegiance. He truly was the Capit Draconis, and if the legends were true, he would magically be able to call the band together now from all across the planet. He wouldn't even need to try. The crown was like a beacon to ships lost in the fog, and slowly, assuredly they would come from all over, pulled by the magical draw of the head. They were the body of the dragon, and they would obey its call.

"Enough prancing around, lets get this stone before that mage does. Master Cheiron said my magical abilities would take some time to grow, and I don't think I will be able to fight that mage if we meet face to face. Our best chance is to get in and out before he even gets there. With any luck we can be back within the safety of the Dragon Temple before he even knows what's going on." Cheiron ended his last statement, and ran over to his mount, jumping into the saddle with the agility and dexterity that left even Cat's mouth hanging open.

The rest of the party gathered their things, mounted their horses as well, and they were once again racing off toward where Master Cherion's map said the stone lay.

* * * * *

The wild riverfront tavern called the Raging Boar was not so inappropriately named as one might at first imagine. It was a sizeable place where travelers might find some food and drink, and the upper floors held many rooms. The rooms were for sleep or other such activities as the numerous women trolling the crowd might suggest. The front and long hallway off to one side was full of tables and generally was for the more sober individuals who required food and drink in moderation. The wide doorway into the adjacent barn-like structure held other adventure and gambling for those who were willing to risk coin and life.

The Scorpion entered this affair after gently bumping into many patrons and serving wenches on his way. For those with keen eyes, one might have been able to almost see a web of sickening green strands being left in his wake as he efficiently and methodically spread the curse with his passing.

The adjacent barn was a large three-story building with an open central area that extended from the fenced in arena all the way to the rafters far above. The place was literally mobbed with drunken revelry from the floor level, to the second and third level balconies where a better view might be gathered of the coming events. Already money was changing hands and the odds were always in favor of the house. It had been many moonths since anyone was able to ride a mutated boar the entire duration of the hourglass and then escape over the fence with his life. Never the less, there was always that chance that someone would, and so the crowd inevitably gathered and spent their coin on the latest foolhardy rider.

Off to the side near a portable bar/sign-in-table was a small line of riders. They were there to sign up and to get enough liquid courage to actually go on with the suicide ride. Without even thinking twice about it, the Scorpion got in line and quickly counted the stolen money he had acquired while passing through the bar proper as well as his previous stash. 596 gold, not bad he thought. The odds board showed 15 to 1. He would be fairly wealthy if he actually lived through the event.

The first lad in line looked like a sailor type in short pants, bare chest, and a gold hoop earring. The second was an aristocrat's son or some such, dressed in his fine velvets and gaudy attire. He wouldn't last long the Scorpion thought. The third in line, the boy right in front of him, was a merchant's son or some such, he smelled of foul chemicals and pungent odors. Then the Scorpion looked down at himself in his low ankle boots, cotton pants, and short-sleeved shirt. He didn't look too promising either, but his wits and dexterity had gotten him out of many misadventures, and if this demon prospect didn't work out, he wanted to have enough cash to head far to the west where he might find a ship to nowhere.

Finally amidst the cheers and drunken slurred hoots of blind ambition, the Scorpion came up to the table and signed his name. The man taking the "Death Roster" as it was called looked at the written name and back to him questioningly.

"The Scorpion, what kind of name is that?" The burly guy asked. Apparently he also served as a bouncer at other times when the boar riding wasn't in full swing.

"Well I got stung by a brain killer when I was a baby, and the local cleric called it a miracle. Ever since I was called the Scorpion. Beats me, its just a name." He shrugged humbly and took a long pull off a bottle of whisky. He rasped, squinted his eyes, and shook his head. Then he took another pull.

"Well sounds like a good name to me, hell I don't think I ever heard of a grown man that was stung by a brain killer and lived to tell about it." He smiled a smile that was a little shy of a full rack. The Scorpion just smiled back dimly, shaking his hand before he moved on.

The riders were all lined up in a little corral next to a gate that was adjacent to it, where a sliding door was placed leading into a gigantic pen.

As the mutant boar was led out, the rider was suppose to jump onto the beast and hang and for dear life in whatever fashion he was able. An hourglass was tipped over that lasted about three breaths and then the rider was supposed to jump off and make for the nearest fence. If he could climb over and live he essentially won. In all reality, the spectators came to watch a few people get gored to death and get drunk along the way. It was just that plain and simple.

The prospect of living or dying didn't really matter too much to the Scorpion just now. He couldn't fully explain it. He was either feeling damn lucky, or he knew the demon or curse or whatever was going on would look after him. He was always one to push limits, and this was the ultimate test to see if his demon guardian was going to look out for him. That and he couldn't help the little ego thrill to think he could handle one of these mutant boars. He had seen these rides before, and the boars were pure anger and rage, bloodthirsty and demonic in their own right.

Suddenly the event was about to begin and he felt a little excitement as the first rider, the sailor, got ready to ride. The entire barn grew silent except for a few giggles of flirtatious pairs, and a belching contest going on in one balcony corner.

The sliding door was lifted and with great speed the bristly boar entered the staging pen. It was roughly as tall as a man with powerful legs and tusks as long as arms. Its beady eyes were red like fire, and the stench of its breath wafted out arguably for draws in all direction. It grunted and kicked with its powerful legs, splintering several boards. For a moment the Scorpion thought that the sailor was about to back down, but his liquid courage prevailed and in a fatal moment he leaped onto the beast's back.

The outer gate was instantly flung open and the beast charged out with raging speed, twisting and bucking as it went. One would have to hand it to the sailor, for the hourglass was actually loudly slammed over and he lasted half a breath before he was thrown painfully off to the side where he rolled and wearily tried to regain his feet. In a quick turn and a charge the boar had the man impaled by it's tusks and wickedly flung the man's corpse over the fence in triumph.

Many of the betting audience groaned and booed as one as several boar keepers jumped the fence with long, magically charged staffs. With the staff's electrical charge they were able to lead it out of the arena on the far side, and the next rider got ready to go.

The aristocrat's son was a little unsteady, but one of the gate hands handed him a silver flask and he greedily drank most of it down in one swallow. He wiped his mouth with the back of his hand and happened to look over at the Scorpion. He winked at the kid and shook his head as if to say, "you can do it kid, go for it." That seemed to do the trick, and as soon as the inner gate was lifted and the boar charged into place, he plopped right on its back grabbing the bristly spines to hold on.

Again the outer gate opened and the boar charged out. The hourglass slammed over to emphasize the point, and the crowd went into a veritable frenzy. The boar jumped left, twisted, redoubled on itself, and twisted far to the right, and the poor lad flipped right off. The boar did eventually come around and gore the corpse, but the fall had broken his neck outright. Beer and wine went flying from cups from the upper balconies in disappointment, raining down on the broken shell of the man. The boar keepers once again herded the beast back to the far side of the pen and another mutant boar was put in place.

The last boy in line was truly wetting his pants at this point, and ran away as fast as he could. Many people yelled and threw food, and even struck him as he went past, but he would live to see another sunrise.

"Hmmm, I guess I'm up." The Scorpion got ready.

{So, you want to play do you.} The thought came into his mind, with authority, but a hint of amusement as well.

[Well, you have to admit this does look like fun.] He said with similar humor and baiting to see if the demon was going to play along or let him die here and now.

{All right, I never could resist a good boar-ride. I'll stick you on like you were part of the beast, but as soon as the ride is over get out of here. Do your job, spread the curse, and get to the tomb. Don't worry about your measly gold, you'll have as much money as you could ever want, whenever you want it as long as you don't try and test me again. Deal.}

The Scorpion liked to have fun, but he knew this was the deal, no negotiations. [As you wish my Lord].

The gate was lifted and a new boar charged into the holding pen. The Scorpion didn't know if they saved the best for last, or because he happened to look like the most capable rider, but this thing looked like some devil-spawn out of the abyss itself. It was similar to its previous cousins, but it was a dull black and a ferocious heat emanated from it.

Great, now I'm gonna burn my ass, the Scorpion thought to himself wryly. And without further adieu to the world as he knew it, he jumped onto the hellish monstrosity.

At the moment he landed on the beast he felt fused with the animal, and its bestial mentality was mind numbing. The Scorpion looked down and saw that he was literally fused at the leg and groin to the monster, but the image wavered and he suspected that none of the other onlookers could tell that this transformation had taken place. The outer gate was lifted and with a gnashing of teeth he was out on the arena floor dancing a macabre ballet, that only ghastly beings from the nether void might ever witness and know with any clarity.

The hourglass slammed over with a cracking of hard metal on dry wood. The breath was ripped from his lungs and he felt as if his skeleton might simply be separated from his meaty self. All he could hear was some distant chanting and cries, drinks and spittle, paper, and women's undergarments were rained down upon him in a shower of gratuitous offerings.

He was thrashed about, twisted, contorted, and slammed in every imaginable way and he still felt no pain, only pure and raw excitement. This was what life was like. He emitted a triumphant, "Yaaaaaaaaaaaa!" as the beast continued to bob and weave, dodge and jump on the floor, but in vainness to eject the interloper who sat so joyfully upon it's back.

And as quickly as it had begun the ride was over. He was suddenly free of the beast and with a move he knew would never happen again as long as he drew breath, he flipped right off the mount, did two elaborate spins in the air and landed nimbly on the fence in a wide-legged stance. His arms were outstretched to both sides as if welcoming the cheer, and a smile spilt his face from ear to ear.

He didn't wait long. The barn went from shocked silence and came alive with stomping feet, thumping weapon hilts, and a chorus of screams and yells. He took a glorious bow, and darted for the nearest exit, touching as many fans as he could on the way. Yes he thought, this was the beginning of a new life and it was truly exciting. Hell, he'd do just about anything for the demon if he could get such another grand performance, pig and all.

* * * * *

The dwarven army was impressive if not massive in its numbers. There was a line of horsemen five wide and a hundred long standing before the gates of Rockshome ready to move out and protect the demon gate at Grathmoor. Most were fighters in either heavy plate or sturdy chain armor wielding large battle-axes, the favored weapon of their race. There were also a total of five priests and two mages scattered amongst their ranks. Ironoak had tried a scrying spell on the region of Grathmoor, and apparently it had been shielded so all he saw was a dull gloom over the area. The mages and priests had enlisted to go at his behest.

The lead dwarf was Velneb Skullcrusher, a veteran of much renown, and with out elaborate farewells, motioned the procession forward, leaving the clan chiefs, Ironoak, and many tearful women behind.

The ride to Grathmoor was not long, and the group hoped to be there within two nights. They should have left sooner Velneb thought, but moving a dwarf was like moving a mountain, and when 500 were involved it was next to impossible to stay on task. Regardless, he was happy they were en route now as it was and didn't want to spoil anything by casting bitter regrets. The hammer was already missing, and he suspected this was going to turn into much more than a watch dog duty. He suspected action, he could feel it in his bones. He'd seen far too many battles to read the signs any differently, and the signs were reading trouble with a capital T.

The procession rolled away from the mountain gate, and once they were clear from the view of spectators, he began looking at his crew trying to figure out who would be trustworthy in the coming battle. All of his dwarven comrades were trustworthy, but he wanted born leaders to help him organize a front when things got hairy. This last minute assembly was mostly volunteers and there was no said hierarchy other than the fact that he was in charge. Over the next two days he needed to establish some order, designate rank, and let everyone know who should listen to whom, when, and to do so without question. Any deviation from this plan was going to get everyone killed. Ironoak was a trusted friend, and a sage to the community, and if he said trouble was brewing he was not about to question it.

Velneb Skullcrusher looked back over his shoulder, as the most prominent of the group rode near him hoping for some authoritative assignment. With a careful look he picked out two, but the rest weren't much more than rich metal smiths trying to get a name for themselves in this little adventure. Velneb spun completely around in his saddle and rode backwards for a while, and many of the would be leaders began whispering to themselves. After a time, Velneb found what he was looking for. About half way back in the line, one fighter was helping out a friend. Then he went over to check another's harness. He scooted around catching one axe before it fell to the ground. He was a genuine leader, regardless of what social status he had. He took care of those around him, and knew how to keep things moving. He might not be all that great in battle, Velneb warned himself, but he did have two days to train him, did he not?

Velneb spun back around in his saddle, and told his aid to go and get the young dwarf. It took some commotion and disruption of the line, but finally the dwarf was brought up to the front. "What's your name," Skullcrusher asked at last?

"Darrel Hammertoe,..sir," the young dwarf replied.

"I see you carry your grandfather's namesake. The old coot never could fight all that well, and inadvertently smashed many of his toes with his warhammer each time he dropped the darn thing. He was a great guy though, he and I had many conversations over the years. It's a shame to have lost him in the latest troll invasion, he was a hero to his family and the clan. If you're anything like him, then you're definitely an asset to our little expedition." Skullcrusher eyed the youth with expert eyes, and could tell the grandson may carry the family name, but he looked like a strong and able fighter.

Darrel wanted to prove himself to Velneb and instantly set two warhammers spinning in his hands in a quick whirlwind. The sight was dizzying, and the leader was truly impressed. The lad stopped suddenly, and took aim at a distant maple tree. He let the hammer in his right hand go sailing end over end and it hit the mark with a loud crack shaking the ancient tree. A second later, the hammer materialized in his outstretched hand. He smiled confidently, but not cockily to Skullcrusher.

"Very well, I want you to help keep an eye on the group and keep things running smoothly. If any problems arise, report to either Thrasher, he pointed toward a huge burly and seasoned dwarf, or Trollbait, he pointed to what could have been Thrasher's identical twin. Understood?"

"Yes sir," he snapped proudly, saluting, and turned away back into the formation.

"We may actually be okay if we run into trouble," Velneb Skullcrusher mumbled to himself.

The long procession came down the mountain's side and came upon a wide trail leading toward the lands to the south. They continued with some minor discussions and young boasts of war. A hearty song rose up, and Velneb let it go, hoping to boost everyone's morale. They were still far from Grathmoor and precious little time to bind the small army together. For dwarves, singing war hymns together was often more effective than weeks of rigorous training. And so they rode until dusk, 500 deep male voices rumbling through the countryside.

BEATING AS THE HEART I NOW POSSESS
DOING AS THE HOLY AS I BLESS
WINE AND SALT; NEVER FAULT
RITUAL OF LIFE AS OLD AS THEE

RESOUND THE CANYON WALLS
SOLDIERS STANDING TALL
NOW TO FIGHT; THOUGHT AS RIGHT
AS WORKERS IN THE HIVE SHALL BEE

FIRE IN THE THOUGHTS OF SOME
WHAT HAS NOW BECOME
A BLOODY WAR; DEEPENED CORE
OF SOLDIERS THAT WHERE ONCE FREE

SHADOWS ON THE OAKEN DRUM
BATTLES STILL TO BE WON
EXCITES THE BLOOD; BEGINS THE FLOOD
CALLING POWER FROM THE TREES

WHAT THEN IN TIME SHALL RING
AS HEROES FALL AND SING
MEMORIZE; A DATE AND PRIZE
AND SHIPS ARE ALWAYS SHE

FLUTES TO ACCOMPANY
A BRIGADE OF SOLDIERY
TO TAKE THE LANCE; DARE A CHANCE
AND CALL IT BRAVERY

FIRE IN THE THOUGHTS OF SOME
WHAT HAS NOW BECOME
A BLOODY WAR; DEEPENED CORE
OF MEN THAT WHERE ONCE FREE

* * * * *

"Just over the next rise is the entrance," Silverworm proclaimed, rearing his horse to face his companions. There was no mistaking his elven heritage. The fading light cast his shadow like that of a nail, slight and hard. He had pointed ears, a trim nose, and hypnotizing amber eyes. His fine silvery hair was held back by a crimson band and his leather armor looked much like himself, supple and strong.

Darkwolfe leaned over holding out the map so all could see. "It says here the Lava Falls," he said questioningly to see if anyone knew anything about the place. If the place any kind of official name like the map indicated, then chances are one of his friends may have heard a rumor or story about the place.

"I've heard of the falls," Little Sunflower offered. "Really only a bunch of twisted stories about horrible traps and monsters. Apparently no one who has ever entered got out alive. Of course I don't know how true any of this stuff is, it might be just a bunch of fantasy. You know how dwarves like to tell a good story."

Sir Gedrick cleared his throat. "Most myths are based on some tidbit of fact, and then embellished with a little liberal creativity with each telling. The next thing you know every temple is haunted, every graveyard is crawling with undead, and every cave has a wicked dragon protecting unimaginable hordes of treasure."

"Just so happens this cave *does* have a dragon!" Cat added with some exasperation. "I didn't know we were going into *the* Lava Falls, this is suicide. Now this is a cave that just *wants* to be left alone."

"Well the deal with this dragon, is that its here to guard the stone. In a way the dragon is on our side. I'm hoping once it sees Darkwolfe's crown it might be willing to relinquish the stone so that we can take it back to the temple." Silverworm concluded with a wry smile, looking over his shoulder distractedly and examining the top of the mountain face.

"You're *hoping* that the dragon *might* give up the rock? This is nuts." Cat was making a show of it, in fact he was looking forward to getting to meet a dragon.

"You're welcome to stay here thief." The elf ended the little debate and started off up the steep rocky incline.

"I was just joking," Cat said. "He's so uptight."

Charlemette and Little Sunflower both smiled and said in unison, "he's an elf."

The rest of the party followed the elf up the rise. Suddenly Silverworm motioned the party to halt, drew his bow, and leaped into a crouch on the rocky slope.

The companions could tell by Silverworm's vicious intent that a fight was imminent. They dismounted as quietly as possible and tried to find some cover behind a few of the larger boulders. All became extremely quiet in the blanketing gloom of falling night, holding electric anticipation.

Out of the silence came the sound of chimes. The companions were near enough to the elf that the magic of his bow would have effected them too. The bows of the Deadly Chimes were created for use with small scouting or raiding bands. The magic of the bow would acclimate to those near to it, sensing in a way who was friend and foe. The sound was lovely followed by a thit-thit-thit as three arrows sped off into the night in rapid succession. The party could only guess at what the elf was shooting at. It was too dark to see much of anything.

"There are snake-men up there, shaithen, hiding behind some rocks. The elf has already taken two out, but it looks like there are at least another six or so." The bard's nasally voice reported as the fight began. "He got another one in one of its eyes." A screeching hiss came rolling down hill in agony. "Get ready, it looks like they're getting ready to come charging down the hill."

Darkwolfe knew his magic wasn't what it was back when he was training with Master Cheiron in the training hall outside of time, but he thought he could muster enough for a simple spell at least. He waved his hands about in front of his eyes and spoke a few arcane words. Suddenly he could see again as if it were twilight again. He could see the snake-men coming from behind rocks, unsheathing their curved blades. Noiselessly they charged down the hill.

Silverworm continued to let his arrows fly, and took out another two before they got too close and he was forced to draw his fine elven blade. Immediately on the draw he leaped up to the side cleaving half of one of the snake-men's heads in a bloody spray of hissing red. He then entered melee with two of the beasts, dodging blades and snapping fangs with graceful ease.

Darkwolfe charge forward to help his elven friend. He drew forth both of his swords, and immediately the sentient sword called into his mind.

{Careful warrior. The shaithen have poison in their bites, and also wield clerical magic from their god Anu. Mostly healing spells, but they may also try and paralyze you with fear.}

No sooner said, then a wave of fear crept over his being and down the hill toward his friends below. He saw one of the shaithen waving his arms in spellform. He could sense and feel the magic, and knew it was a test of will, and so he called upon the element of fire, his will itself to battle the fear. In an instant, even as he was still running, the magical wave broke around him. The companions below were not so blessed, and the lot of them stood frozen, paralyzed with fear.

Then head on, Darkwolfe met the only two not already fighting head on. He met one blade with his long sword, and jumped back as a dagger came slicing in. A hop and a sharp kick to the side low and toward the knee found home with a loud crack of bones snapping like dry wood. He was quickly dodging and jumping again to avoid the second ones' blades. Out of the corner of his eye he saw Silverworm thrusting his blade home into the chest of one of the creatures.

Then for the next few seconds the only sounds in the night was the ring of metal on metal. Surprisingly, the creature whose leg he had broken, was now standing and coming in to attack again. It had healed itself, and now it was closing with its sword and dagger, and it was all Darkwolfe could do to hold the one at bay.

{Quickly, cast through me, attack darts now.}

Before he could think, he extended his short sword toward the approaching shaithen yelling the command word for the spell. Instantly a barrage of missiles roared out of the end of the sword and slammed into the charging creature. A storm of flesh and smoke followed, and the snake-man fell dead to the ground. Darkwolfe didn't actually witness this last, because immediately after casting, he brought his sword back on guard to defend against the other attacker.

Silverworm had taken a leg off his second attacker, and then followed up with a slash across the monster's throat. He grabbed his bow again, looking up the hill, but saw no other creatures coming.

Darkwolfe severed the off-hand with the dagger of his opponent. In triumph he stepped forward to finish the job. He slipped, falling flat on his back. The snake-man leaned over wickedly to impale the pagan king. Then there was the chimes again filling the air again with their melodic intent. The shaithen then seemed to go to sleep with its weird eyes still open and its sword extended. Then all at once there appeared three arrows sticking through the thing's head and it fell in death.

Again the night fell to silence.

Darkwolfe looked back down the hill and could see Cat, Charlemette, Sir Gedrick, and Little Sunflower standing like statues. Slowly, they began to twitch and move, and then the spell was broken.

The Pagan King came back down the hill and greeted his friends, making sure everyone was okay. Sir Gedrick felt embarrassed for having succumbed to the effects of the shaithen magic. Silverworm held his bow taunt, in case any more of the priests were still about. Apparently they had exhausted their immediate forces, and the party led their horses to the top of the rise.

There was a fire still burning and many horses tethered to some scattered trees. Silverworm seemed to relax a little once he found that the number of horses and dead were identical, eight. There were more tracks, and two humans with another band of snake-men as far as the adept tracker could tell, but they were long gone.

"We'd best get going as fast as we can, for all we know they may be in the dragon's lair itself even as we speak." Silverworm said, tying his horse among the others and preparing to enter the cave.

"I agree," Darkwolfe said, "let's get going, this place is creepy. I feel like we are being watched."

Charlemette sat off to the side with Little Sunflower near the fire. "I don't feel well, I'm gonna wait here."

"Me too said the bard," quietly. "I think that spell upset my nerves as well."

"Well we can't just leave the women sitting out here unprotected," Sir Gedrick said valiantly, "I'll protect them."

Cat shrugged his shoulders as if saying me too, I'll stay and protect the women. He took a seat over near the bard, trying to look down her top again. Silverworm shook his head, met Darkwolfe's gaze, and the two headed into the Lava Falls.

3

Lair of the Dragon

The cave entrance was set in a huge depression of smooth rock. It looked as though it was made by intense heat and forced inward like the forming of a vase that a glass blower might make. It was low in the depression, so it was more of a hole in the ground than a cave set in a cliff face. It was dark and a smell of sulfur emanated from the ghostly pit.

They entered the cave, and after immediately taking a sharp downward slope, it formed a large open entry chamber. The elf with his night vision and Darkwolfe with his spell of Twilight Eyes easily navigated the dim cavern. The place was deathly still, and many old skeletons in armor still desperately clutching their weapons lay strewn about. Darkwolfe hoped he and Silverworm weren't soon to be added to the macabre collection, slumping in some glass-blown hollow inside a hill of volcanic rock.

A great tunnel led down and away from the entrance hole. They followed it walking slowly and cautiously.

"Wait," Silverworm yelled, but it was too late. Darkwolfe had triggered some magical trap and a beam of light, or non-light as would be a better description, shot out and hit him.

Nothing happened.

Darkwolfe looked at his arms and hands, over at the elf, then back at himself again. Whatever may have happened somehow didn't effect him. He thought of Kiriana his sentient sword and drew her.

{So now you understand. I have much knowledge, all you need to do is ask.}

[What happened with that light thing that hit me? I thought I was a dead again for sure.]

{This place is warded against plunderers and evil creatures. Because you are good of heart, and more specifically, because you wear the crown, the magical traps won't harm you. I'm not sure if the elf will be so fortunate. You may want to tell him to wait here.}

"Silverworm, you should wait here. The aura of my crown will protect me from the magical traps. I'll hurry." Darkwolfe could tell that the proud elf Lord was not happy about staying behind, but he was intelligent and wise and knew never to let pride get in the way of caution. If he was dead, who would look out for the well being of the new young king?

Darkwolfe wove around the littered bodies of previous fools and adventurers, occasionally triggering a trap, but each time the deadly ray would hit harmlessly and disappear. The cavern went down further, twisting and turning, and finally he could see into a gargantuan chamber that he could only imagine must be his destination, the lair of the dragon.

[So Kiriana, what do you know of this dragon? Is it evil? Is it going to eat me for dinner or what?]

{Well, the answers to your last two questions are no, and no. Dragons you see are creatures of magic spawned from the web of the universe by the great goddess of magic Hecate. They are not evil, but not necessarily purely good either. Think of them as neutral, always seeking balance and to maintain the structure of your *reality* as it were. Will the mighty Eleanor help you on your quest? Probably, since you are in fact in opposition to the demons of which the dragons and they are sworn enemies. The demons strive to destroy the balance and the dragons to maintain it. Oddly enough they are a form of balance in themselves. Now you may see the quandary present in merely destroying the demons. Would this somehow effect the balance?

By wearing the crown, you became the Capit Draconis. In some ways you are a part of these dragons, especially since being revived in the dragon pool and assuming their blood. There are however what are called renegade dragons. These dragons have broken from their essential neutrality and now fight blindly for good or evil.}

[Blindly?]

{Yes, for they no longer see the need for balance. Of course good and evil being somewhat subjective, but referring to order and individuality in their extremes. We need individuality and in fact it is the very premise of free will, but without any order everyone would be stealing and killing without heed for their fellow man and races. If we have too much order and law, we have restriction, stagnation, and no expression of will. Like all things and every aspect of life there must be a balance.}

[I see. It is perfect, but really a constant struggle between opposing forces and achieving a balance through their eternal tension.]

[I see.] Darkwolfe began walking again and entered the dragon's lair.

There were heaps of armor and weapons and coins. There were mounds of gems and semi-precious stones. Strange magical items and vials of potions were scattered here and there. Yet no dragon was apparent. Straight against the far wall in a throne made of gold and jewel studded glory sat a beautiful woman with flowing red hair. Her features were perfectly chiseled, from the prominent cheekbones and graceful chin and shoulders, to her more womanly curves. She sat idly, twirling a fiery lock of her magnificent hair around a finger. A smile was etched on her hard face, but in amusement rather than anger at his sudden intrusion.

"Greetings Darkwolfe of Grathmoor, wearer of the Pagan Crown, leader of the Dragon Band, and the Capit Draconis." She spoke with a profound lilt, sounding more like she were singing than merely addressing a stranger. The mere sound of it was glorious. It flowed into and through him, bringing him great peace, loss, and wanton desire. His whole life he had felt empty somehow. Even with Charlemette in all her love and beauty, being resurrected with a goal and purpose, finding the warrior and the magic in him, none of these things had truly made him complete. Somehow the mere sight and sound of this veritable goddess before him did. It made him feel whole.

"You seek the stone of Za'Varuk?" The lady asked.

"I do." He stared at her again in a moment of captivation. "Who are you?" Darkwolfe spoke granting more emphasis to his query than that of his original mission.

"I am Eleanor."

"A dragon?"

"Perhaps. Maybe less, maybe more." She opened her hand, and it lay a fist-sized ruby of unimaginable wealth. "I give it to you."

Darkwolfe tried to question his sword Kiriana in his mind, but either she wasn't in the mood for talking or the dragon was somehow blocking their mental communication. Tentatively he stepped toward the throne and the mysterious woman. He had envisioned a dragon to be less beautiful and more,...scaly. He was before her, looking fully upon her radiance, losing himself in the waves of her fiery hair. She looked him full in the eyes with her green and red flecked orbs, red lips curved up to the side in a curious and wry smile. He took the stone, brushing her velvet skin, knowing for the briefest of moments only pure ecstasy.

With total willpower and instant loss, like his heart being torn from his chest, he looked away and started walking out of the Lady's lair.

"Beware of treachery," she warned, calling after him with that golden singing voice.

He stopped and turned, facing her once again. "And what of you now that the stone is gone?"

"Fate as a funny way of keeping me occupied. I will stay here for now. In time we will see each other again. Remember your purpose for being brought back. No matter what happens, you must go on. Fare thee well young king."

With that he gave her one final look. He tried to memorize every line and feature so he could recall her image to mind later on. Their eyes met one last time and then he left.

Silverworm was still standing where Darkwolfe had left him. In fact the king would have sworn the elf hadn't moved a muscle, and he didn't until Darkwolfe came up beside him. They both turned to leave. Darkwolfe held up Za'Varuk's stone for the elf to see. Silverworm grimly nodded.

The elf wasn't sure this was such a good idea. The dragon he thought was the best guardian of the stone. It had been safe for thousands of years, and now they were taking it out in the open for any thief or group of bandits to take. It didn't make a whole lot of sense, though he had to admit the Dragon Temple would also be an excellent place to hide the stone. It was just that the trip from here to there wasn't sitting well with him. Darkwolfe was having similar thoughts, but both men did have complete trust in Master Cheiron's judgement and would unquestioningly follow his will.

The exit to the dragon's lair soon came in sight and the two companions were relieved to be getting out into the open air once again. Cat, Little Sunflower, Sir Gedrick, and Charlemette could be seen sitting where the two had last seen them. The waved cheerfully and got to their feet in expectation of the good news.

Darkwolfe held up the ruby for them to see, smiling happily as he walked over with the elf by his side. Silverworm was looking around in his usual agitated, protective self.

"That's it?" Charlemette asked, eyeing the ruby with curiosity and a hit of awe. "How do you know it's the right one?"

"I don't know for sure, but the dragon did give it to me herself." Darkwolfe responded. "We'd better get going, the sooner the better. There may be more of those snake-men about. We've got to get back to the Dragon Temple with the stone."

"It's so pretty, can I see it?" Charlemette pleaded, looking into her lover's eyes.

Darkwolfe absently handed her the stone. She examined it with a grin and quickly stuffed it in a sack.

"What...," Darkwolfe began, but instantly the illusion was broken and Charlemette turned into a man in robes, a mage. The paladin, bard, and thief turned into snake-men. Before the illusion was even completely dispelled, the elf had dropped back and began unleashing the fury of his deadly bow. Two of the shaithen were already pin cushioned and dead before a loud booming voice yelled "Hold" from the other side of the hill.

Silverworm and Darkwolfe snapped their heads instantly in that direction and took in the stranger. It was a Black Paladin. Flanking him were five Shaithen. In front, bound and gagged, were his real friends.

"You see," Sabbath began, "you really can't win. I must thank you for getting the stone for us, the prospect of fighting the dragon myself didn't really sound all that appealing. Once we realized you were also after the stone, it just seemed easier to take it from you than the dragon. You can fight me to try and get it back, but your four friends will certainly die and most likely you and the elf as well. Or, we take the stone and you all live. That sounds rather nice of me. What do you say?"

Darkwolfe looked to his friends in fear and agony. He couldn't just let them die. He remembered the dragon's words. He was here to save the Pleides, not to save any one person, even if it was Charlemette, his beloved wife. He was ripped with indecision. Somehow he controlled his raging emotions and also the image of the tarot card, *The Charioteer*, came to him.

He needed to be in control at all times. His will, his mind, his emotions, and his desires all needed to be tightly reigned to do the right thing and make the right decision no matter what his lesser self wanted. His greater self, his higher will, his spirit is what needed to be in control and make the decision with a certain degree of objectivity. And so he did.

"We can't just let you take the stone and release the demon. Do you realize what that would mean? Total destruction of the world. Absolute chaos. Millions of innocents would die at the hand of that fiend. Is that what you want?"

"I had a feeling you'd say something like that," the mage replied. He clapped his hands together and a burst of deafening thunder erupted. The concussion sent Silverworm and Darkwolfe hurling through the air. They landed in a bloody and disoriented mess. The mage and the lone snake-man joined the larger group. "Here," Sabbath tossed Anteas the sack containing Za'Varuk's stone. "You and the shaithen start back, I'll catch up."

Without question they ran to their horses and started down the hill and onward to Grathmoor castle. Soon the fleeing group was far enough away, and silence claimed the hill one last ominous time.

The moon had risen and cast an eerie glow of silver over the scene, like some dark play or opera waiting for the beginning notes. Sabbath stood behind the four tied captives, hood drawn up in the semblance of an executioner. The friends struggled and tried to speak around their gags, but to no avail. Silverworm and Darkwolfe were then just starting to stir. Darkwolfe was first on his feet and stumbled over toward the group with murderous intent. A horse whinnied like some gleeful apparition eager to have some new dead to converse with.

"So who is it going to be," Sabbath questioned, toying with his dagger dangerously behind Cat's head. "This one?" He moved behind Sir Gedrick. "Maybe the dwarf?" He came behind Little Sunflower.

"Perhaps the priestess of Levanah?" He brought the tip of the blade to the base of her skull on her neck.

Darkwolfe was still stumbling over to the mage, horror in his blood smeared vision, the Pagan Crown more red than platinum, sitting at an odd angle. This time there was no way to dive in front of the boulder and save her life. Pain, anger, confusion, and hatred boiled into one as he went to call for his magical energies. He fought through the dizziness and nausea created by the blow he had taken to the head when he was thrown to the ground. He managed one measly attack dart that was easily deflected by Sabbath's shield. He drew both swords and continued to close the distance.

"You see I was willing to let you all go. All you had to do is give me the stone. Fighting is useless, now their blood shall be on your hands." Sabbath was playing with him, enjoying every moment. Suddenly the mage's shield lit up with blue and purple lightning as several of Silverworm's arrows were harmlessly repelled.

A trio of attack darts flew out from the mage's hand, whizzing across the hilltop and slamming into the elf. He stumbled back several steps and fell to the ground, unconscious and barely breathing.

Then, Sabbath mercilessly thrust his dagger through the back of Charlemette's neck and the point protruded from the front in a gurgling spew of gore. She fell forward hitting the ground hard, dead. Tears trickled from the corners of her eyes even after she was gone. She wept not in pain, though it was excruciating, but in the loss and emptiness of leaving her lover, friend, and husband behind.

"Noooooooooo," Darkwolfe screamed hoarsely and charged the last little distance to the mage swinging wildly. The mage's shield deflected the first few, but began to weaken under the forceful onslaught of the magical weapons.

Sabbath quickly unleashed another spell allowing him to assume ghost form. Just as he did so his shields failed and Darkwolfe's swords drove through, but they didn't connect and went harmlessly through the wispy image of Sabbath. With a cackling laugh of victory to rival any banshee, the ghost form darted away on the wind in the direction of the fleeing Black Paladin and the shaithen.

Darkwolfe slumped by the side of Charlemette's corpse. He laid her head in his hands and cried out with total unrelenting agony at his loss, oblivious to the pleadings of his other companions to be released from their bonds. Nothing existed at that moment but pure sorrow, the lonely moon, and the intrusive image of the dragon Eleanor.

4

Convergence

Some time later the Pagan King gathered enough sense of his surroundings to at least untie Sir Gedrick. The paladin also wept as he went about freeing the others and hurried over to see if Silverworm was still alive. The elves were a hardy race and Silverworm's constitution proved enough to pull him through. The paladin gathered him up and brought him over to where the rest of the companions were, trying to make him as comfortable as possible. The paladin cast a minor healing spell, and soon the elf slept deeply and soundly.

No one knew what to say about Charlemette's death. They wanted to comfort their new king, but also wanted him to know the solace of quit contemplation. In fact Darkwolfe didn't know what he would prefer either, he was just simply in shock and functioning within a numb existence, where buried lay a flame. It would soon surface consuming all his enemies in unrelenting revenge.

{Come. Bring her body to me.} The voice of Eleanor beckoned.

Like one of Sabbath's undead servants he picked her up and without explanation to his companions he headed back into the cave. His friends and followers did not say a word or attempt to follow. Again the magical traps flashed around him like some strobe effect and he entered the lair of the dragon once again.

The ornate throne was gone, and in its place was a precious sarcophagus. It was gold and inlaid with lapis lazuli and mother of pearl. Emeralds and rubies and sapphires and diamonds were set in intricate patters, most prominent was the symbol of the goddess Levanah indicating her faith and devotion as a priestess. The interior was of rich velvet and sprinkled with rose petals. Darkwolfe came over and gently laid her within.

Eleanor waved her hand over the body and it was instantly dressed in the regalia of a high priestess. There were no bloodstains and the hole in her neck was gone. A shimmering field of magical energy sealed the top.

"This shall be her tomb." The dragon stated, looking the young king in his sad, tear-streaked eyes. In a surprising display of affection Eleanor wiped his tears away and kissed him gently and tenderly on the lips. "You must go on. I know you grieve, but how many men's wives will also be slain if you let these murders get away; if the demon escapes?"

"You knew?"

"Dragon's sometimes get hints of the future. We see time more circularly not linearly as humans do. In time you may also come to see. Remember that your love once given can never be lost. It is the transcendence of time and the twisting of memories that make them grow faint. Remember we live and die and are reborn. Group souls often reincarnate many times over and over." She took his hands in hers and he felt the distortion of time. He heard her voice, yet saw great visions.

"Time and again you two have been together over the millennia." There were images of men and women, children playing, many races and ethnic flavors. Sometimes he was a man and she the woman, and at other times he was the woman and she the man. "We experience many things in each life. Always different. Different races, sexes, poverty and riches, various trades. Sometimes a farmer, then a miner, then a bard, a poet, a king, a soldier. When we finally are complete we merge back into the consciousness of the creator. This is how it knows itself; through our experiences. So you see your love is not lost, Charlemette is not gone." There came before him an image of his love. He knew it was her spirit. At first it looked like just Charlemette, and then it became more abstract and he looked into her eyes. They were intense and powerful, something he did not at first recognize as his wife. "What you see is her true self, her essence. The sum of all her incarnations. When death finally claims us and we heed it's call and not cling tenaciously to life like lost spirits or undead, we see our higher purpose. Each incarnation is nothing more than an expression of who we really are, ever changing, ever evolving. Know peace dear king for some day, at some time you two will be together again. Time bends and it will seem like now. The past, present, and future exist simultaneously. We have the vision of the now, but it will pass, and there we will have what remains; what has always been."

Magic raced through him and he could feel the essence of his dragon blood. His tears were gone and he felt strong and healed and ready to battle his enemies. Not in revenge, but in pure purpose of stopping those who would stand in the way of the divine plan. He was their chosen warrior, their voice. He was the Pagan King

* * * * *

The dwarven contingent had come to a halt some time after dusk. The small army had simply stopped on the road when Velneb gave the signal and readily grabbed the nearest piece of dirt and laid down to rest. Velneb, Thrasher, Slayer, two other notable leaders, and Darrel Hammertoe sat off by themselves by a small fire to discuss the coming confrontation at Grathmoor castle. It wasn't a sure thing, but they were treating it as one in case it was. Their plan evolved as if coming into Thor's Hammer and dealing with a huge force. At the point of contact, they would change their plans accordingly, and of course if there was no force to meet them, all the better.

Thrasher and Trollbait sat close to each other, veterans of the latest troll invasion. They both wore heavy plate and were short stocky characters with brown beards and matching hair. It would even be fruitful for one to distinguish the dirt marks one from the other in naming the two. The only noticeable difference that one could claim, was the slight raking scars that ran down Trollbait's right cheek. He was particularly happy of the wounds, since in the last invasion of the dwarven stronghold he had been a scout primary to drawing out the enemy and had inadvertently acquired his present name.

"I don't care what happens this go round," Trollbait said emphatically, "I'm not gonna be no one's bait in drawing out any trolls. I'll fight goblins, demons, and snake-beasts, but I'm not gonna sit around waiting for some trolls to come out of their mountain caves to come gnaw on my face like last time." He crossed his arms as if to emphasize the point and spit into the fire with a sizzle.

"Don't worry," Thrasher said, "this time we're just guarding a gate." He took a huge bite of his chaw and offered some to Trollbait who waved it away with an angry arm.

Jessup Stingwater leaned forward over the flickering fire. "Here, take a swig of my latest concoction, it'll make you forget about those trolls."

"Yah, the last time I drank some of your inventive potions, I couldn't get out of bed for a week," Trollbait offered with another spit into the fire.

"Well you're only suppose to drink a little of my brews. This isn't some beer or wine, but real potent stuff." Jessup tried to explain, offering Velneb a swig, which he took gratefully.

Skullcrusher took a steady pull and passed it on to Cory Mealntor at his right. "Look Trollbait, we probably won't be encountering any trolls this time around. Ironoak said the worst case scenario would be some undead zombies and skeletons and whatnot. But realistically

Grathmoor's gonna be untouched and we'll just roll in and secure the gate with Lord Noblin still in control of the region. If he's somehow been deposed, then we have to gain control of the town. Either way, I don't see any trolls in your near future, just some fodder for your axe. We only used you last time, because you were so good at drawing them foul creatures out of their holes that's all."

Cory took a swig and passed the flask on to Darrel Hammertoe, who looked at it askance and smelled it with a wrinkling of his nose. "This stuff is gonna curl my nose hairs," he proclaimed, and took a sip anyway. He coughed, but held the vile brew down and passed it on to the next victim.

"That's not all it'll curl boy," Thrasher said draining the rest of the flask. "Is this all you got Jessup?"

"Ha," the maker snorted, "I brought about another twenty!"

"Now listen," Velneb began with some sincerity and authority in his voice. "I want to look at this as a worse case scenario. We go in to town thinking the entire place is overrun with undead and some interloper has assumed the right of Lordship. I personally don't believe it, but Ironoak thought it was the only plausible conclusion in regards to his failed vision spell. I want to be optimistic, but I also trust that old coot. He's been around since my great-great-grandfather's time, and he knows what he's about. If he says there's gonna be some trouble, then by gods there's gonna be some trouble. You men are what I feel are the best leaders amongst the bunch." He stopped taking the newly offered flask from Jessup and took a long pull and passed it on.

"Now chances are as soon as one of these lads," he pointed over to some sleeping youths who didn't look over 50, "get a look at a zombie, they're gonna go running back to Rockshome. We don't want that to happen. If it does, we're finished. Thrasher, Trollbait, I want you two to go charging in and make some kindling out of them, that out to liven the bunch up a bit. Jessup, Cory, I want you two to push from the back so there can't be a retreat. Darrel, I want you to stick with me. We're gonna drive through the middle and fight and yell and whatever it takes to bring us to the gates of Grathmoor. Now the gates might be closed, but Ironoak gave me this magic ball. If we set it at the gate, and run away as fast as we can mind you, it should blow the gates open. If it comes to that, we kill everyone in sight who looks like an enemy and head for the secret passage." He took the opportunity to pass the castle diagram around so everyone could familiarize themselves with the layout.

"Remember, our goal is to protect the gate. Get in, find the gate, and establish a wall of steel to deter anyone from getting in. If you recall how the hammer was taken, there will inevitably be a mage with them."

"No problem," Thrasher said in his deep bass voice, patting his trusty crossbow. "My bolts have never been stopped by a mage's shield before."

"I don't doubt it, with every priest in Rockshome and Ironoak adding their little magic to them," Velneb smiled sternly trying not to get too friendly and to maintain his sense of acting general of the army.

"Sounds good to me," Jessup concluded. "Now let's get drunk, have a fine campout nap, and then get on to war."

As one voice the group responded raising their weapons, "By Thor's blessing, amen."

* * * * *

Out on the street the Scorpion felt much better. The air on the open street was sweet with incense and numerous ladies lining the alleys trying to grab passers by to view their wares and indulge in a little fun. The chorus of cheers slowly died down within the barn, and slowly he could hear the rise of angry shouts and fights breaking out as the curse slowly spread and came to a violent head.

The Scorpion didn't want to be too close, for inevitably the blood would spill out to the street. He quickly touched and fondled many of the scarlet women as he made his way down the street. He took several quick turns and headed into another section of the city, leaving this part to its own demise.

* * * * *

Za'Varuk was relatively content in regards to the way things were going. Sabbath had retrieved the stone and was in route back to the castle. His army was readily amassed and hidden within the northern edge of woods waiting to receive the dwarven army. As well, the mage had dealt a blow to the Capit Draconis by killing his beloved. Any slight against his sworn enemy, especially an emotional one would weaken him and better the demon's chances in their forgone confrontation.

The demon was secure in the way things were going, and sat in the Lord's chair within the dining hall amidst his undead servants; a conqueror waiting for the season to come in full; A time of death and dissolution of the entire fabric of life and existence.

* * * * *

The next portion of the city was somewhat more respectable and there were no easily approachable targets lining the streets as in the district of the scarlet light. The Scorpion did however see a tavern coming up on the left. The sign labeled the establishment as the *Mermaid's Kiss*. It seemed like a good enough place as any to continue his work, so he went through the swinging double doors into the smoky barroom beyond.

The Scorpion strolled in and headed straight for the bar. He ordered a whisky and dropped a few coins into the barkeeps outstretched hand brushing it lightly amidst the swirling green mist. "Thanks a lot," he said turning and gently bumping the guy next to him. He came around the end of the bar. There was a three-step drop into a sunken parlor where various games of chance were currently underway.

"Come, come my friend. Try your luck tonight, the stars are aligned for good fortune." The weasel-like man patted him on the back as he passed. "There is wealth to be had, yes." Then as if suddenly considering something, the man shut up. The Scorpion thought for a minute the guy might attack him, but the demon had told him he probably wouldn't be attacked while spreading the curse unless he outright provoked a fight. The curse itself would offer him some protection.

The weasel guy then pulled his dagger. He walked right around The Scorpion and headed toward the boss's office doors where two burly bodyguards were blocking the entrance. Shouting started to occur back in the main room. The Scorpion had a great vantage point of both events, so he decided to stay put and enjoy the entertainment.

The barkeep Jim had enough of the drunk, drawling slob sitting at one of the tables. This drunken retch had been coming in for the past few fists, begging for money and booze, and Jim only allowed him to stay because the barmaid Alice felt sorry for him and as it turned out Jim had a thing for Alice. Now in his curse induced rage, Jim thought since Alice wasn't willing to sleep with him unless they were handfasted, which Jim had no intention of doing with the barmaid, then he would just find someone else to keep him warm at night and enjoy throwing the slob out of his bar. He grabbed a big club from behind the bar which had *The Law* burned into its wooden handle and made for the poor unsuspecting drunk.

The guy at the bar who The Scorpion had bumped into was a member of the Poisoned Daggers, a local thieves' guild. He had thought of brawling with The Scorpion for his carelessness, but thought better of it after recognizing the king's mercenary. He took a swig of his drink and started staring at Alice's nice curves again. How dare she ignore his affections he thought, I'm the best thief in all of Thor's Hammer. His anger boiled over and he marched toward the barmaid with dangerous lust and rage in his eyes.

"What do you want Ruskin?" One of the burly guards said as the weasel-like man came before them with a dagger. They were blocking the door to the boss's private rooms. "The boss ain't expecting you, so get lost. And put away that knife before we have to hurt you."

"I want the money I'm due, now stand aside you ogre-brained dolts."

Both of the guards raised their eyebrows in concert and one of them moved to punch Ruskin in the head. The little guy ducked underneath the big arm and slashed the bodyguard across the inner thigh and groin with his curved dagger. The guard yelled and fell back on his rump in a pumping spray as his femoral artery faithfully shot forth with each heartbeat.

The other massive guard drew his sword. Ruskin knew there was no chance to win with his dagger against the warrior's huge blade. The weasel man fondled a necklace about his neck briefly morning the loss of his magical item and pulled it from his neck, breaking the leather ties. It was a small smoothed out quartz crystal, but the glow it emitted drew the eyes of many bystanders and the guard drew back in fear. Ruskin hurled the stone like out of a sling and the magical rock struck the chest of the cringing warrior.

With a squeak of mousy doom, like a rodent in a feline's maw, the guard slowly hardened, freezing in place as a crystalline statue. Ruskin sauntered up with a dignified face of superiority and victoriously slammed the butt of his dagger into the chest of the dead man. He shattered loudly to the floor in a pile of rocky-clear crystals.

Next, Ruskin turned the door handle, and while jumping to the side flung open the door to the boss's office. Instantly there flew out of the doorway several darts with wicked barbs on their heads. The harmlessly flew past the dodging man, but hit a lady in a blue dress standing off to the side. They hit her in the arm, breast and neck. She slumped over the table and died in a widening pool of blood. Her life's essence splatted to the wood-planked floor as it ran over the sides of the table's edge.

On the other side of the bar, Jim had come up behind the drunk and collared him with his big hand. The man yelled and kicked as he was lifted to his feet.

"Stop moving will ya." Jim bellowed angrily and the drunk was instantly cowed. Yet it had the opposite effect for the barkeep. Seeing the drunk still and frightened even made him more outraged at his worthlessness and pitiful existence. Jim took his club (*I am the law)* and smashed the poor man's head in. He tossed his corpse like a traveling pack effortlessly into the dusty corner.

The Poisoned Dagger thief was now upon the barmaid Alice. In one strong grab and pull, he had torn her blouse open and she stood there in shock naked to the waist. Many of the male patrons in the place whooped it up and applauded his brave stupidity. Everyone knew Jim had taken a liking to this one, and they anxiously awaited the action that was soon to follow.

They didn't have to wait long. Alice's scream made Jim snap his head in her direction and he took in the scene with bloody rage. Jim came charging in with a wide overpowering swing. The thief wasn't a small man either, so he ducked in and shouldered the barkeep hard, knocking him back into some of the drunken spectators. The curse quickly spread, and the personal fight soon erupted into an all out barroom brawl to the death.

Unfortunately Alice was still standing in the middle of the room screaming when an annoyed man shut her up by slamming a short sword between her breasts. Jim followed this up by breaking the guy's neck and the Poisoned Dagger thief hurled his knife into Jim's unsuspecting leg before he threw himself out the nearest window. The poison soon took effect and the barkeep died with horrible convulsions on the floor.

Self-preservation seemed like a good idea just then, and so did murdering a few of the Terra Paladins. The paladins have always been there to keep the Poisoned Daggers in check, and tonight Murdock had the guts to do something about it. Several other of the cursed barflies escaped into the street as a fire broke out, burning more than one man to death.

Ruskin charged in low before the boss had time to reload and stabbed him in the gut, pulling upward in a ghastly mess. The boss hit the floor amidst his own entrails while Ruskin went about quickly grabbing a few sacks of gold and precious gems. He then dodged out the door. The bar had ignited into total pandemonium and everyone was either fleeing or killing each other. Ruskin eyed the Scorpion curiously and then ran over to him.

"He, what's your deal man," he asked looking about warily.

"You want more of what's happening around here, and a few more boxes of gold?" The Scorpion questioned nonchalantly.

"Hell ya, this is more fun than a boar-riding contest." The Scorpion suppressed a chuckle as he thought of his own boar-riding experience and motioned for the man to follow him.

In the street, Murdock was still brushing himself off. He looked at the duo as they emerged from the burning building and considered his options. They looked like they could hold their and he could use a little help in his exploits. Chances are the guild itself wouldn't back his rash attack on the paladin's headquarters. "Safety in numbers and all that," he said holding his palm up in peace.

The Scorpion could tell the man had an agenda, and a murderous curse induced one at that. "You help us, we help you." He offered.

"Deal." Murdock came over, watching as the flames were quickly consuming the building and firefighter bells were ringing close by somewhere down the street.

"Follow me then," The Scorpion said and headed off toward St. Thagle's Cathedral and the crypt of Sciloren. At least he thought, it wouldn't be so bad dying with a little company.

* * * * *

The companions hadn't waited for long at the cave entrance when Darkwolfe appeared along with some red headed lady wearing white robes. They were taken aback by her grace and beauty. As well, they could only guess as to who she was and what she was doing with their king climbing out of a dragon's lair. The night was slightly crisp and moving on. With each moment the fleeing enemy was getting further and further away.

"Come we must take pursuit. Get your horses and let's be on our way." He turned to get his steed and then as an afterthought said, "oh, and this is Eleanor, she'll be traveling with us from now on. Please make her feel welcome and treat her as a friend."

The companions said their brief hellos and introductions and then were shortly tearing down the hillside and off in hot pursuit. Their speed was too swift for conversation, so they rode in silence. Tree whipped by like blackened giant spectators to their midnight passage.

Eleanor took the time to examine each of her companions and to see and feel their spirit, their sorrows, and their joy.

On the outside Darkwolfe appeared to be steady and in control, a perfect facade of a strong new king. Underneath this visage however Eleanor could see the turbulent energies of his aura. It shifted in color from green and red to green and darkening to blue and purple and then back to red and on again. He kept changing between his love and loss and the hatred and overwhelming anger he held toward Charlemette's killer. Thankfully the spirit of the dead priestess flew along the side of her living lover and helped to smooth out his aura with her spiritual energies. Their combined efforts were enough to help Darkwolfe hold true to his quest and continue in the name of the Pleides. For now the spirit of Charlemette would still look out for her widowed husband. They were never formally hand-fasted but the heart is all that truly matters and they had consummated their marriage that one night of the drawing of the tarot cards.

Silverworm was a regal and proud elven Lord. He looked as though he were a part of the horse they way he moved with it so peacefully. The elf's face was stern and devoid of emotion, but the dragon Eleanor could tell the elf felt great guilt for the death of his king's wife. He felt it was his solemn duty to protect the ding and his consort and he had failed. The mage would die he repeated over and over in his head and Eleanor listened telepathically.

Sir Gedrick, the Terra Paladin of Thor's Hammer, felt in many ways akin to the way the elven Lord felt. He felt guilt as well. He was weak in succumbing to the shaithen spell. Which then allowed the mage to steal them off and with an illusion take their positions. He couldn't believe he had been taken prisoner. Then he was tied and gagged and helpless to stop the mage from stealing Za'Varuk's stone and his friend and king being brutalized. Then of course the death of Charlemette was too much. The paladin could not conceive of how anyone could murder someone, especially a helpless woman. His belief structure and morals were so different than that of the mage, that the paladin was having a hard time even imagining how someone could do such a thing. A goblin or troll, or even a giant had it in their nature to do such wicked things, but for a human to do it was…, well totally inconceivable. Sir Gedrick vowed to himself that he would remain strong and fight the demon with his bare hands if need be to restore his honor.

Cat rode along side the dwarf. He was more interested in the bard than anything else, and the dragon was slightly amused. At least he wasn't wallowing in his own sorrow. He seemed merely pleased to watch the dwarf's bouncing bosom as she rode.

Little Sunflower hadn't been with the group very long, but she had grown fond of the priestess of Levanah in that short span. She didn't really feel guilty per say, but wallowed more in a fit of sadness for the loss of the wonderful and beautiful woman. Periodically tears would trickle from the corners of her eyes.

The party rode long through the night but never caught sight of the fleeing mage, Black Paladin, or shaithen. Some time near dawn both groups stopped, though many draws from each other, to eat, drink, rest, and care for the horses. The rest wouldn't last long, and they would soon be riding hard again.

* * * * *

The Scorpion, Murdock, and Ruskin stood outside the fence of the massive structure of St. Thagle's Cathedral. The place was constructed and dedicated to the founding high priest Thagle himself, and with it the worshippers of Osiris had gained a foothold in Thor's Hammer. The fence was of long black bars with spearhead tops and the looming mountain of a building lay beyond.

"Come on," The Scorpion whispered, creeping along the outer edge toward the back of the building. A sturdy oak had not been attended to in several years and a large limb hung out over the gate with a nice drop inside the grounds. While the gates were readily locked at sunset, other diligence in security was obviously lacking.

The Scorpion scaled up the tree with great ease, and with Murdock pushing from below, Ruskin made it up as well. Then Murdock climbed up and the three murderous thieves went out on the limb one at a time and dropped into the ground of the cathedral of Osiris.

Osiris was a sacrificial god, like many others, who had been slain and later resurrected. His cathedral had high buttresses and intricate carvings as well as many gargoyles siting high up on the walls. Murdock hoped they were just statues and not real ones that would silently descend upon their heads and eat them for a midnight snack.

The three men made their way to an isolated side building that was marked as an ancient crypt and entrance to the catacombs below. The left noticeable prints in their wake as they crept along the moist grass. The crypt was dark and extremely foreboding. There were even warning signs to ward off stubborn trespassers, but The Scorpion merely ignored them and forced open the sealed doors. He created a horrendous racket and thought the whole priesthood would soon be coming to kill the intruders, but no lights shown in the cathedral after several moments, so he finally entered the dark chamber beyond. Cobwebs were strewn about but appeared old and out of use. The spiders had long since moved on for better homes and food sources.

"This place gives me the creeps," Ruskin admitted through chattering teeth and bugged-out eyes. He drew his dagger and looked about the eery gloom in fright and uneasiness. "I'm not so sure this is such a great idea."

The Poisoned Dagger held his tongue and watched The Scorpion to see what he would do.

"Don't worry, I'm on good authority that we'll be safe here." The Scorpion moved to the back of the short hall and found an old dusty set of stairs leading down into the lower catacombs. He pulled out a short stick from his pack, which grew into the size of a fat torch, and then burst into flames. "Come on, let's get this over with."

Reluctantly the other two followed. The stairs weren't terribly long or deep and soon they found themselves in a very dark and chilly cavern. Caskets were lining both walls in tiered dug out holes in the rocky wall. In The Scorpion's head Za'Varuk was guiding him, so to the other two men it appeared as if he knew exactly where he was going. They turned to the left, went down a long hall, took another left, a hall, and there they were at their destination. There was a barred door at the end of this hall with more symbols of warnings to would be thieves and intruders.

Murdock examined the lock thoughtfully for about a minute, and then stepped back eyeing it some more. He motioned for the party to stay clear. He then slowly disarmed a poisonous needle-dart trap from the lock with great relief. Then with a couple of small tools he pulled from a concealed seam in one of his gloves, he set to work on the lock itself. The scratching on the lock sounded like scurrying rats and the flickering of the torchlight sent wavering shadows across Ruskin and The Scorpion's determined features. The curse had settled into a steady throb with the two new hosts, and while they were agitated and eager to do some more killing, some inexplicable fate and bond now bound the three.

Finally with a loud click the lock popped and their heads jerked in surprise. With a slow and steady push the door creaked open revealing a chamber of total darkness. In the center of the room was a stone slab and o the slab was a husk of a corpse, really not much more than a skeleton.

"Is this…Sciloren?" Ruskin asked hesitantly, almost afraid to name it and invoke the doomed man's spirit.

"It is," Murdock concluded. "I know the story well, though I can't say how much of it is truth and what make believe. At any rate, mages and priests often will take a quest of the spirit to gain great powers. For some religions it is a rite of passage, for mages often just the next step in their training. However sometimes these aspirants try too early or simply aren't strong enough to survive the ordeal. It was told that Sciloren had tired of the slow climb to power necessary in the priesthood of Osiris, and without permission of the high priests drank of the potions of initiation and failed. When they found him he was like this in his rooms. Now like others of a similar fate he is trapped for all eternity in the abyss, in the City of Pyramids. Out of respect his dead remains were placed in the catacombs, but legends say that sometimes these cursed priests and mages come back, escaping their horrible imprisonment and become vampires of energy." Murdock stopped, licking his lips. "Did you hear something?"

All was deathly still.

Suddenly three priests of Osiris were at the doorway brandishing heavy maces and glowing in magical spell protections. The three thieves backed away from the door to the far wall. Murdock and Ruskin were saying whatever prayers they could thing of. Desecrators to the dead of

Osiris often became permanent residents. Ruskin glanced up at The Scorpion who was wearing a goofy grin.

"The funny thing is," the king's mercenary said, "is that story is true."

Just as the priests were coming around the platform where the cursed cleric lay, it sat up with swirling yellow eyes, like phosphorescent sand being shaken in an hourglass. The priests were startled and stepped back away from the vile thing, but not before the abysmal creature lashed out a skeletal claw and grabbed one by the shoulder. A wave of energy seemed to leave the priest and enter the skeleton. As the priest shriveled up, the cursed cleric became whole again. He looked like a normal naked man except for his turbulent saffron orbs.

One priest swung with his mace, but the creature caught it effortlessly in mid-air and with his other hand palmed the priest's face. Again there was the energy transfer and the priest fell withered and dead to the cold stone floor. The sight by the torchlight was truly astonishing and horrific. Ruskin and Murdock thought to flee, but at the same time were riveted by the macabre spectacle.

The last priest turned and ran, but the vampire was not done feasting just yet. With a startling leap the creature rocketed out through the door and smashed into the back of the fleeing man, knocking him to the ground. By the time the three thieves made their way out to see what had occurred, the third Osirisian was drained to a husk and the healthy naked man was donning the priests robes and tying it with a belt. The creature had short-cropped black hair and a golden complexion. He moved with incomprehensible speed and grace, and radiated some kink of immense raw power.

"I am Sciloren, I believe Za'Varuk sent you."

5

Shadows Thicken

The sky had barely begun to lighten when Velneb Skullcrusher had ordered his men to mount and get back on the move. He thought that if they pressed on and make good time, they might just make the outskirts of Grathmoor at, or shortly after dusk.

The dwarves were a grumbling lot by nature and this morning was no exception. With Trollbait, Thrasher, Velneb and Darrel all prodding and pushing it took no less than half an hour to get the crew up and moving (an effort worthy of commendation for any dwarven army). However, once their inertia had been broken, they were full speed ahead and talk of crushing the enemy quickly began amongst the filed ranks.

"Fifteen I tell you. This time out I'll get me fifteen kills." One of the dwarves yelled, bragging of his future deeds.

"Ha, you'll be lucky to keep your head intact, let alone kill anything."

Another one yelled back bringing a chorus of baritone laughter.

The announcements of heroism and kills went on through the morning and day, driving the dwarves into a veritable frenzy for blood. Many hefted axes and looked ahead with growing interest and anticipation. The excitement was pushing Velneb from behind and he was forced to quicken the already speedy pace. Soon the column was racing ahead and Velneb's hopes of a dusk arrival seemed more likely by the minute.

* * * * *

As if on cue, Sabbath and Darkwolfe's parties mounted up and continued on their course. The day was hard and the intensity of the ride was wearing harshly on both groups; they had been in action for several days and while their blood still pumped with exhilaration and adrenaline, their bodies and minds were tiring.

Sabbath planned to use this to his advantage. He knew his pursuers were just as tired as him, and so he thought he might throw a little block in their path to test their resolve. "Anteas, do you think we could enlist some more of the shaithen to get rid of our tail for a while?" They slowed their horses so the mage and Black Paladin could converse more comfortably.

The whole group came to a halt on the wooded trail. Normally the snake-men just did their own thing and since the paladin and snake-men worshipped the same god Anteas let them do so, but now more direct communication was required. He called upon the power of his god Anu to produce a language spell and while Anteas could readily tell he had succeeded, Sabbath watched on with intrigue to see the outcome.

The Black Paladin faced what he presumed to be the shaithen leader by its black sash and spoke in a hissing and breathy voice. The snake-man responded in kind. The strange dialogue went on for several moments and then the leader did a quick bow and led his group off the trail and into the surrounding woods.

"What happened?" Sabbath asked. "What's the plan, are they going to help us?" The mage stretched, trying to get a cramp out of his lower back and looked in the direction that the shaithen had gone.

"They said they must converse with their leader, Prince Lachesis. They suspect he will grant another 20 or so of their kind for your little ambush, but must go to the underground complex and submit their request in person, though they have surely already done so telepathically by now. Don't worry, I doubt they will actually succeed in stopping this Pagan King, but they will slow him down enough for us to release the demon before he gets there."

"Good," Sabbath replied, "Za'Varuk wants to eat this Darkwolfe's beating heart and add his power to his own. Killing his lover has insured that he will follow, but I don't want his journey to be too easy, and I don't want it to look like a trap." He unsheathed his dagger and looked at the dried blood there. The mere sight of it brought a sinister smile to his eyes and lips.

"Well maybe I shouldn't have told the shaithen to kill them all. They may be more competent in their job than you believe." The Black Paladin replied wryly.

"I trust this *Pagan King's* resourcefulness. A few of his friends might die, but I doubt he'd fail to get through somehow himself before he took a stab at revenge." The mage looked over his shoulder in the direction of where they had come from, expecting to see the party appear at any second. He knew they were much further behind than that, but his uneasiness was such that he couldn't help an idle look. "Come, let's get going. We should make the castle at dusk."

* * * * *

The shaithen complex was an intricate web of tunnels and large cavernous rooms beneath the forest floor. Several levels down, Prince Lachesis sat upon his obsidian and ruby throne. He was flanked by several adept mages and esteemed priests of the order who functioned as counselors to the prince.

Lachesis looked similar to many of the snake-men race, but was taller, more heavily muscled, and had a more coppery color to his scaly head. He wore finely made strapped sandals, a waist wrap of quality linen, and the customary scimitar and curved dagger. From left hip to right shoulder he wore a crimson sash as a humble display of his powerful position. His mage advisors wore saffron sashes and the high ranking priests emerald ones.

The shaithen were a very ancient race, some say as old as the dragons and demons. They held a strong bond with their god Anu. All of the snake-people possessed certain fundamental clerical magics, being bred from the god himself many ages long past. Telepathy was a common way to communicate, as the race had an aversion to loud noises and was prone to irritable attacks against woodland intruders for no other reason than for their noisy trespass.

Communication with the party accompanying the demon's pet mage had already come about. Already 20 warrior/priests and one mage were ready and lined up at one side of the throne room. The request for a war party in person was more of a formality, for in truth Prince Lachesis had already granted it.

Down an incline and several stairs came the party who had been traveling with the mage and blessed Black Paladin. The party spread out before the throne in a fan-shape with the leader several steps out in front of his warriors. In unison they bowed deeply. The leader then issued forth his request in a series of hisses and breathy sounds.

"Great prince, the enemy known as Darkwolfe approaches our forest. I ask that we not miss the opportunity to kill this young king before he comes to full power."

"I hear your request Solomon, a leader amongst the shaithen, respected and wise in our ways." The king responded, waiting for his counselors to chime in.

"Should we not pit this Darkwolfe against the demon?" One mage asked.

"True, perhaps we should test both their strengths, and what better way than an open confrontation?" Another mage agreed conspiratorially.

"Yes," the prince concurred. "We should test this Darkwolfe's powers through our ambush and in his dealing with the demon. The more we watch how he does battle, the better prepared we will be when we finally capture him for sacrifice to Anu. For now however, he stands as a balance to these accursed demons. We can let him do our fighting for us, let the demons weaken the cities and throw all into chaos, and when the time is ripe the shaithen will rule all the lands. If this Za'Varuk should happen to kill him, well so be it. I can always have Anteas bring me his corpse and he can serve as my family's wraith-slave for all eternity." The room erupted in a chorus of hissing laughter, all present finding the plan marvelous in it's sweet wickedness.

The warrior leader Solomon wasn't as convinced as the rest of his peers. "My prince, I still feel we would be better off having the blessed Black Paladin Anteas to simply smash the stone with Thor's hammer and be done with it. We can then kill this Darkwolfe and leave nothing else to chance."

"Patience," Prince Lachesis chided. "In due time all will be made clear. Anu works in mysterious ways. I confess even I do not know his plans in their entirety, but this is the path we will take. You will do as I say. Add this group to your own and in the forest wait. Hurry now, they come. Set the trap before it is too late. We will see as death occurs and read the blood trails to tell of our next course of action. Let the Pagan King through to Grathmoor, but kill the rest mercilessly." The prince slammed his scepter on the stone floor indicating that the meeting was at an end. Quietly the large group moved out for the kill.

* * * * *

Sciloren had led the three thieves away shortly after his rebirth to Alcyone from the abyss. He hungered to suck the energy out of their pathetically weak and mortal shells, but for now he agreed to work with the demon and use his henchmen to help bring his evil plans to fruition. The four had escaped the catacombs and cathedral grounds without further incident and had holed up in an abandoned house for the remainder of the night. Several homeless had the mistake of being present when Sciloren entered the residence and he quickly fed on them to sate his endless thirst.

Now it was daylight and the vampire needed to stay within the protective darkness of the old house. He was a creature of the abyss now, a being of negative energy, and the searing fire of Ra's eye would readily banish him back from whence he came.

"Do what you need to do this day in preparation for tonight's fun. I will meet you near the Terra Paladin stronghold at dusk. The prophecies say they will aid this Pagan King in his fight against the demon horde. I don't need a prophet to tell me this is so however. Za'Varuk has informed me that he already has one of the Terra Paladin's at his side. I'm sure this is more than some random coincidence. Now go, I need to rest before this evening." With that Sciloren seemed to freeze in the standing position he was in, and the swirling sandy eyes of his went black and still.

"Alright then, let's try and spread some more chaos and see if we can get to one or two of those paladins before tonight. We should split up, and remember to only go for the squires for they won't have their god's immunity to the curse. The squires should likely assassinate the paladin's for us if we're lucky, but if nothing else should stir up the hornets nest for us, eh?" The Scorpion thought well of his plan, and as they headed out of the abandoned building, he couldn't help but wonder if any connection had been made yet between him and the dead boy.

Lord Bastion entered his study followed by an aged wizard. "I thank you for coming Lazareth," Lord Bastion said with stern sincerity. I'm certain there is more going on here than meets the eye; I just can't figure it out. It would appear like some robbery or such, as some of my magical potions and scrolls are missing, but it looks staged in some fashion and there were a few drops of blood on the stairwell which would indicate that the murder had taken place there. Your reputation for magically reenacting a crime and helping bring the criminal to just precedes you. If you can help, I would be most thankful and of course pay you accordingly."

Lazareth smoothed out his russet robes and gave only a distracted nod. His senses and mind were already working the case, taking in every detail and speculating on what they could mean. He would certainly resort to his magic, but it was a game in some way to see how close he could approximate the truth with his senses alone. He paced the room methodically and finally came out to the balcony where the birds were caged and cooing restlessly. It started here he thought.

"Do you notice anything unusual about the birds?" The mage inquired.

"Well," Lord Bastion pondered tugging on the ends of his mustache. "This bird here must have been a recent arrival from Grathmoor, but I never received any word or message. Do you think the note had anything to do with the murder? What could be going on there that people would kill over?"

"That is precisely what we are going to find out." Lazareth loved a good mystery. With that, he took a tiger's eye rock out of his pocket that had been polished to a smooth gleam. He placed the rock in the center of his forehead and began chanting in the arcane tongue. Once finished, he took his hand away from the rock and it stayed attached to his forehead projecting out light radiance around the balcony. "Just stay quiet and watch as I do. The scene will play itself out now."

Suddenly Clive was standing there, but it was more of a ghost-like image rather than a solid one. He was going about his duties with the birds when a lone pigeon came flying in to roost. Clive put him in one of the cages and took the little tube from its leg. Lazareth noted the little transfer of magic and the swirl of almost imperceptible green tendrils of smoke. Then Clive went into the study and the mage and Lord followed him.

The pigeon boy made his way to the stairwell and then went down.

The two followers were hard pressed to keep up with the image and they nearly missed the collision with The Scorpion. Just as they came around the bend in the stairs, they witnessed the incidence and once again Lazareth made a mental note of the transference of magical energy. There was a brief exchange and then the boy was dead. When the killer read the little note, the mage positioned himself so he could get a glimpse, but the paper was blank. The king's mercenary picked up the corpse and then made for the Lord's chambers.

Again the two older men hurried to keep up and when they arrived in the rooms above, The Scorpion was already going about tossing the room. He took the invisibility potion and then the show was at an end.

"First thing is first," Lazareth said walking back out to the balcony. He began chanting before he even reached the balcony and Lord Bastion's mouth dropped open as the mage sent fire shooting out from his fingertips burning every single bird into a crisp.

"What in the god's names…" the Lord began.

The mage came back in passing the Lord. "No time to explain fully Bastion, but your birds there just unleashed a curse on Thor's Hammer. I must go warn the king." In a swirl of russet robes and a whoosh of magic the mage had disappeared.

The massive throne room of King Charles was beyond imagining. The ceiling was several stories high and had paintings depicting battles and loves between the gods and goddesses. It must have taken a painter an entire lifetime on his back painting the ceiling in its entirety. Yet no mastery of beauty could compare. The floors were tiled in fantastic patters and color and the walls were mixed with tapestries and mosaics. There was a great raised dais at the far end where sat the king and queen in all their glory and splendor. The gold contained in the thrones alone could have fed the poor within the city for several decades. King Charles certainly wasn't the most vicious of kings in the city's sordid history, but he was ruthless in his dealings with his enemies and any peasant uprising. There was a long line of petitioners this morning reporting heinous crimes of the night before. There were an unprecedented number of murders unheard of within the city. The king was in a foul mood and on the brink of issuing martial law.

"Your highness I do believe we are having an epidemic of sorts, the reports of violence and murders are increasing even as we speak." One Lord noted.

"I fully agree," Lazareth said popping into their midst. "I have reason to believe we are experiencing the effects of a mage-curse."

"Really," Thuja proclaimed, "and where do you come by such information my *friend*?" The court mage used the term friend loosely, as the two mages had never been such. In fact Thuja had always been jealous of Lazareth and the favor his powers brought him from the king.

"I have discerned that a courier pigeon from Grathmoor has brought this curse to us. The boy Clive is now dead and I believe your man The Scorpion is responsible for the spread in the city."

"Even if this were true your majesty, the last thing we want to do is openly blame a mage for this outbreak and have a full blown mage-hunt on our hands. I suggest we use the militia to contain the violence until which time we can validate this story and/or facilitate a way of counteracting it." Thuja was a highly intelligent man and he didn't want to outright deny Lazareth's words for far too often he was right and had in the past made Thuja look the fool. No, he would play along, take control of the situation and if he was lucky get to disintegrate a few peasants just for fun.

"So be it," the king stated. "Call out the militia and our reserves if necessary. If any resistance is met in containment have no hesitation in killing those who cause trouble."

"I suggest a quarantine on the castle grounds until we know what we're dealing with. I believe the curse is spread by touch, so I caution anyone from snuggling with any strangers if you get my drift." This last comment was indirectly sent to the king since he was known to have a new wench every night in his bed. The queen was unable to bare children so in order to gain an heir, the king was making the most of his predicament. Two women were already reported to be with child, but the king wasn't about to stop his activities any time soon. However by the look in his eyes, Lazareth could tell that the message had gotten across.

"Fine it's settled then, I believe I should head to my labs to see about finding a spell to counteract this curse of yours." Thuja stated with self-importance and prepared to leave the throne room.

The king motioned for his messenger who was waiting off to the side. "Get me Captain Riley boy and do hurry." The messenger was out the side door before the king had even finished with the hurry part.

"If you'll excuse me your excellence there are some other matters I need to attend to. I don't like the prospect of this Scorpion fellow running around. I'm gonna see if I can track him down. His actions belie a man with ulterior motives. He doesn't appear to be acting in a curse-induced state. If this is true, then I need to establish what his real plans are and find a way to stop him." Lazareth was turning to leave and be about his business when Thuja intervened.

"Well perhaps I could track this man down for you Lazareth. I think spell creation might be more up your alley and missing persons mine." The mage had far too big of a forced sincerity for Lazareth's liking, but before he could put the other mage down the king decided for them.

"I like this idea. Thuja you track down this ex-man of mine and make sure he doesn't cause us any more trouble, and Lazareth you find the counteracting spell." It was as a commander to his soldiers and no room for debate.

The two mages went about their work as the militia was preparing to take full control of the city.

Ruskin hid behind a water trough acting as though he were kneeling down to fix his boot lace. His quarry was a young squire by the name of Timothy about to fetch some water and perform some other duties for his patron paladin. It was a boring apprenticeship as these things go, but he hoped to begin his sword training by next summer when the sun was at its brightest.

Timothy came around with the jugs and began filling them. Ruskin popped up quickly, bumping the boy and then hurried away. The young man teemed with anger amidst the swirling fingers of the curse. Water boy? He who grooms horses? Nay, I am a knight he thought. I'll show Sir Boroff a thing or two. With a deadly grin he hurried away leaving the forgotten jugs behind.

This was Ruskin's third squire he had infected and the morning was still young. If only Murdock and The Scorpion were as good. With a playful smile and catching a whiff of what could be now considered a competition, Ruskin ran off in search of other prey.

In fact the other two thieves were doing as well in the subtle warfare. Before mid-draw more than 20 of the Terra Paladin's squires were planning to murder their patron paladin's come the ceremonial ritual at dusk. When Ra's eye was taken by the body of the Goddess Nuit, an even greater darkness would fall upon the city than her starry splendor.

Thuja had left the royal palace that morning after casting a tracking spell, which much to his discomfort had been taught to him by Lazareth before their troubles began years before, and set out after The Scorpion. His trail had taken him to the tavern where the boar riding had occurred, and later to the remains of The Mermaid's Kiss. He came after a time to St. Thagle's cathedral and found out that several priests had been killed in an unusual fashion and the corpse of Sciloren was gone. Speculation as to the deaths and missing body went unsaid, but even a court mage knew of the legend and thought there might be some portent in this connection with other stories he had heard during the day.

He came to an old abandoned building and noticed a strange statue, but felt some evil presence and quickly left it alone. He didn't want to call himself a coward, but he rationalized that finding The Scorpion was his mission after all, not hunting down a vampire from the abyss.

The morning wore on and he ignored his want of food. The spell was telling him that his target was somewhere close, but he couldn't tell exactly where. He hid off in an alley and watched the nearby street for a time to see if he could pick up the mercenary and take him out with an unsuspecting spell. He did think of himself like an assassin, but he used magic instead of a dagger. He loved to shoot someone in the back, and he only awaited the day when he would get the chance with Lazareth.

The shadows of the alley were cool, but he had to keep a scented cloth to his nose to keep from gagging on the rotting garbage and scurrying rat infested gutters. His vantage gave him a clear view of a line of market stands, and other tents where wares and crafts were sold. He even noticed a couple of squires of the Terra Paladins sitting at a booth. The were both selling goods to raise money for the order, and to enlist young men to join their cause. Thuja leaned forward expectantly when a hooded man came up to their booth, but he had seen The Scorpion on many occasions and easily denied this man to be him.

The stranger talked to the two squires briefly and then shook both their hands and turned to walk away. The mage instantly could see the trails left by the curse as it took control of the two lads. Thuja prepared a spell to blast the stranger.

Suddenly there was a hand on his shoulder. "Good mid-draw to you mage, and how is the palace in my absence."

Thuja would have responded in kind to the cursed dog, but he was too busy dealing with the surge of anger and other mixed emotions that the curse was boiling up within him. His greatest thoughts of course went back to Lazareth and real murder lay where only idle fascination was a moment before.

"Come now Thuja, we both now what kind of man you are. Join us and you may even be the next king of Thor's Hammer. I myself had first dibs, but I have my sights on other kingdoms." The Scorpion had moved around to face him and look him in the eyes.

Part of the mage fought the curse spell, but he was really never good at heart, and this part began to take hold and blossom. The soothing voices of the vampire Sciloren and the demon Za'Varuk were like a lullaby in his brain, and like so many others over the ages when offered riches and power, he succumbed to the dark path of true evil.

* * * * *

The horses unfortunately could not keep the relentless pace and so Darkwolfe called for his group to slow and walk the animals for a while even though he knew it would allow the mage to further his lead. "Just a few minutes," he said, "if our rides die from exhaustion we'll have to walk all the way to Grathmoor."

No one complained of the break, but Silverworm felt that they could have pressed on, horses be damned. However had they not stopped, he might not have noticed the movement in the trees up ahead. "Everyone down he yelled," and as several dozen arrows whizzed toward the party, the companions dove for cover. Thankfully no one was seriously injured in the first shaithen assault except Little Sunflower who had twisted her ankle slightly when she jumped from the large horse.

A second volley drove in killing two of the horses, and a mage-thrown lightning bolt blasted a third apart. Eleanor began chanting and a huge shield of energy sprang up between the party and their attackers with a loud buzz. Several arrows and attack darts were harmlessly repelled.

Darkwolfe saw one snake-man edging around to the flank with a drawn bow and he released his own attack darts driving the shaithen back into a tree with half its head burned and blown away.

The trees weren't terribly thick in this portion of the woods and most of the snake-men were crouching behind bushes, fallen trees, rocks, and several drapes of hanging ivy. The companions were pretty much blocked from proceeding forward, and trying to move around the ambush would be too long and dangerous. Retreat was entering into all of their minds.

Eleanor grabbed Darkwolfe's shoulders, "I can only get one person through, and it must be you." Her hair and eyes, the mere sight of her beauty banished the pain of Charlemette and he longed to reach out and touch her, but somehow felt guilty and turned his head away looking for more enemies to blast with his magic. "We'll catch up as soon as we can. Remember your swords! Kiriana will advise you, and if you do face Za'Varuk, the Demon Slayer isn't just a fancy name. Now ride, my magic will protect you."

The Pagan King didn't argue and he jumped on one of the surviving horses and prepared to bolt down the path through the shaithen ranks. Several more arrows and a small ball of magical fire were deflected by Eleanor's shield. Just as Darkwolfe kicked in his heals to charge, the dragon covered him in a shower of glittering magical dust and light. One moment he was facing a flurry of arrows and charging, sword-wielding snake-men, and the next he was a draw up the trail riding hard on an empty path with the sounds of battle far behind.

Darkwolfe was amazed at the way the spell allowed him to jump such a large distance, but with out further thought he rode ahead vowing to reach Grathmoor by dusk. He would stop this demon and evil mage if it was the last thing he did. He didn't stop to consider it very well might be just that.

Several of the snake-men had then rounded the edge of the big magical shield. Their swords and daggers were drawn and they were boxing in the remaining companions. Sir Gedrick held his huge two-handed sword out before him and stood on one side of the path. Silverworm had his long sword out and took a small shield from one of the dead horses. The two women were in the center of the road, protected at least for now by the Terra Paladin and the noble elven Lord.

It was very long ago that Eleanor had been outside the Lava Falls. She had a limited source of magic like any mage or magical creature, and much of it had been spent in putting up and maintaining the shield. Without it they would be dead. Sending Darkwolfe jumping ahead had also terribly zapped her reserves. She would wait and see how things went, but she had a last resort option in case things didn't go well for the two fighters. It had been so long, 2000 years in seclusion and sacred duty in protecting the stone of Za'Varuk. Granted she slept most of the time like a human would. In that time of sleep where a person may seemingly lose eight hours, Eleanor would lose decades at a time. Of course until some foolish adventurers would come in and disturb her sleep, and like a hibernating bear devour them before going back off to sleep. Yes, so long. Now she was free once again to the world and it's crazy machinations. In time a balance might be found and the young Darkwolfe would be useful in fulfilling this need.

As two of the Shaithen came into close range fighting, Sir Gedrick called on his god and in a flash of divine radiance he had cast both a protective aura about himself and blinded his two closest attackers. Before they could compensate for their blindness, the Terra Paladin ended their existence in a spray of blood and crunching of bones. Another two came rushing in for the attack.

Silverworm was being pressed back into the street by three of the snake-men. Swords and daggers were slicing in from all angles in a deadly whirlwind. Thankfully the elf had thought to grab the shield, for with it he was able to deflect most of the attackers' blows. Even still he had several cuts and knew he was fighting a losing battle. Behind these three were even more of the deadly enemy with their shining weapons, bobbing heads, and flickering forked tongues.

The bard felt so helpless watching her friends fight and to top it off her ankle was throbbing painfully. She considered the ring Ironoak had give her and then pulled out the flute instead. It was well made and appeared as just an ordinary instrument, but upon examination she saw that there was a word inscribed in small letters on one side. She put the flute to her lips, whispered the magic word, and then began to play a tune. There was no light or fire or anything much to her dismay, but she played on hoping something might eventually occur.

Unknown to the dwarven girl, the flute's magic was working wonders upon some of her enemies. Several of the shaithen had been charmed by the lovely sounds and were overcome with a great desire to protect the bard and her companions at any cost. Just when Silverworm thought he was dead for sure by the overwhelming numbers, a number of the snake-men turned on their comrades and stabbed them in their defenseless backs and sides. Many fell dead, but the remaining engaged with their kin or succumbed to the elf's deadly accuracy with his enchanted blade.

Sir Gedrick was still faring well; with his longer weapon he was able to keep the enemy at bay, and with his greater strength was occasionally able to bash through one of their defenses and diminish their numbers one at a time. He too was being pushed slowly back by sheer force and quantity of the attackers, and the circle was ever tightening. He only hoped he could hold out long enough to deplete their forces and save the women from an awful fate.

The shaithen mage began chanting in his hissing language and then released two spells, one after the other. The first one slammed several of the magical attack darts into Sir Gedrick. His plate armor took most of the impact damage, but the force was enough to send him tumbling back onto the dirt road.

The second of the mage's spells was a magical arrow modified to breach the barrier that Eleanor had erected and prevented the snake-men from using a frontal attack in the first place. The arrow burned through the air, sliding easily through the shield, and lodged into Eleanor's right thing with a sizzling thud. She issued forth a cry and sank to the ground on her good side. She had had about enough and thought it time for her back up plan.

With a mighty leap, beyond any human capability, she soared high in the air above her companions and turned into her dragon form. She had wanted to wait and prevent startling her traveling mates, and had even wanted them to treat her like a human being for a while before they realized her true identity, but if she didn't intervene they would all be dead so then what would it matter.

The creature was huge. The head alone was twice the size of a full grown man. Great jagged teeth were abundant in the gaping maw. Hard glistening reptilian scales covered her body from snout to long whipping tail. Vicious claws sprang from thick fingers. The wings were like that of a bat, translucent and leathery. Her color was reddish-orange like a setting sun boiling away in the ocean on the horizon before it disappears.

The sudden appearance of the dragon sent everyone into a second of shock. Thankfully the way Sir Gedrick and Silverworm were positioned with their backs to the dragon they weren't affected. Their opponents were, and in that second or two the elf and paladin took a few free shots and lessened the opposition by three more. Similarly the charmed snake-men weren't distracted and fought on for their bard felling two of their brethren.

The shaithen mage made the mistake of conjuring up a spell. This only brought him to the attention of the hovering wyrm and Eleanor gracefully extended her long serpentine neck and blasted the mage with her fiery breathe.

Prince Lachesis had been watching the event through the eyes of his mage, and when the vision suddenly ended, he sent out a telepathic retreat to his warriors. There was no sense in wasting any more of his soldiers fighting a dragon that much was sure. At any rate, he had gotten the information he needed and the Pagan King had gotten through as planned. However with a dragon at his side this did complicate matters.

The stakes were rising and the prince weighed his options carefully. This was a dangerous game he was playing, but if patient and prudent he knew he would eventually win.

Suddenly all the shaithen turned from the fight and fled into the surrounding woods. The charmed ones gave chase, still under the influence of the spell until it either wore off or they were killed. Silverworm and Sir Gedrick looked to the dragon suspiciously, wondering if it would attack them as well, but both men knew well the nature of dragons from myth if not in person, and this one was apparently in league with them and their king. As the dragon landed Eleanor assumed her human form again lightly landing on her feet. The shield spell finally dissipated with an eerie silence following the incessant insect-like buzz.

"Save your questions for now, just know that I am the dragon Eleanor and I am on your side. Put the dwarf on the last horse, she has injured her ankle. I have enough energy left for one spell that will allow us to run more quickly." She was about to begin casting when Cat appeared out of nowhere.

"Hi there," he smiled brandishing bloody sword and dagger. "I've been a little busy. Nothing like a little invisibility potion to help a thief and an assassin." He sheathed his weapons and helped the bard on to the horse. She beamed him a fond smile and flicked her blond mane in a flirtatious manner.

Once the spell was cast the party was making their way once again toward Grathmoor but even with the spell Sir Gedrick in full plate armor could only run so fast. In all likelihood they would miss the castle's evening fireworks. So they sped away leaving behind a bloody mess of shaithen corpses. Soon the survivors would come and take the bodies back to their underground complex where they would be made into zombie-slaves, used as food, or if held in high esteem in the eyes of the society buried with ceremonial rites. None present were of this last category.

6

Showdown in Grathmoor

Dusk began to descend like a dark cloak over the western continent of Glazeer on the planet Alcyone. One continent among many. One planet among a spiral of eight sisters. One string among many in the galaxy. One galaxy among many in the universe. On and on into what the human mind would conceive of as infinity. Yet in this place, like a single piece of rice or wheat in a silo, disease and corruption was about to be spawned that could ultimately destroy the entire universe. The elder gods would watch and hope that balance would be struck, all except for Anu who had been playing his hand all along. Even this god was perhaps nothing more than a puppet in an endless line of strings, and like a chain reaction once one moved so did they all.

The clouded sky was dark and ominous. The purple and black contours of the billowy clouds looked like bruises and obscenely complemented the blotchy black and blue flesh of the cadaverous undead. They took their positions to intercept the dwarven army as they came into the wicked town of Grathmoor. The Lord of the region controlled these monsters and by decree of the Lady Heather it was Sabbath. Za'Varuk possessed the woman, and while at first she was fond of the power that boiled in her veins, over the past couple of days she learned to fear her decision in naming this evil mage Lord. The ruthless and chaotic intentions of this demon were horribly clear to her and millions would be dead because of her actions. Of course now it was far too late, and she could do nothing more than cower in the recesses of her own mind and pray to the goodly gods and goddesses to repent her terrible acts and she spent her idle time setting grueling reparations for herself.

Velneb Skullcrusher called a halt to the army of 500. Through the trees he could see the town of Grathmoor and the castle beyond. All appeared still and deserted, but a rolling breeze brought the horrible stench of rotting flesh to all of their senses and the seasoned warriors knew that undead were about. Velneb knew it was some kind of a trap and called his mages and clerics over to seek their council. Darrel ran the length of the column and told them to fan out. Within minutes the two columns opened up like a two arms held together above the head and brought down to the sides at shoulder level. Velneb had planned for a wide sweep through the surrounding woods and town, and a small group itself would head for the castle and gain entrance to the gate.

"What do you gentlemen suggest," Velneb asked, looking at the men around him, up at the darkening cloud cover, and then on toward the town ahead.

"I smell undead as sure as I'm a dwarf," a cleric of the mountain god Thor said. "Our spells of protection can help, but by the stench I'd say there must by thousands of the things hiding in the woods and town, our spells will only help a little bit."

"I can battle with my magic as usual," a mage offered, "but I certainly can't win the battle for you, my magic is limited. If the priest's estimate of their numbers is accurate, then you're going to have to fight them the old fashioned way."

"That's just the way we like it," Trollbait and Thrasher said in unison. Thrasher was hefting two battle-axes and Trollbait wielded a thick mace and a deadly flail. The two were more than ready for some carnage.

"Alright. Let's start a slow sweep straight-ahead. I want the clerics and mages to use as much of their powers right of the bat to force them back as much as possible. Hopefully if we do that we can keep up the momentum and smash our way straight to the castle. Once we get close, I want Thrasher and Trollbait, myself, and Darrel to head for the gates with a few other men. I'll use the thing Ironoak gave me to get in the gate and we'll head in to secure the demon portal. Until then, I want you all to work as leaders and motivate, prod, and whatever it takes to keep the rest of the men moving forward. If we lose our momentum we're doomed. Let's go."

The gathered leaders spread out and dispersed themselves throughout the ranks of the common soldiers, offering words of encouragement as they went. Many of the dwarves present were young warriors out on their first real battle, and fear and trepidation could be seen in their eyes and trembling hands. The priests began casting their spells of protection and bravery, and the mages also began summoning forth elementals to fight by their side. "We call to the elemental watchtowers to aid us in our fight," the mages yelled. These creatures were pure energy specific to their nature. A muscular earth gnome sprang up made of pure rock and compact dirt. A fiery salamander burst forth, essentially living fire. A watery undine appeared, made of water but compact and a single blow could kill an armored warrior. An airy sylph materialized from nowhere, it could also deal a great deal of damage with its forceful strikes.

Once all the preparations were in place, Velneb took up a long spear with a pennant displaying the markings of Rockshome on it, and held it high over his head so all his men could see it. Then in a military snapping motion he brought it swiftly down and handed it to his aid. The long line of horsemen slowly made their way forward and Velneb pulled out his own mighty axe.

* * * * *

Of course none of the guards present at the royal palace would think that the quarantine would apply to the court mage Thuja. In fact as he came through he applauded the guards for their diligent service in such a time of need and patted them on the shoulder as he went by. He continued to do so all the way to Lazareth's private laboratory, spreading the curse throughout like high-sun wildfire.

The mage Lazareth was busy bent over a workbench when Thuja came in. He was mixing vials and sniffing them. One cauldron was boiling on a wood fire and steam was wafting up. Several animal cages were kept against the far wall, and on a perch sat a multicolored bird which the mage had explained once as being called a parrot. Thuja watched for several moments, allowing his anger to boil like the water in the cauldron, but his steam had no obvious outlet.

"So are you going to stand there all day, or are you going to tell me if you found The Scorpion or not *my friend*?" Lazareth continued working and didn't offer the younger mage the satisfaction of looking at him when he spoke.

Thuja crept in like a stalking panther and finally gave in to the curse, pulling a wand from his belt and firing a lightning bolt at the older mage. Thuja only became more furious when the lightning bolt fizzled away, burning through the illusion as the real Lazareth stepped out from a nearby alcove.

"Now, now, why such the temper? I must confess that I don't know why you've always been so bitter. I have always tried to be like a father to you when your family sent you here from Northpoint. You have been a good student, and as an apprentice I even treated you with more respect than perhaps I should have. What is it that ills you?"

"You are nothing but an old man," Thuja sputtered, firing the wand again but only managing to dispel yet another illusion. "I will beat you and be the greatest mage in all the lands." He continued to fire at each new image as they stepped into view, but each time not hitting the real

Lazareth. Finally the wand was spent and Thuja threw the wand across the room in frustration.

Finally a corporeal form of the old mage came into view, and Thuja confirmed it by hitting it with a few attack darts. The old mage stumbled back by the shock and had burned and torn away portions in his robe where the darts had hit. "No you must not get the potion, it will give you too much power." Lazareth ran toward a table with potions set about its top. He grabbed one close to his chest and then threw it toward the wall hoping to smash it and rob the young mage of its properties.

In mid-air Thuja telekinetically guided the vial to his outstretched hand. The label read *trial of the abyss.* "You would try to rob me of the desert walk old man? I shall become magus before your dying eyes!" He hurled a fireball at the old mage blasting him into a wretched lump of flesh, but somehow he still breathed. Thuja uncorked the vial and drank down the bitter liquid.

Instantly he was hurled into darkness, ripped from his fleshly body and thrown into the abysmal plane. He found himself in a vast desert of indigo sand and the sky was a curtain of midnight stars without a moon. He knew enough of the desert walk to not literally walk, but to will himself ahead, and he floated across the great expanse. Psychically he was being drained though. He had foolishly entered the trial and the dark forces made him lethargic and drew him to the city of pyramids. Out of the endless nothingness emerged hundreds of gigantic pyramids the size of mountains sprawled across the rolling dunes of purple and black. It was here that he laid down in exhaustion and entered that endless sleep. Before he lost consciousness however he glimpsed approaching shadows, hungry for his energies. He heard the unnatural screams of torment and the damned.

Lazareth suddenly became visible in the corner of the room he had decided to let this inevitable confrontation play out. With a ray of death he ended the life of his agonizing clone and turned his attention to the body of Thuja. The young mage lay in a deep sleep while he was in trial, but the older man knew Thuja would not survive long. Just then the young man's body began to shrivel as it was drained of its life energy and with that Thuja was dead. Lazareth was saddened to have let his apprentice go in such a way, but it was a test and the young one had willfully taken it. Thuja had fallen from the proper path and would have only brought pain and destruction if he had ever become a true magus. Now he would suffer for his mistake. At least Lazareth thought, I will send his corpse back home to Northpoint and tell his family he died well.

* * * * *

As they neared the town, and really not to any of the dwarves surprise, thousands of zombies and skeletons emerged from the trees and outlying buildings. Even with the foreknowledge of the attack, many of the younger warriors were losing their nerve. Thankfully there were some veterans and clerics and mages nearby to steady their calm and reinforce their conviction.

The mages and clerics soon tired and fell to the back, fending off "Forward," they yelled, "crush the enemy. Onward to the gates. Smash the undead!" When they finally met head to head, there was no more time to think, and their warrior instincts kicked in. Mighty axes slashed, clubs and maces crushed. Mages unleashed wave after wave of fire and lightning. The priests also called forth their magic, destroying many with their divine radiance. The elementals thrashed through the ranks leaving huge swathes of room, which many of the dwarves jumped in their wake and followed.the many monsters with their staffs and war hammers. But still there were just far too many to fight, and the dwarves began suffering heavy losses. To make things worse, when the dwarves died, they were instantly revived as undead and began fighting their former comrades.

"Go, ride to the gate," Velneb yelled, tossing Thrasher the magical bomb. He and Trollbait rode off with Darrel at their side for the front gate of the castle. They dodged between houses and shops in the northwestern quarter of the town, smashing through the undead ranks with the sheer force and momentum of their horses. The zombies clawed at their legs as they went past raking the metal dwarven armor, and in most cases losing more of their own flesh and causing themselves more damage than that which they inflicted.

They forged on into the richer part of town. Trollbait was enjoying the hideous game of polo, as he continually sent heads flying with his mace and flail. Thrasher smashed in with his two wicked axes. Darrel Hammertoe rhythmically split skulls with his dual hammers. Before them loomed the great gates to the castle. They weren't shocked by the fact that the gates were closed, but they had to dodge rocks and other thrown objects that skeletons on the walls hurled their way. Thrasher looked at the "bomb" and generally had no idea how to use the thing. It was essentially a fat metal wand, but heavier than normal magical devices. Several rocks banged off his armor and his horse pranced around in agitation. They had left most of the monsters behind them at the outskirts of the city. The few on the ground were being disassembled by the might of Trollbait and Darrel.

Thrasher shrugged his huge shoulders and said, "Abracadabra", hurling the magical device at the gates. The wand spun end over end and hit the huge wooden gates with a dull thud and fell to the road. Several more of the stones, and now spears were being hurled down at the trio. Thankfully these undead creatures were horrible with projectile weapons and the spears hit the ground no where near the party.

The next thing they knew, the three dwarves were laying on the road next to their horses.

The Pagan King Darkwolfe rode his horse toward the back entrance to the castle of Grathmoor. The stag crown sat atop his head. He wore the dragon armor and his magical blades remained sheathed for now. He had met no resistance on his journey since leaving his companions in the battle with the shaithen. He was curious as to his approach, but he could pick up the sounds of battle on the other side of town. He pulled Kiriana from her sheath to see what thoughts she had on his present situation.

{Greetings my lord. I do believe the fun has already begun. As you can hear, the dwarves have already started their attack on the town and are making their way in to guard the demon gate.}

[How do you know these things Kiri, are you all knowing or something?]

{I have a certain amount of clairvoyance, but unfortunately the inner castle is warded against such intrusions and I can't warn you about what may be inside. I would think that the mage and Black Paladin have a nice trap waiting for you though. I would proceed with caution.}

"Thanks for the tip," he said out loud and made his way for a back entrance that he knew servants often used in taking the chamber pots out to the pit to dump. The king found the door open and unguarded. This was even more unsettling than a ferocious welcoming by trolls and giants.

{I don't sense any magical or mundane traps.}

Right as Darkwolfe entered the keep a loud clap of thunder resounded throughout the stone walls. For a minute he thought he was dead again, but then realized it must have been some kind of magic blast out in the courtyard or in front of the gates themselves. He proceeded with caution and crept through the place hallway by hallway, still he encountered no resistance or enemies.

The dwarves picked themselves up from the dusty road. Their horses did likewise and ran off back toward the town leaving the dwarves standing alone before the castle gate. The three checked each other for damage, assured that their weapons were good to go, and charged into the now gaping hole where the gates had previously been. The bombardment of rocks and other projectiles had ended, but they did meet some undead warriors in the courtyard and easily hacked them down. Before them loomed the great doors to the castle itself and they ran forward. Their mission was to secure the demon gate in a hurry and it was there that they must go.

{Proceed down this hall and to the back of the council chamber. You will find a secret door against the wall with stairs leading down to gate. Beware, for if there is a trap it will mostly likely be there. I can cut the flesh of the demon, but I suggest you use the Demon Slayer, of course it was constructed for such purposes and will serve you better than I if the demon has already been released.}

[What about magic. Can I hurt it with magic? What powers does it have? How can I defend myself?]

{All very good questions, but arm yourself, I sense movement coming this way.}

With that, Darkwolfe drew his long sword, The Demon Slayer, and stood ready with his dual blades.

The three dwarves had entered the main entrance hall and by the time Darkwolfe had drawn his blades they were entering the same hall leading to the council chamber. All of them jumped back at the sight of each other and stood frozen for several seconds.

"I bid you no harm dwarves. I am here to stop the demon." Darkwolfe lowered his weapons slightly trying to show them his good intent.

"Fair enough. I see you wear the crown. No one in their right minds would wear such a thing unless they were for real. Come on then."

Before any of them had a chance to continue the conversation, roughly 20 undead ambled out of the council chamber in their odd gait, apparently trying to block their path. The three dwarves charged right ahead. Darkwolfe followed suit, hacking into the creatures with both his swords. Dead flesh and bone and even the foul odor flew through the air as the four warriors crashed into the next room in the middle of combat.

Again they were hit by another wave of the foul creatures as they entered the room. These men and women wore the regalia of woodland thieves and it became apparent that the mage Sabbath had also rooted out their guild in search of soldiers to fill his army. However as much dexterity as they may have had in life, these undead still moved mechanically and in a disjointed fashion. They were no match for the ruthless power of the four heroes and they were soon at the secret entrance and the stairs leading down into the demon's pit.

The city and even the palace were in a chaotic uproar. The Terra Paladin's were a holy order and though their efforts would soon be needed in maintaining order, the high general had declared that the evening ritual would go on as planned. It was a symbolic rite, honoring the setting sun and the dark contemplations of night. In the morning the eye of Ra would come again and bless the world with its holy light. The squires were in private quarters with their patron Paladins, helping them dress in their ceremonial armor, and to cater to their every needs. In time, they too would learn the ways of the warrior and priesthood, but for now service was their gift to the cause.

Reports had been coming in about the declaration of martial law. But it seemed that over the day, even the guards had somehow come unruly and were killing with the same ruthless abandon as the commoners. Rumor was spreading of a curse and the paladins were prepared to go out and help maintain order in the coming night following the ritual. They would go forth in their shiny ceremonial armor like beacons of good and righteousness in the lawless dark of Thor's Hammer.

Little did they suspect that the three over-achieving thieves had infected nearly all of the squires with the curse. As the squires helped their patron paladins into their sacred suits of armor they bore daggers as well as hatred and silently slit their throats and stabbed them in their unsuspecting hearts.

On the street before the Terra Paladin stronghold waited Murdock, Ruskin, and The Scorpion. The screams of rage and murder filled the gloomy night. Then Sciloren appeared with his shifting sandy eyes and beguiling speed and dexterity.

"Greetings gentlemen, I must compliment you on your days work." You may have done too good of a job, I can sense that most of the paladins within have already been killed by your squires. Very fine indeed, but I wish to feed on the energy of these paladins so we must make our move now. With that the vampire raced toward the front door of the place, smashing into the door and through it in an explosive force of splinters and supporting beams. The very foundation of the place seemed to shake and the high general emerged from his dressing quarters half dressed and the ceremonial priests stood agape. One had been impaled by a large piece of wood and was propped at an odd angle against the altar.

"An altar of blood, how appropriate." Before any of the priests could move to defend themselves, the vampire grabbed one in each hand and almost instantly drained them of their life's energies. He tossed their husks away and turned on the High General of the Terra Paladins.

His attendant tossed the General his broad sword and he took a stance ready to face this unearthly creature. An aura of protection surrounded him and a few of the surviving paladins raced to his side in defense. The three thieves had entered the building at this time and also stood by their leader ready to do battle. The paladins didn't take into account the squires and they also didn't suspect that the other paladins had been killed. So when the young men came out of the adjoining rooms and began stabbing them mercilessly, they were taken aback and mortally wounded before they could defend themselves. Sciloren easily went from one to the other, draining them of their energy. He saved the General for last and savored his soul for a second longer, but in the end the Terra Paladin stronghold had fallen and the city of Thor's Hammer lay in chaotic ruin.

Down the stairs they went, as quiet as plate and dwarves could be, and emerged in the hallway leading to the gate. Several torches burned brightly throwing the hall in flickering light. Before the gate stood Sabbath with the huge ruby, Za'Varuk's stone in his hand. He had a sardonic grin and magical lightning crackled at his fingertips. The huge gate behind him seemed to throb in anticipation of the nearness of the stone and a stirring wind began to drift slowly about the huge hall.

"I see you have arrived just in time to great the demon in person Darkwolfe." Sabbath had a lilt and humor in his voice that told he had the upper hand even though there were no other foes in sight. Along the hall were many darkened alcoves and Darkwolfe assumed there were present surprises for him *if*, no *when* he charged to attack.

The three dwarves beat him to it and in unison the three went running forward with their weapons. Sabbath merely waved his hand and they went flying back and stuck helplessly to the stone wall as if it were made of the stuff they hung to catch flies. They struggled with all their might, but to no avail. They were held fast and any hope of stopping the mage before he released the foul demon rested in the hands of the new king.

With both swords out and ready, Darkwolfe began to move slowly forward eyeing the many alcoves as he went expecting something to jump out at any moment. Sabbath only watched, amused and made no attempt to quickly put the stone in the proper socket on the door to release Za'Varuk.

Then of course the inevitable happened, out from one of the alcoves stepped Anteas the Black Paladin, one in the service of Anu the snake-headed god. He was wearing his blackened armor and a similarly colored helm in the semblance of a snakehead. In one hand he held his broad sword, the other was the Hammer of Thor, a truly awesome and magical weapon. Darkwolfe could only speculate what kind of damage it may inflict if he was hit by the dreadful thing.

"So it is you and me." Anteas stated matter of factly, taking on a fighting stance. "Get on with it will you mage. This has gone on long enough."

"I agree," Heather said stepping from a different alcove, the timbre of her voice revealed that she was in fact in the demon's grasp. "Now mage, let's do this thing, I have waited long enough."

Somehow Sabbath's resolve to somehow control or betray the demon fell apart, and he used his magic to lift the stone up to the height, many men high, to where Za'Varuk's stone would fit. Like a key it would release this demon, but the others would remain sealed until their stones were found and similarly put in the appropriate places. It was a gate, a door of sorts, but not in a normal sense. It was a portal to the inner core where the demons had been banished. It could be standing up, lying down on the ground, in a river, on a mountain, in a house, or wooded glade, it really didn't matter. It was a magical device and could have been placed essentially anywhere. The dwarves were now thinking their choice of placement was poor and now the universe would be destroyed because of their faulty decision making.

Darkwolfe charged forward to stop the mage, but Anteas blocked him and attacked with his weapons. The young king dodged and parried. Anteas's magical hammer slammed into the wall issuing forth sparks and taking out a huge chunk. They danced back and forth and no matter how much Darkwolfe tried to push forward, he couldn't reach the mage in time without losing his life in the process.

{Don't be foolish. Take out the paladin if you can, but don't get yourself killed. You are the only hope for Alcyone. Use your head and your training.} Kiriana whispered in his brain as he blocked the sword, thrust, parried and lashed out with a quick kick, then another. His feet didn't do any damage because of Anteas's protective armor, but it knocked him back for a second. Darkwolfe cast a defensive spell. His image wavered and now the paladin saw two of him as if he were cross-eyed, which would certainly make hitting him much more difficult. Darkwolfe then pointed Kiriana at him and sent forth a few attack darts, but Anteas had erected a protective shield with his clerical magic and they were instantly dispelled.

Again the two met head on weapons flailing, and the paladin scored a minor hit with his sword, but thankfully the dragon armor deflected most of the damage. Darkwolfe responded by spinning about with both blades and driving the sword from the paladin's hands. Anteas was left with just the short warhammer and he retreated, assessing his best plan of attack. The Pagan King had had enough. His head was filled with magical rage and out flew a ball of fire the size of a huge melon. It slammed into the paladin and sent him flying backward. He smashed off the gigantic demon gate and fell to the stones out cold.

But then time was out.

The earth itself seemed to sing in such a low bass tone that everyone present felt their teeth rattle and bones shake. The gate crackled with blue electricity and the giant ruby burned brightly to a lava color and then shattered with a loud whip cracking snap.

"At last…" Heather said and fell to the floor, free of the demon at last but weakened by his presence.

Then there was a swirling gray smoke and a haunting baritone laughter echoed in the hall. Then a shape began to form from the smoke and Za'Varuk the Conqueror materialized, at last free from his banishment.

He stood at least twice the height of a man and easily four times his width and weight. His skin burned a reddish-black around bulging muscles that could easily snap a horse's neck. His head was somewhat elongated and wide at the eyes, which were oval-shaped and burned with unimaginable fiery hatred and anger. He had wickedly sharp, curving claws and great teeth the size of fingers and yellow like a burnt lily.

"Now I will eat your heart dragon-kin." The demon rushed forward.

Somehow his rush was vastly more predictable than the talented paladin he had just been fighting. Darkwolfe dodged to the right side at the last second and slashed the backside of Za'Varuk's leg as he passed with the demon sword. There was a sputtering like bacon and the monster bellowed like no sound any living creature could ever want to hear and live another day. Darkwolfe spun another half spin with a backhand and pointed Kiriana at Sabbath's feet and the ground erupted in a minor quake of spitting rocks and splitting earth. The mage flew to the side, landing at an awkward angle with his leg bone sticking in shards through his leg and robes.

The demon was then rushing in again and Darkwolfe used the speed of his boots to take several steps and then launch himself into a diving roll that brought him back up again to his feet. He was then facing the beast as it turned around again for a more slow and careful attack. Sabbath was moaning in agony and fumbling for a healing potion. Darkwolfe nailed him with no less than 7 attack darts for good measure before the creature was close enough for his sword work.

Thankfully his training had given him enough agility to dodge the cumbersome size and relatively slow swings of the monster, and Darkwolfe was also able to score several minor hits to the legs and lower abdomen. Each hit sizzled and the demon issued forth that gods-awful howl each time. Then unfortunately the young king's luck ran out. Anteas rose to his feet, although somewhat unsteadily and still smoking from the fireball. The slight distraction was enough for the demon to land a blow, and the awesome hit knocked the breath from the man and sent him tumbling back to the end of the chamber where his dwarven warriors were still helplessly stuck to the stone wall.

With a suction cup pop the trio fell to the ground, free of the spell.

The demon stopped his forward progress, seeing the dwarves free. He could easily take the four he thought, but that accursed sword the Pagan King wielded was draining his physical energy. He paused to consider. Then another bunch of dwarves emerged from the stairwell. In a frenzy they yelled to Thor and charged the demon. Thrasher, Trollbait, and Darrel were up and charging too. Darkwolfe was still trying to make sure his head was still attached.

Za'Varuk began tearing into the dwarves as they took their swings. He ripped a couple apart, but he was taking many hits. Some of the weapons didn't even affect him, others stung bitterly, but none like the king's Demon Slayer. As much as the demon wanted to finish this with the king now, he didn't think he could take them all out, and he could see more dwarves coming out of the stairwell and the pagan king rising to his feet. No, he would live and fight another day. He was patient.

In a furious outburst of energy the demon took down four more dwarves before he turned back in the direction of the gate. With a wave of his hand a dimensional hole opened up. Anteas was helping the barely living mage to his feet and stumbled though the hole. The demon jumped through and the hole zapped shut before anyone could pursue.

"We let him go!" Darkwolfe yelled at no one in particular, as he waded through the dwarves and came before the huge demon gate. There were still many, many sockets left unfilled and potential demons to be released. He thought this a minor victory in reclaiming the gate, but he was also bitter at letting Za'Varuk and his lover's killer escape. He straightened his stag crown and turned back toward the waiting dwarves.

"Hail Darkwolfe, long live the Pagan King!" The dwarves yelled, bowing awkwardly as dwarves were want to do.

Heather crawled over to his feet and kneeled with what little strength she had left. "Yes, hail my Lord. Lord of Grathmoor, King of the pagan folk." She kissed his feet and fell unconscious.

He picked her up in his arms and was thankful she still lived. He was sickened at the sight of the mutilated corpses of the dwarves. He wiped away a tear from Heather's cheek and cradled her to his chest protectively. Upon the girl's decree, Sabbath had lost control of the region and all of the undead fell, never to kill again.

About the Author

Adam holds a M.A. in Psychology and draws from many backgrounds in his writing: martial arts instructor, ceremonial magician, Wiccan priest, musician, poet...

He is married with two children.

9 780595 200344